I KNOW YOU

ALSO AVAILABLE BY ANNABEL KANTARIA

The One That Got Away

The Disappearance

Coming Home

I KNOW YOU

A Novel of Suspense

Annabel Kantaria

CROOKED
LANE

NEW YORK

Copyright © 2018 by Annabel Kantaria

Published in the United States by Crooked Lane Books, an imprint of The Quick Brown Fox & Company LLC.

Crooked Lane Books and its logo are trademarks of The Quick Brown Fox & Company LLC.

Library of Congress Catalog-in-Publication data available upon request.

ISBN (hardcover): 978-1-64385-110-5
ISBN (ePub): 978-1-64385-111-2
ISBN (ePDF): 978-1-64385-112-9

Cover design layout HQ 2018
Cover illustrations © Trevor Payne / Arcangel Images (window); all other images © Shutterstock.com
Book design by Jennifer Canzone

Printed in the United States.

www.crookedlanebooks.com

Crooked Lane Books
34 West 27th St., 10th Floor
New York, NY 10001

First North American edition: June 2019
Originally published in Great Britain by HQ, an imprint of HarperCollins Publishers Ltd., June 2018.

10 9 8 7 6 5 4 3 2 1

For Sam

PROLOGUE

I stare at the computer screen, my eyes flicking as they keep up with the feeds rolling down the pages like ticker tape. The only movement in the room comes from my hand clicking on the mouse, and the occasional staccato burst of my fingers on the keyboard ringing out like gunfire in the silence of the house. Everything around me is still, which is exactly how I like it. The curtains are drawn, and just one beam of sunlight escaping through an imperceptible gap illuminates dust motes suspended in the stale air. Not that I notice. My attention is focused entirely on the 24-inch monitor I've angled to face me, the iPads on the desk next to me, and the screen of my mobile phone. All show live social-media feeds, internet searches and live chat rooms.

My fingers flick over the keyboards, the key strokes rattling in the silence of the house as I follow the fast-moving feeds. I lean towards the screen, my attention focused 100 per cent as I scroll, click and type, and then the printer whirs into action, spooling out a colour picture. I pick it off the tray and stare at it almost lasciviously: new material. Even though there's usually something fresh each day, I'm pleased. It's a good one. I roll my chair over to the filing cabinet and locate the right scrapbook from the top shelf, then I flick through it, smiling to myself as I go through the familiar images. While the other books all show pictures of people, this one has images of things: cars, streets and houses. Some are older now, their corners starting to curl: I didn't used to laminate.

I run the new image through the laminator, picking it off the machine while it's still hot, then carefully fix it in the book using corner mounts. Without the images of her blonde hair and his easy smile, this mightn't be as interesting a scrapbook as the others to a stranger's eye – but you have to trust me: it's way more valuable.

I remember well the day this story started. It was the day I joined the walking group: the day I met Simon; the day I met Anna. It was a wintry December day – dry and bitterly cold. People had their Christmas trees up and fairy lights hanging in their windows but it wasn't close enough to Christmas for the real excitement to have begun; for people to have started realizing just how few days they have left to rampage through department stores, grabbing aftershave and perfume, leather gloves, lingerie and watches.

The day I joined the walking group marked the beginning of a cold snap that lasted well into February. December to February. By March, when tiny green buds were starting to form on the trees, and flowers were beginning to push their cheerful colours through the earth, by then it was all over. Three months of brutal cold before spring started. That's all we're talking about here. Three months.

So let me begin. My mother always told me to be choosy. She's not really in this story, though I feel she should be.

'Be choosy with your clothes, be choosy with your make-up, be choosy with what you put in your mouth and with whom you share your bed,' she used to say, leaning back against the kitchen counter, her arms consumed by marigold gloves. 'But most of all,' she would say, 'be choosy with whom you make friends.'

It was good advice, and I was thinking about it as I pulled on my socks that December morning. I tied the laces on my walking boots and hunted around for my gloves, my hat and the warmest jacket I owned – the one stuffed with ultra-light down, like everyone seemed to have in those days. In my head, there was nothing more serious than the need to keep warm and the need to make some friends.

'All very well, Mum,' I said out loud. I was talking to myself a lot back then. 'But beggars can't always be choosers.' If only Mum could see me now, two months into married life in London with no friends to call my own, she'd tell me to come straight back home, that's what she'd do. And maybe I should have gone home: for sure, if I had, things would have turned out differently. That's easy to say now. But that day, I zipped up my jacket, found my purse, and set off for the park, my head full of plans.

I still remember how, despite the jacket, the cold hit me the moment I stepped out of the house, the door slamming shut behind me in a gust of wind that must surely have blown in directly from the Arctic. I paused for a moment, unused to those British winters: unused to those blue-sky days that looked so inviting when you were cosy inside but felt as if they'd strip raw any uncovered flesh the moment you stepped outside. I adjusted my scarf to cover my cheeks, pulled my woollen hat further down onto my head, and took in the bare-limbed trees, the parked cars, the cracked, grey paving slabs, the litter blowing in the gutter, and the cans rattling against the kerb. I took in next-door's fat tabby cat licking its paws, and the tired-looking, grey-coated people, their faces turned down, hurrying to work. I remember feeling jealous then – of their jobs, their purpose, and of their colleagues; of their silly water-cooler chats, coffee runs and birthday whip-rounds.

'This is it, babe,' I said out loud. 'This is London.'

I set off down the street looking, I hoped, more confident than I felt. I was on a mission to meet people because, as Jake joked at that point, I had exactly three friends: Facebook, Twitter and

Instagram. It was difficult to believe that I should have no real friends in London and, hand on heart, I was having trouble to adjusting to the fact that I knew no one. I'd laughed at his joke but it had hurt. There were days back then when I'd thought the loneliness would surely drive me insane; when I felt as if the darkness inside me was going to explode out and flood the house, engulfing me like a seabird caught helplessly in a slimy slick of oil. It makes me squirm now, but back then I'd see myself floating down the hall, arms and legs glued to my body, eyes bulging, choking on loneliness, and I'd have to breathe into a paper bag to stop myself hyperventilating. I never told Jake about that. Maybe I should have done – who knows? – but, ultimately, that's why I decided to join the walking group.

At the end of my street, I turned a smart right, crossed the main road, headed towards the park, and arrived bang on time. And so the story begins.

* * *

I see the walking group at once: a mish-mash of people gathered beneath a huge old oak. Some, in sportwear, are stretching hamstrings and quads, others are clutching take-out coffees and, had I been worried about what to wear, I realize right there that there's no need: there's a whole range of active wear between the two groups. I turn my back to the group and snap a smiling selfie with them in the background, then upload it to Instagram as I walk towards the group. 'Hiking, London-style! #lloydpark', I write for the caption, adding a little heart emoji, full of the knowledge that my friends back home will find the image everything it's not: cute (Taylor in a hat!), quaint (London parks!), and moody with the dark sky and bleak trees (weather!). Hollywood Hills it isn't. Already my phone buzzes with Likes.

They say you judge a person in seven seconds, and I'm perhaps even quicker than that. I scan the group as I approach, my eyes sweeping right and left through them, ruling out those standing with friends and those too old. I've nothing against the elderly, don't get me wrong, but I'm looking for a specific type of person – a new best friend – and, for that, there are criteria.

I wonder now what would have happened had I turned up earlier or later in the year; had I gone to a different supermarket, seen an ad for a different walking group; read a flyer for a different kind of hobby. I go over and over how things might have been different. But this is the day I join this walking group, and I spot a potential friend at once. There's something about her face, her hair, her clothes, and the way she holds herself. She looks like one of my friends – my real friends back in the States. What I feel is familiarity: that woman standing there in the skinny jeans, the brown boots and the olive-green coat looks like she should be in my tribe. I take a deep breath and wend my way through the other walkers, smiling politely, until I get to her.

'Hi,' I say. 'It's Jen, isn't it?'

She looks at me and purses her lips. Squints her eyes.

'You don't remember, do you?' I give a little laugh and shake my hair back as I lean in towards her as if we're sharing a joke. I have the kind of face that's generic to a lot of people: a symmetrical, pretty face, with a smile so friendly you think you know me. You've 'seen' me, you've seen thousands of me, and this 'do I know you?' tactic often works. But not on this day: the woman shakes her head slowly.

'I'm sorry. Head like a sieve. Remind me,' she says.

'I'm Jake's wife. We met at dinner at Richard and Kate's the other week . . . ?' I falter. 'At least, I think it was you!' I laugh again, and shrug. 'Or have I made a huge mistake? I'm rubbish at faces.'

She tuts and shakes her head. 'Sorry.'

'Oh god. No, I'm so sorry. I can be such an idiot!'

Now she's smiling but it doesn't reach her eyes. 'No worries. It's okay.' She's already looking past me, towards the gates of the park.

I thrust out my hand. 'I'm Taylor, by the way.'

'Polly,' she says, giving my hand a limp shake, and I picture myself telling Jake that I'd met a real, live person called Polly. It's such an English name. There's something so pure and sweet and rosy about it. It's like I hit the English-names jackpot. In my head, I fast-forward our friendship like a movie: Polly and Taylor. I imagine nights out, holidays together, us telling our other friends how we met at a walking group 'way back in the day'. I've already said that I lived in my head a lot in those days, haven't I? Loneliness is a bitch.

'Glad to meet you,' I say to Polly, changing the subject. 'So what's the deal here? It's my first time.'

'Oh, it's fairly relaxed,' she says. 'We sign in with Cath over there . . .' she points to a woman with a clipboard, 'and then we all start walking. It's about an hour's walk.'

'Great. And we end up back here?'

'Yes. Sometimes we go a different route; Cath tries to show us different parts of the town and park but, yes, we end up back here.'

'Hi!' We're interrupted by a fresh-faced woman who approaches behind me.

'Hey!' says Polly. The other woman turns out to be called Bex. And this is where it all goes wrong. From the moment Polly and Bex start talking to each other, two things become clear. One, that this is a weekly date for the two of them; and two, that I'm the gooseberry. I make my excuses, turn around and fall into conversation with a tall man who's standing behind me: that's how I come to know Simon.

2

By the time we get back to the starting point of the walk, I feel as if I know the vast majority of Simon's life history. It's not his fault, and I'm not complaining – it's just I've been so starved of conversation since the move that I don't stop asking the poor guy questions. I don't ask him how old he is but I'd guess from the greys starting to lighten his hair at the temples, from the crow's feet that line his face, and perhaps from the self-deprecating maturity with which he talks about his situation, that he's in his late forties, maybe even just gone fifty. He's divorced but is 'fine about it' because it means he can live with his dad – he's the only child and pretty much his dad's full-time carer. The dad, whom he curiously refers to as 'Father', has a lot wrong with him. Simon uses technical terms with which I'm not familiar but I imagine his dad being housebound, perhaps even confined to his bed. I can picture Simon bending over him, tending to him with never-ending patience – though maybe he's not like that at all. Maybe he's impatient, snapping at his father, resenting the fact that his life's ebbing away as he wipes dribble from his mouth, shampoos his thin, grey hair, and trims his yellowing nails. Some external carer, a volunteer or something, comes occasionally, and that's when Simon slips out to do things like go to the library, and walk with this group.

'I come here for the company,' he says as we trudge, head-down into the wind, so I ask him who he usually talks to.

'Oh, no one specific. I just come to be among other people. Not necessarily talking to them.' He laughs. 'You're honoured I've put up with you for a whole hour.'

We both laugh then because surely it's as obvious as day is day that he's done all the talking.

'So tell me about you,' he says. 'Have you lived here long?'

I open my mouth to reply but am rendered mute by the memory of that evening when Jake had sat me down on Santa Monica beach, the huge, red sun kissing the horizon and the soft air balmy against my skin, and suggested a fresh start in Britain.

'London!' he'd said, arcing his hands as if to embrace the entire city, and I'd pictured the lights, the shops, the buzz and the bars of the West End, not exactly Croydon.

'A smart little townhouse,' Jake had said, 'for us and this little one . . .' He'd patted my tummy where the baby was then about the size of a lime. 'What do you think?' Only it hadn't been a question, it had been an ultimatum, and we'd both known what he meant: move away and give our marriage a fighting chance, or stay in Santa Monica and let it flounder on the rocks of his infidelity.

I'd plumped for the dream. Jake's dream. My marriage. But I'm not about to tell Simon that.

'No, I'm new to the area,' I say finally.

He asks when the baby's due, which I think is a brave question given how subtle my bump still is for thirty-two weeks, especially under the Puffa-style jacket that muffles every dip and curve, and he doesn't even pass comment on my American accent.

I'm just saying bye to him when the walking group finally does cough up the result I was hoping for. Maybe it's a payment from the universe or something for me for giving so much attention to Simon, but I see a woman I didn't spot at the start, and she's exactly what I'm looking for. With blonde hair and wearing a bright blue jacket, she stands out from the crowd and I wonder why I didn't see her before. I make my way over to where she's standing alone.

'Good walk?' I say, giving her my best cabin-crew beam.

'Yes,' she says, smiling back in a muted way. I forget how wary English people can be of strangers. 'It was good. I was a bit late arriving, though. Thought I'd have to run to catch up.'

'Have you been before?'

'Oh, one other time,' she says, 'but I've only been in Croydon a month so I'm still finding my way around.'

'Me too!' I say, perhaps too enthusiastically, then I stand there wondering how I can keep her longer; how I can make sure I see her again. She looks nice. I toy with the idea of asking her out for a coffee but it seems too forward and if there's one thing I've learned about Brits, it's that they don't do 'forward'.

'Will you be here next week, do you think?' I ask in the end, and she shrugs.

'Maybe.'

'Okay, cool,' I say. 'Maybe see you then.'

That's Anna, by the way. About to become my new best friend.

* * *

I still remember how the afternoon of that day had yawned ahead of me, an Atlantic Ocean of emptiness and boredom; me alone on a pea-green boat, rowing my way towards six o'clock when Jake was due back from wherever it was he'd gone that week. Shrewsbury, I think it was. I changed into some comfy lounge clothes, hauled myself back downstairs while holding tight to the banisters because I was always slightly paranoid about falling down the stairs and killing the baby, made myself a cup of tea, and opened up the iPad.

Here's a confession: I spent a lot of time online in those days. Not so much any more. But back then I did.

Jake didn't like it – not that he knew the half of it. I used to wonder – I still do wonder – what he'd have done had it been him who'd had to sit at home alone all day in a foreign country with all his friends halfway around the world. If he were in my position, I doubt he'd have been able to amuse himself 24/7 without a bit of online chat. So, as I said, he didn't like me being online – yet it clearly didn't bother him enough to tell me that; to talk to me about his concerns. Had he done so, things may well have turned out differently. But the most he ever said at the time was, 'Join some groups or something,' and I tried, honestly, I did.

I saw a 'Bumps and Babies' group advertised, and I went along to a coffee morning full of pregnant women. But that's where I discovered that, despite needing friends like most people need oxygen, my mother's advice to be choosy really had been absorbed into my DNA. Over the course of those ninety minutes, I learned that I'd rather be alone than be with people I had nothing in common with bar a foetus. I'm not going to say anything more about that morning. Let's just say I never went back, and park it there.

Instagram's my favourite social media, but Twitter was my go-to place for chat. I know there are people who say it's had its day but, love it or hate it, there was always something going on on there. My news feed moved fast and I loved clicking through interesting articles and joining in the banter with my regular group of mates. What did we talk about? A lot of things, I guess: pregnancy, parenting, babies, airline chat, relocation, expat life and, as Donald Trump came to power, a bit of American politics. I loved that you could duck out if you didn't like the way a chat was going, and I loved that you could block people who annoyed you. Imagine doing that in a coffee shop.

But the day of the walking group – the day I meet Simon and the girl in the blue jacket – I'm after something different. I grab the iPad and click onto Facebook. Like a junkie desperate for a fix, I systematically search groups specific to the area, scrolling through the members one by one for her blonde hair and smiling face. I have a good memory for faces and dismiss ten, fifty, a hundred similar faces and then, finally, on a buying and selling page that doesn't have too many members, I see her. I click on the profile picture and expand it. It's her. I'm sure it's her: Anna Jones is her name.

I KNOW WHERE YOU LIVE

You think you're so discreet, don't you, so internet-savvy, never posting your details online, hiding behind a screen name. But you leave a trail wider than a jumbo jet streaking across the summer sky. You leave a trail so clear I could follow it with my eyes closed.

You probably don't remember taking that picture, do you? The one of the oak tree with the winter sun rising behind it back when you first found the house? *Très* arty. I agree, the image was stunning, the austere branches silhouetted against the sky like some prehistoric monster rising from behind the row of roofs. You could almost feel the frost in the air. It really deserved all those Likes. But what you forget, my sweet, is the double whammy of Instagram location services and Google Maps, and how useful they are to people like me.

It takes me half a day. In the general scheme of things, that's not long. It's seconds. Milliseconds. Insignificant. Edging along Street View, looking for that tree, in front of those houses, those parked cars, that bus stop, that crack in the road, those paving stones, that manhole cover, I even find myself enjoying the challenge. Do you remember those childhood games of hide and seek? I loved those, too. But this is way more fun.

And then, when I think I've found it, I spin my point of view around and there I am, looking at a house. Your house. The upstairs

13

window from which you took the picture. Is that your bedroom? I think it is.

A door and a window downstairs, two windows upstairs. That's all. Nothing in the windows to give a clue: no picture frames, perfume bottles, nothing. A few terracotta roof tiles cantilevered out above the step to give shelter to callers. Below those tiles, a navy front door that could do with a fresh coat of paint. It's on your to-do list, isn't it, to get out there and paint it yourself? Oh, come on, admit it – you're already imagining the Instagram shots: a paintbrush balanced across a tin of paint; brushstrokes of paint on wood; a close-up of the smudge of paint on your adorable little nose. What else can I see? New PVC windows not in keeping with the style of the property. White paintwork. A garden fence that could do with being re-stained. Dirty-grey paving slabs in the front garden. A big, black wheelie bin. Outside, oh look, there it is: your car.

Nothing remarkable but, to me, it's gold.

I walk the Street View back down the road, check the street name, then examine the map of the local area. Nice.

3

Anna Jones' Facebook page was private, and she had only had one profile picture and one generic cover visible to the public. I still remember how it annoyed me at the time, in the way that anyone who buttoned up their privacy settings on social media annoyed me – and I'd flung the iPad down – but then I'd found her Instagram, and practically yelped with joy to see that that was wide open, my screen suddenly filled with gorgeous square shots to pore over.

I'd scrolled through them like a child opening a Christmas stocking, lifting and examining each one, and starting to feel as if I knew Anna Jones inside out. In one, there was a tall bear of a man and I stared at it, wondering who he was. Her compositions were careful; her pictures way more than just snaps. Lots were of details: her nail polish; a piece of jewellery or an accessory; a plate of food. I don't know how long I spent looking at her pictures but after some time – half an hour maybe? – my back had started to ache and I'd gone into the kitchen. I remember wondering if the clock was broken, its hands stuck at 2.30 p.m., but my watch confirmed the news: the hump of the day wasn't even broken; the afternoon still stretched ahead like a road through the Mojave Desert.

I looked for Anna on Twitter but ended up spending the bulk of the afternoon in an online discussion about whether or not you should find out the sex of the baby. Inevitably perhaps, someone got pissed with me. She – or he, I suppose it could be – sent me a rant spread over three Tweets and I sat there wondering if there was any point in defending myself; if there was any point in anything. I just felt so beaten. Lonely and beaten. Remember that before you judge me later; remember that this story is born from loneliness. Unless you've experienced it, you've no idea where it can lead you. Do I sound defensive? You can blame Jake for that.

* * *

Around six that day, when Jake's due home, I start to get restless. I get up from the sofa, go to the front door, and squint through the peephole, disappointed when I see the emptiness of our parking space. On the hall table, tanned versions of Jake and me smile up at me from a photo frame. It's a casual picture from our wedding day. Standing above us, the photographer caught us laughing as the guests showered us in dried rose petals. I close my eyes – the day had been perfect. Jake and I had had the barefoot beach wedding I'd always dreamed of, on an island off Key West. Although that picture's now in a box in the basement, just thinking about it brings back the warm caress of the sun on my skin, the sound of the palms rustling in the gentle breeze, and the blaze of glorious colours: the turquoise of the sea, the white sand, and the vibrant pinks and purples of the bougainvillea that trailed around the resort, dripping off the white plantation-style balconies of the guest cottages. Easy days. Simple times.

Waiting for Jake to get home, I remember the way he'd grabbed my hand and led me and our friends barefoot down the beach to board the catamaran for our sunset drinks reception . . . I sigh – it seems a lifetime ago – then I leap as the doorbell rings. I didn't hear the car.

I've a smile on my face as I open the door, and it's on the tip of my tongue to ask Jake why he didn't use his key, when I realize it's not Jake at all, but a smiling woman wrapped in a raincoat. Her brown hair's shoulder-length and streaked with honeyed high-lights, though at the roots I can see a hint of grey, and she's wear-ing red lipstick and a foundation that's slightly too tanned for the pallor of her winter skin. Still, she's attractive. I'd guess she's ten years older than me. She tilts her head sideways.

'Hello!' she says cheerily. 'I just wanted to pop by and intro-duce myself. I live at number twenty-six.' She nods her head down the street. 'Saw you and your hubby moving in. Thought I'd give you a bit of space before saying hello.'

'Thank you,' I say. 'Nice to meet you. I'm Taylor.'

She extends her hand. 'Sarah.' The wind gusts and she tucks her hair back behind her ears.

'Would you like to come in?' I ask. 'It's just I'm expecting my hus-band home any second but you're welcome to step in for a minute?'

'If you don't mind, there's actually something I'd like to ask you,' she says, so I lead her into the front room and we stand awk-wardly on the carpet. Dinner's pretty much ready so it's a funny time to offer tea. Wine? Should I offer her a glass of wine? I don't think we even had any in those days.

She gives a little laugh. 'To be honest, I have to admit I've come here with an ulterior motive.'

'Okay,' I say.

She glances around the room, spots the bookshelves. 'Oh good,' she says. 'You do read!'

Should I have been more guarded with a stranger at my door? Probably – but, 'I love reading,' I say. 'My books were the first thing I unpacked when we moved in.'

'Fantastic! I know what you mean! Well, I'm not so embar-rassed to ask you now, but basically, I'm starting a book club – like a little reading circle. Just a couple of girls in the area where we can get together and have some drinks and nibbles and talk about books. When I saw you moving in I couldn't help noticing all those boxes marked "Books" and I just wondered if, maybe, it'd be something you might be interested in?'

'Oh! What sort of books do you read? It's just . . .'

'Oh, nothing too highbrow,' she says with a laugh. 'Please don't worry about that. Contemporary fiction. Latest releases. Anything really.'

'Oh, okay. Sounds good. Obviously, I might not be able to be in it for long . . .' I pat my bump in case she hasn't noticed it.

'Oh!' she says. 'Very compact! How far are you?'

'Due late Feb.'

'Aww.' She smiles at my bump for a moment, then looks back at my face. 'Well, look, you're very welcome. We'd love to have you, and the bump.' She smiles again. 'Bring a friend if you like.'

'Thanks. I'd love to join,' I say and out of the corner of my eye I see Jake parking the car outside so I start to usher her towards the door. At the hall table, she stops.

'Oh wow, is that your wedding?' she asks, picking up the photo and running a finger over the glass.

'Yes,' I say. What else can I say?

'What a beautiful picture,' she says. 'You both look so happy.'

'We were,' I say. Outside, I hear Jake walking up the path. 'We are! Anyway, here he is now . . .' I pull open the door. 'Hi, darling.' I widen my eyes at him to show I'm as surprised as he is at our unexpected visitor. 'This is Sarah. She lives down the road. Sarah – my husband, Jake.'

Sarah steps back to look at Jake, then leans into him and gives him a showy kiss on the cheek. 'Mwa. Even more handsome in real life,' she says with a laugh, wiping her thumb against his cheek to remove a smudge of lipstick, then she's off down the path. 'Bye, Taylor! I'll let you know when the next meeting is. Byee!'

I'm smiling when I close the door.

'What was that all about?' says Jake.

'That,' I say, puffing up a bit, 'was my invitation to join a book club. I think I've got a new friend.'

4

When I look back, it seems Jake was away more than he was home in those days. I can't imagine why I didn't just tell him I wanted him to spend more time at home. It seems so obvious now, but it didn't occur to me even to question his work then; to ask 'is this really necessary?' Maybe it was necessary. Maybe it wasn't – but I didn't want to make an issue of it. The truth is, I was walking on eggshells with him at that point and I didn't want to smash the lot of them.

Anyway, after Sarah had invited me to join the book club, Jake and I spent the weekend together. I don't recall what we did – maybe some sort of preparation for the baby's arrival, or maybe we just had a lie-in and did some Christmas shopping. The point is, they weren't perfect, but they were innocent days; days before everything fell apart. I can't look back at photos from that time now.

Jake left again the following Wednesday.

'Look after yourself,' he says as he throws his bag into the trunk. 'Go back to the walking club.'

'Be good,' I say to him and the weight of the words hangs heavy between us.

'I'm back late on Saturday,' Jake says. He slides into the car in that graceful way of his, and my smile doesn't falter as I lean in to smooth a piece of his hair that's escaped a heavy gelling.

'Bye,' I say, waving as the car recedes down the street, leaving nothing but a lingering smell of petrol exhaust. I turn back to the house and a cavern of emptiness hits me in my chest. I still get that feeling sometimes now, if I'm home alone, early in the morning. That day, though, it feels as if the emptiness inside me might actually physically explode, and I have to lean against the doorframe for a moment while I catch my breath.

I was in a bad way back then. Neither Jake nor I saw it at the time but, looking back, I guess I could have been depressed. I've read a lot about it since what happened and, as I said, I think I was. I'm not making excuses, just saying.

But that morning I don't question it. I go back into the kitchen: it's silent bar the whir and occasional shudder of the fridge. The scent of Jake's cologne still hangs in the air, mixed with the morning smells of eggs, toast and coffee. His cup, cutlery and plate sit unrinsed on the counter. Four days he'll be away this time. Not long, but it includes half a weekend, and before I can get my defences up, the thought thunders in like a runaway train: why does he need to be away on a Friday night? A Saturday? It's his fault I question these absences now. I used to trust him. In my head, that ever-recurring snapshot of me picking up his mobile phone; of me clicking on the last conversation in his WhatsApp and finding a sex chat with 'her'. My heart thuds at the memory, as it did that day. His denial. His tears. My trust broken.

Why did I look?

I take a deep breath and give myself a pep talk as I put the dishes in the sink, squirt detergent onto the sponge, and wash the plates by hand, carefully removing all traces of the coffee and food that's touched Jake's lips: *It doesn't mean anything. You're going to have a great week,* I tell myself. *He's learned his lesson. He won't do it again.* But a smaller voice persists: *Once a cheater, always a cheater,* and I squash it back down, visualizing it spiralling down the sink with the dishwater.

Jobs done, I turn to face the kitchen and sigh again. It doesn't help that I have no friends to distract me. You can't cut people away from their natural habitat and expect them to pick up just like that in a new place. Even while I'm thinking this, I'm denying it: as cabin crew I'd been constantly moving and never felt lost. Maybe that's the problem: here in Britain, I've lost more than just my friends and family. I've lost my identity.

And then there's the reality of what life's actually like in Croydon. Not in my head, but down on the cold, hard ground. My previous experiences of life in London, staying at smart hotels within a stone's throw of the city lights, were galaxies away from the reality of life in a street of two-up two-down red-brick terraces. I laugh out loud at my own naivety – a bitter laugh that echoes through the empty house like the cackles of a witch. I wonder when the book club is. What number did that Sarah woman say she lived at? Twenty-six? I make a small detour to walk past her house on the way to the park: peeling paint, a messy front yard, and drawn curtains that prevent me from seeing inside.

*   *   *

At the park, I see Simon at once. He's taller than most of the others, his red beanie easy to spot. He gives a little wave so I make my way over to him.

'Hey, how are you?' I ask. 'Good week?'

'Up and down. Up and down. Father had a turn this week. Been in hospital.' He sighs then smiles, his eyes peering intensely into mine through heavy glasses I can't decide are geeky or cool. 'I shouldn't burden you with this. He's out now. All's well. Looking forward to the walk?' His voice is reedy, thin.

'Of course.' As I say the words I spot the woman from last week in the blue jacket: Anna Jones. My heart skips.

'I'm just going to register,' I tell Simon, and head towards her. As I get close, I catch her eye and smile.

'Hey,' I say. 'How are you?'

'Good. You?'

'Yeah, good, thanks. I was just going to sign in. Have you?'

'Not yet.'

We walk together over to Cath, where I watch her write her name. At least I can admit I know it now.

Anna watches me write my name, too. 'Taylor. That's unusual,' she says.

'It's American. I'm from the States.' I want to add 'obviously' but sometimes people don't pick up on my accent and, sometimes, those that do are quite hostile. 'Just don't hold it against me,' I say.

Anna laughs. 'It's okay. I lived there for a while.'

'Really? Whereabouts? I'm from California!'

'Houston. My husband works in oil and gas.'

'How was that?'

She shrugs and we both laugh.

'I hear you,' I say, then I flounder for something else to say. 'So, do you live around here these days?' is all I can come up with even though I already know the answer. And, as I say it, I realize what a stupid question it is. People aren't going to travel far to come to a local walking club. But Anna smiles again.

'Yes. But I moved here a couple of months ago. I've been all over the place. Most recently, Bristol. It's down in the west,' she adds.

'So why Croydon?' I ask.

'I wanted to be closer to London. It ticked my boxes.' Anna shrugs. 'Good connections. I have friends in Brighton. And I like to be relatively close to an airport.' She laughs. 'I feel trapped otherwise. I blame it on my flying days.'

I do a double-take. 'You flew?'

'Yes. Once upon a time.'

'Oh my god. Me too. Delta. I quit because of this.' I pat my bump. 'And obviously moving here. Happy days!'

'Yeah. Happy days,' Anna echoes, then she nods at my bump. 'How far are you?'

'Thirty-two weeks.'

She puts a hand to her own tummy. 'I'm twenty.'

'Congratulations!' I say, and I feel as if Christmas has come: not only is this woman nice, she's pregnant!

'Thanks! Anyway, look,' Anna says, her eyes suddenly looking past me. 'Seems you're needed.' And I see Simon approaching with his gangly walk, head tilted to one side and a smile on his face.

'Ready?' he says, nodding towards the rest of the group where the first people have started to move off.

Anna puts both hands up. 'Don't let me stop you.'

'It's fine,' I say, 'join us,' but she's already walking away, looking for someone else to talk to, and irritation towards Simon surges through me.

'How was your week?' he asks, and all I can think of is the connection I feel with Anna. How I can't let her get away. Yet, as I watch, she wanders over to Polly, who seems to be without Bex, and the two of them chat for a minute before starting the walk together without a backward look at me. Am I jealous? Am I ever.

I KNOW WHAT YOU READ

#throwbackthursday (#tbt) is your most-used hashtag. Did you know that? You really do love your throwback shots. But let me give you a friendly word of warning: so many throwbacks makes people think there's nothing interesting about you now; that the only interesting things you did are in your past. You ought to think about your feed, sweetie-pie; think about how you come across to other people.

Can you guess what your second-favourite hashtag is? It's actually two, which, up until Friday last week, were tied in second place. #amreading and #nomnom. Go figure.

We're actually friends on Goodreads. Do you know that? Probably not. You just say yes to everyone who wants to follow you – never check them out; never check their own pages – you just assume they want to follow you because, well, you're so fucking marvellous, who wouldn't?

And guess what? Every time you rate a book, I get an email. Right into my inbox – sometimes I have to pinch myself, you make my job so easy.

But, dear god, I wish you would read something more interesting. I called you 'Mainstream Meg' for a while. Yet you go around telling everyone you have 'eclectic' taste; that you read 'a bit of everything: biographies, non-fiction, romance, thrillers, self-help'. Why do you make out you're so much better than everyone else?

And yeah, I see you on Twitter, rapping with the book bloggers, Tweeting publishers and authors like you're part of this literary circle when really, sweetie, I have to tell you they've no idea who the fuck you are. They don't care. They're not interested. They Retweet for PR, it's a publicity thing; you're doing their job for them. So here's a tip: give it a rest, and go read some interesting books. Loser.

5

don't remember what I spoke about with Simon that day at the park. I wonder if the hour passed quickly or slowly; we probably talked about the weather – the cold, dry snap had gone on longer than usual, as I recall. People were talking about it, desperate for rain; the reservoirs were empty, and there was talk of a hosepipe ban in the south that summer. I'm bound to have asked Simon if it was always that cold, and we probably spun that out for a good twenty minutes. I certainly didn't know then what he did for a living; I was still under the impression that he cared for his dad full-time, since that was all he'd mentioned. It's funny what people reveal to you; how they slowly unpeel themselves. What I do remember is that, as we headed back into the park at the end of the walk, I couldn't wait to make a beeline for Anna.

'Good walk?' I ask, touching her arm so she spins around, surprised.

'Oh, yes thanks. It's good to get moving. I'd never be motivated to walk for an hour if it was just me alone. So, mission accomplished.' She checks her FitBit. 'Yes! Step count complete.'

I ask what her goal is. Ten thousand, she says. That's the figure that sticks in my mind anyway, but ten thousand is everyone's goal, is it? Maybe I'm putting words into her mouth. Maybe it was more, or less. It doesn't matter.

'Do you usually make it?' I ask, telling her that mine's set on eight thousand, and that I struggle even with that.

Anna sighs, a heavy sigh, as if the whole world's conspiring to prevent her from reaching her step goal. 'Not usually. Not unless I make an effort, like this. Which I guess is why I'm here. I hate the gym.'

'Me too.'

There'd been an awkward pause then. I suppose it was a cross-roads moment when the friendship – or lack of friendship – could have gone either way and, to this day, I remember how desperate I was to stop her from leaving. Maybe there's always a connection between those who've flown; those who've known the same excitement, fears and physical demands of constant air travel – a bond, I suppose, with our siblings of the skies. I remember scratching around for a way to keep Anna talking; clocking the plain gold band of her wedding ring, and wondering if I could ask something about her husband. What I really wanted was to ask for her phone number but it seemed too forward to ask for her contact details given we'd only exchanged a few sentences. But, even from that early on, I felt a connection with her, and I was always a good judge of character: it was one of my selling points. Already I knew she could be the friend I'd been searching for. I remember having the ridiculous idea that meeting her was like seeing food when you've been starving, only being asked to wait before you eat it.

'See you next week!' Simon calls from where I've left him a few feet away. He gives me a cheery little wave, his hand up by his face, and his smile some sort of silly munchkin-type thing.

'Bye,' I call back. 'Have a good week!'

'Right,' Anna says. 'I suppose I'd better get going.'

'Would you like to grab a coffee?' I blurt. 'If you've got time?'

She doesn't say yes as quickly as I'd like. I hold my breath while I watch conflicting thoughts move across her face, then finally she says, 'I really should get going,' and my heart literally hits my boots.

'Sure,' I say.

Perhaps she notices that my smile's flat, because then she dithers, looks at her watch and says, 'Oh, maybe I could come for a quick one.'

'That'd be great!' The words slip out of me in a gush of relief.

'Do you know anywhere near here?' she asks.

I shake my head and we both laugh.

'Okay,' she says. 'I've got my car, and I know how to get to the shopping centre. Shall we go there?'

'Brilliant.'

* * *

We go to Costa. A ubiquitous chain that soon becomes a recurring part of our friendship; a constant. On that first day there are other choices, but Costa's there, safe, reliable, consistent – and, even with the morning bustle, there are tables available. The central heating feels hot on my face after the cold of the park. We take cold bottles of freshly squeezed orange juice from the chiller.

'I'm going to have a muffin, too,' Anna says. 'I've earned it. Oh my god, look at that one. Is that crumble on top?'

She asks for the muffin at the counter then turns to me.

'What I'm really craving is a milkshake, only I don't think you're supposed to have them when you're pregnant. I don't know if it's an old wives' thing or true – I read it in a Facebook mums-to-be group. Something to do with soft-scoop ice cream, I think.'

'Wow, I didn't know that. There's so much to learn, isn't there?'

'You can say that again. I'd be lost without those pregnancy groups. Fountains of knowledge, they are.'

'Yeah. I'm on a couple, too. There's always someone, somewhere, who's just been through what you're about to go through, isn't there?'

'Have you ever tried those mothers' morning things?' Anna asks as we move over to a table. 'You know, ones you see in the cafés?'

'Oh, yes. I did give one a try.' I give her a flat smile and widen my eyes, trying to look terrified. 'Have you been to one?'

'No. Why are you looking like that? What happened?'

I laugh. 'It wasn't my thing. Let's just say that. Twenty women all pushing their opinions on everyone else. Everyone's better than the next person; everyone's got to get one up on the next person. God, they're so judgemental. You can count me out of that. I'd rather jump into a tank of piranhas!' While I talk, Anna slices into the muffin and sets it up for a photo.

'Yeah, same,' she says as she holds the camera above the muffin and takes the picture. 'Sorry. Instagram. Just a sec.'

'It's okay. I'm just as bad.'

I check my phone while she fiddles with her photo then she puts her phone down and leans back in her seat, her attention once more on me.

'There, done. I can relax now. What were you saying?'

'Umm . . . oh yeah, the online forums? They work better for me. You can ignore people there if they're too annoying. Though, bar the odd one or two, they're generally a helpful and supportive bunch. I got into it when I was trying to conceive. There are so many support groups for that.'

'Did you have problems?'

I sigh. 'Not as such. I got pregnant all right: keeping them in was the problem.'

'I'm sorry,' Anna says.

'It's okay. But I did become a little obsessed for a while when I thought it would never happen.' I pat my belly. 'But we're here now, aren't we? And that's all that matters.'

'I had the opposite. This bubba wasn't planned, if I'm honest. My husband – Rob – he works in Qatar.' She pauses. 'I'm not really sure how it happened.' She puts her fingertip into a little puddle of condensation that's dripped off her juice bottle, and traces out the letter 'R' with her nail. Then she looks up at me and smiles. 'But it is what it is, I guess.'

'You can say that again.'

We smile, no words needed, as the gossamer veil of friendship falls over us, swathes us, binds us.

'How often does Rob come home?' I ask, trying out the name on my tongue; a name I hope will soon be rolling off it: Anna 'n' Rob', Rob 'n' Anna – maybe our new best friends.

'He tries to come for a few days every four to six weeks but it's not always possible, and the flights aren't cheap. You can't EasyJet back from Qatar.' She smiles.

'It can't be easy. Especially pregnant.'

She sighs. 'It has its pros and cons. And I take bump photos for him – you know, to show him how it's going; keep him feeling connected.'

'That's nice,' I say. 'What a lovely idea. You're not planning to move there yourself?'

She gives me a look that says 'over my dead body'. 'No point,' she says. 'It's only a one-year contract.'

'Fair enough.'

There's a silence for a minute and I take a sip of juice, wondering what to talk about next. I don't want her to think I'm boring. I'm worrying about this when Anna speaks again.

'So, you seem to have made a friend.'

'What?'

'That bloke you walked with? He seems to like you.'

'Simon?'

'You don't half attract them.'

I squint at her. 'What do you mean?'

'Puppy-dog eyes.' Anna takes a sip of orange juice, raising an eyebrow at me as she does.

'What? The guy's pushing fifty and lives with his father.'

'Doesn't mean he can't have puppy-dog eyes,' Anna says.

'I'm pregnant!'

'It floats some people's boats.' She's laughing at me now. The pair of us are laughing like real friends and I love it.

I tut. 'Oh stop, that's disgusting.'

'Ooh,' says Anna, holding out both hands in front of her, fingers splayed, and licks her lips, 'I love pregnant bellies . . . can I have a feel?'

'Shut *up!*' I ball up a napkin and throw it at her and we both laugh.

'Do you ever get that?' she asks. 'People asking to feel your belly?'

'Yeah, sometimes. And they can F right off or I'll put their feely fingers where the sun don't shine,' I say in a London accent.

Anna laughs, then finishes her juice and pushes the cup to the side. 'Right,' she says, 'It's been lovely chatting but I guess I really should get going. There's a mountain of work at home with my name on it.'

She sees my surprise and I kick myself for assuming that everyone who walks in the park in the daytime doesn't work.

'What do you do?'

'I'm an indexer and proofreader. I do a bit of copy-editing, too. Freelance stuff. Maybe write the odd bit of below-the-line copy for advertising.'

'Wow. It must be nice to be able to work from home. I'd love that. It's the perfect solution.'

In my head, a little movie plays of me dandling the baby in one hand while knocking off some professional paid job on a fancy laptop, and it's at this point that I realize that it doesn't have to be flying or nothing. That if I worked, I'd meet people; have colleagues, friends. I'd be valued for doing more than keeping house. Suddenly I'm flooded with the feeling that the world's my oyster; that I could retrain to do anything I like.

'Is there something you could do at home?' Anna asks as if she's followed my train of thought.

My brain moves at lightning speed: Anna's recently moved . . . I wonder if she needs some help. 'I like interior design,' I say carefully. 'Maybe I could get a qualification or something, and give that a try?'

'Fantastic.' Anna laughs. 'God, I could really do with an interior designer right now.'

Bingo. 'Really?'

'Bloody hell, yes,' Anna says. 'Getting the house sorted is driving me crazy. I don't have a clue with stuff like that. Where to put things, how to pull everything together. It's like I'm interiors-dyslexic. Rob's not bad but he's obviously not here.'

'I could help you if you like.' I smile, trying not to look too keen. 'It'd be great experience.'

'Could you really?' Anna looks so happy.

'Yes!' I say. 'I'd love to. Honestly.'

'Okay,' she shrugs. 'If you're sure, why don't you come over on Friday?' She names a street. 'Give me your number and I'll message to confirm.'

I give myself a mental high-five: nicely done, Tay. Nicely done.

I KNOW HOW YOU MET

On a flight. Because it had to be something different, didn't it? Something special.

New York to London. BA176. Thirty-one flights a day to choose from and you end up on the same one; not just on the same flight, but sat next to him.

It must be fate. How sweet.

Six hours and fifty-five minutes. Neither of you can sleep. A couple of movies? A drink or two. Something to eat. Is it long enough to get to know someone? To fall in love?

I know, I know – but he thinks it is.

From the moment you sit down, he's captivated.

He's so easy, he makes me want to puke. I can see it now. The way you slip your neat little arse into the seat. What are you wearing? Skinny jeans maybe. Flat pumps. A t-shirt showing off your tits. Hair tied up. Lip gloss. You have a pashmina: *of course* you have a pashmina, an expensive one at that. You wriggle yourself back in your seat, look for the seat belt and touch his hand by accident. 'Sorry!' You smile at him – and him, he's such a sucker.

'Hey,' he says. He nods and gurns a smile like a puppet and you giggle. Does he give you that line about being a nervous flyer? Is that why you tell him how much you fly? He picks up the safety card from the seat pocket and says something really dumb like,

'Bet you know this off by heart!' and you laugh and say, 'Actually, I wrote it.' 'Really?' he asks and you laugh, like – you really believed that?

He'd believe anything that comes out of your mouth.

He hams it up during take-off, acting out the charade that he's scared of flying. Little do you know that he probably flies as much as you do. But he thinks it's cute the way you put your hand on his arm and tell him it'll be okay, and that's all that matters, isn't it?

You order drinks: a beer and a juice. Neither of you plugs in your headphones – you play with the wire of your headphones in your lap: shall I/shan't I? But he makes small talk, doesn't he? Where are you from? What took you to New York? Why are you going to London? The food comes; he orders another round of drinks.

You talk the whole flight. I can hear your voices in my head: his deep and smooth, quiet and confident; yours giggly, flirtatious, reeling him in like an open-mouthed fish in the quiet darkness of the cabin. 'It's as if I've known you forever.' 'How amazing that we ended up on the same flight!' 'It was meant to be!' 'Serendipity!'

Spare me the crap.

As the plane taxis to the stand, he touches your hand. 'Can I ask for your number? It'd be cool to stay in touch; meet up when we're both in the same town.'

Because you're both such glamorous jet-setters.

You encourage him. Don't play the innocent here. 'I suppose it's fair enough now we've spent a night together!' you say. Giggle, giggle.

But he can't tear himself away from you. You walk through the airport: through immigration, baggage reclaim together and then you're by the doors and at the front of the taxi queue and the taxi's waiting and the cars all around are honking and he does it, he only goes ahead and does it: he bends his head down and kisses you with his disgusting overnight-flight morning breath.

He does, doesn't he?

I knew it. It's almost as if I was there.

6

When I get home, I go straight to Instagram: I want to see how Anna's muffin shot turned out. It's good, but what I love most is what she's written underneath it: '#post-walktreat #walkinggroup #newfriends'. I'm so pleased I take a screenshot – I don't know why, but somehow I just want to keep it forever.

I scroll through her account again and get an idea. Every week she posts a picture of her growing bump – presumably they're the shots she takes for Rob. I save each of them to my phone and use another app to create a collage showing how she's grown. I think she'd find it interesting to see the photos together – like a timelapse – and I imagine the two of us giggling as I show it to her; her laughing with her hand over her mouth; her saying, 'Oh my god, that's amazing! How did you do this? Can you send it to me?'

I make a sandwich for lunch and take a look through Anna's Tweets while I eat. She tends mainly to Retweet, but still I scroll, searching for the jewels among the dross, and I find a few more clues to who she is: she's not a fan of Donald Trump; she hopes everyone's okay after the hurricane; she absolutely loves white-knuckle rides; she really enjoyed *The Girl on the Train*. I note them down on my phone: things for us to talk about.

I go back to Facebook and am about to send her a Facebook

friend request when I stop myself. We've had a coffee. We've agreed I'll help with her interior design: I should probably wait till we've spent a bit more time together. I get up and stretch, shake out my legs, and roll my shoulders as I realize that all the while I've been hunched over my phone the day's tipping fast towards evening. My phone battery needs recharging, as does my own. But Anna still hasn't messaged to confirm our plan for Friday. I sigh and head to the kitchen to make a cup of tea. This waiting around for a message feels like the beginning of a love affair, all that wondering: was I too forward? Doesn't she like me as much as I like her? Did I say something wrong?

Why hasn't she messaged?

I potter about the house, unable to settle, and the potential friendship waxes and wanes inside my head in a rollercoaster of emotions. I try to put the blame on Anna: maybe the invitation to help out with her house was just empty words. Maybe she's flaky – one of those people who never follows through on what she says. God knows, I've met enough of them over the years.

But then I feel guilty for maligning Anna before I even know her that well. She seems really nice, and I'm a good judge of character. There was a time I saved a teenager from being trafficked on a flight from San Diego, all because I'd got a feeling that something wasn't right about the man she was with. My instinct's usually right. *Oh, come on,* I tell myself. *Have some faith!* Maybe her husband suddenly managed to get back for the weekend; maybe she's busy with work; maybe she's got pregnancy brain and simply forgot.

But still, I can't help but think about the girlie day we might have had. I can't stop picturing it: the two of us chatting and laughing as we slide furniture about and try out different positions for mirrors, tables and drawers. Maybe we'd have gone out for lunch, or shared a pizza after a hard day's work; taken a few fun pictures of the process. God knows, it would be nice to have something interesting to put on Facebook after so long.

Looking back, I have to remind myself of how I waited to hear from Anna; of the negative thoughts I entertained about her. It's almost funny now to think I thought she might not have meant what she said; that I was worried she might not message me. I soon learned that she's one of the most determined people on the planet, and that, once she sets a course, she sticks with it. It's actually very admirable.

* * *

I decide to get some air. Without questioning myself, I put on my coat and slip out of the house. I have no conscious plan in my head but my feet take me, as I suspected they might, towards the street that Anna had named.

I slow down once I reach the road and take my time as I look over each property: they're all the same type. I walk on down the road until I see, parked at the kerb, a car just like hers. It's outside a house that has a broken 'rented' board lying in the garden. It has to be it. I lift my chin and walk on past, trying to look purposeful while squinting with my peripheral vision to see as much as I can from the front of the house, both hoping and not hoping that Anna will see me walking past. Would it look odd to be walking down the street she named? I could just be out for a walk, or on my way to the bus stop. It would be perfectly reasonable. I get to the top of the street, turn left into another road, walk for a minute or two, then turn around and head back, watching Anna's house every step of the way as I near it. I can still see it, imprinted on my memory. Without thinking about it, I let myself in through a gate that doesn't sit properly on its hinges, walk up to the door and knock.

I wait, heart hammering, wondering what I'll say if she does open the door – and what I'll say if it's not her house – but nothing happens. There's not a sound from inside, but then I hear steps – fast, urgent – on the pavement behind me and I spin around, guilty, caught red-handed, but it's a just a woman in a black coat, rushing past without giving me a second look. I knock again. Nothing.

Braver then, I step back and look up at the windows. All I can see is the reflection of the sky and the houses across the street. Her car's outside. Where is she? Then I catch myself. What am I doing? I turn back and walk quickly towards the nearby parade of shops, telling myself I'm looking for somewhere we could grab some lunch the next day.

*   *   *

Back home, I decide to do something constructive. Proactive, that's me. I log on to Pinterest and go through my favourite interior-design websites, looking at the latest trends and getting some fresh ideas. I think about what Anna's interiors style might be: neutrals, brights, shabby, Scandi, modern, contemporary, country? I hope it's not country – I was never a fan of oak – not then, and not now. Jake and I gravitated towards a coastal, New England style in those days. Well, he didn't really mind what we did, to be fair, but, on arriving in England, I'd tried to recreate something reminiscent of the Nantucket holiday homes I'd stayed in as a child, though it was by no means as convincing to reproduce that feeling in a damp Victorian terrace in the cold northern-European light. Still, I tried, and what we had in the Croydon house was definitely a nod to New England: plenty of white, with lots of clean, sleek lines that some-how, just about, managed to transform the long, narrow space into something other than the sum of its parts.

If I had to guess, I'd put Anna down as 'eclectic' – from what I can see on her Instagram, that's the most likely. Or maybe she doesn't have a style at all. Not everyone does. I wonder if she'll let me take her under my wing; introduce her to my favourite brands; show her how to pull together a look with just a few small pur-chases. Girlie shopping trips with stops for coffee and cake. I don't ask for a lot.

At six, she still hasn't messaged to confirm and I'm antsy with not-knowing. 'Come on!' I say to my phone, giving it a shake. I flop onto the sofa with a sigh, click on the television and aimlessly watch a property show. About a year later, it just so happens that I catch the same one on repeat, and the sight of those elderly Brits humming and hawing over houses they were being shown in Florida brings back the misery of that afternoon like a slap. But then, on that December day, with no idea of how events would play out, I simply enjoy the show for what it is. I know the Sunshine State like the back of my hand and just looking at those neat and tidy houses with their lanais over their pools and their green gardens backing onto lakes ('No swimming! Alligators!') brings back the scent of the hot vegetation, the prick of the mosquitoes, and the damp glistening of humidity on my skin. I lose myself in the show for a while, absorbing the sense of sunshine, warmth and belonging that I crave so badly. Only when the show finishes do I take a deep breath and send Anna a private message on Facebook, aware as I do so that it'll probably go into her 'message requests' folder rather than her inbox as we're not connected. Still, I feel as if I've done something, and that makes me feel better.

I wait a bit more and, when it becomes apparent that Anna hasn't even seen the message, I put the phone on the table to charge again. *Fine,* I tell myself. *It's not happening.* I'll find something else to do in the morning. Again, the feeling of empty blackness takes me over, oozing through my veins as if it's trying to extinguish me.

Ping.

I leap over to the phone. It's her.

'Hey.' Smiley face. 'Sorry. It's taken longer than I thought to finish what I was doing. Can you come on Saturday instead?'

Even though I've primed myself for this, I slump against the table. Why keep me waiting all this time and then postpone? All of a sudden, I'm tired, so very tired. Tired of having no friends; tired of trying to meet new people; tired of Croydon, of England, of being on my own; and physically tired from the pregnancy I seem to be handling all alone. With a sudden flash of anger, I type 'Sorry, I'm busy,' and it feels good, it feels so good, but then I delete it, and am instantly glad I do because my phone pings again.

'Can u come around 10? We could have lunch. My treat,' Anna's written, and I smile.

'Sure,' I type. 'I'll bring the coffee.'

Anna sends her address – as if I don't know – and I sink back against the sofa cushions with relief. Finally.

7

I wonder sometimes why I remember so much detail about this period of my life. But I know, really, that it's because I've been over it so many times in my head, for myself more than for the police. I can remember everything from what the weather felt like to which clothes, shoes and accessories – now long-gone – I had in my wardrobe. I remember what beauty products I was into back then, and which shampoo I used – but the perfume is worst. To this day, if I'm walking through a department store and I catch a smell of the perfume I used to wear in those days, it can stop me in my tracks, triggering a wave of emotion that almost knocks me off my feet. The first time it happened, I had to be helped to a makeup counter stool; brought a glass of water; fussed over. I'm more careful these days: I enter department stores through 'Menswear', 'Footwear', or 'Home' if I can. If not, I hold my breath.

My alarm goes off at eight the Saturday I'm meeting up with Anna. I've allowed myself half an hour to lie in bed before I get up, like I usually do, but I'm wide awake the moment it rings. It's the first Saturday in forever that I have a concrete plan involving someone other than Jake and, while I don't want to get to Anna's too early, I simply can't wait for the day to start. It's like waking on Christmas morning as a kid. I get up, shower and put on the clothes I'd spent half of the previous day choosing, then I make a big bowl of porridge and eat it slowly while I check Anna's Instagram. She's added a new image: an inspirational quote about new beginnings, and I wonder if she's referring to me – to our blossoming friendship – but then I realize it's far more likely about the sorting out of her house. My finger hesitates over the 'like' button but I don't press it in the end – it'd look odd, wouldn't it, given I'm not actually following her?

Finally, finally, finally when it's 9.50, I gather my things and leave the house. Despite being full up to my eyeballs with porridge, I don't want to turn up empty-handed so I go via a coffee shop, where I pick up some treats and a couple of decaf skinny cappuccinos. It's an investment, I remember thinking. An investment in our friendship.

As luck would have it, on the day I have time to kill, I'm served quickly and, by the time I walk out, it's on the dot of ten. I figure a few minutes late is perfect as I don't want to look too keen, so I walk really slowly to Anna's. It's not easy – even then, even heavy with the baby. I've always been a fast mover, a no-nonsense walker whose life mission seems to be to get from A to B as efficiently as possible. Flying was an obvious career choice to me. Walking slowly reminds me of the slow-bicycle races of my childhood, when the bike's going so slowly it's practically falling over. As I turn into Anna's street I check my watch: the hands are spread wide like they're holding a yoga pose – 10.10 – so I walk up to the front door of her house, ring the doorbell and step back, suddenly, after all the build-up, a bag of nerves. I clear my throat and fluff my hair, put down the bag of treats, then pick it up again, run my hands though my hair again, and then I hear a bolt shoot, then another, then a key turns and the door opens. Anna's in skinny jeans, a blue sweatshirt and socks. Her hair's scraped back in a messy ponytail, and she looks pleased to see me. I think of her Instagram post '#newfriends'.

'Morning!' she says in that English way that still makes me smile. 'Come in!'

She opens the door wider and, as I cross over the threshold, the first thing that hits me is the musty smell of an unloved building, and I feel sorry for her having to live somewhere so beaten. Already I'm mentally in there, opening the windows, flushing fresh air through the place, and positioning scented oil burners and reed diffusers in each room. Sometimes even now I catch that smell in a building and, if I shut my eyes, I'm back there, standing in Anna's hallway, the coffee and croissants in my hands.

'I'm sorry it's a mess,' Anna says, motioning to a pile of junk mail and free newspapers in the corner. The wallpaper's faded and peeling; a painted wall dirty with the scuffs of a family long gone. No wonder she didn't put this on Instagram.

'Understandably!' I say. 'You haven't been here that long. It took me weeks to get through all my boxes.'

'Almost. There are still a few.' She shrugs. 'You know how it is. We don't have a lot of stuff, to be honest, but there's also not a lot of storage, so I've been agonizing over where to put everything.'

'Tell me about it. Why do these places not have basements?'

'Wouldn't that be amazing?' Anna leads me into the front room, which I'm gratified to see is a knocked-through lounge-diner like mine. The furniture's been placed, but badly, and there are still a couple of packing boxes in the corner – I recognize them from her Instagram and smile to myself. Already I'm assessing what I can do to make the room look better.

'Most of the furniture's in the right rooms, I think,' Anna says, 'but it's just making it homely that I need help with. I've never been good at positioning things.' Anna pauses, then waves her hand at the room. 'So what do you think? Be honest.'

'It's nice,' I say, 'but we can make it better. Oh, I brought coffee, by the way. Decaf, of course.' I carefully extract the two coffees, put them on the table and hand the bag to Anna. 'And some chocolate croissants. To keep our energy up.'

'Ooh. I'll get a plate.' Anna disappears off towards the kitchen and I have a better look around. Like the hallway outside, the room has rather knackered stripped floorboards. A tatty red sofa dominates a mish-mash of a room. I narrow my eyes and try to reshuffle the furniture in my head; what would go where; what would fit where, then Anna's back with the croissants on a plate.

'Thanks,' she says, 'they look delish.'

'You're so welcome.' I rub my hands together. 'Right, shall we start with your dining table? Is that where you want it?'

Anna sighs. 'I don't know.'

I purse my lips to make it look like I'm thinking when clearly it's a no-brainer. 'Well, if it's of any help at all,' I say, 'I have a similar layout and I've played around with it a *lot*.'

'Oh wow,' Anna says. 'Same house?'

'No. Same living area but we have the extra room downstairs which I don't think you do? Shall I show you what I've done? I shan't be offended if you don't like it.'

'Really? That would be fantastic.'

'It's no problem,' I say. 'Right. So, I have the dining table in this section, closest to the kitchen, so you can separate out a food/eating area.' I look at Anna and wonder if, like me, she ends up eating dinner on her lap in front of the television when her husband's away – or skipping dinner because cooking for one's such a depressing activity – but she nods.

'Okay.'

'Then the sofa really looks like it should go there,' I say, pointing where it currently is, 'and I had mine there for, like, forever but if it's there the light from the window means you always have to close the curtains to watch TV. Not an issue if you only watch it at night, but if you're partial to a little daytime TV – though you probably aren't since you work,' I look at Anna, suddenly embarrassed, 'then it's better to put the sofa here.' I point to the mid-section of the long room. 'You can create a divide if you put the bookcase behind it so it backs onto it. What do you think?'

Anna's shaking her head with a big smile on her face. 'It sounds amazing. Shall we give it a go?'

8

'What do you think?' I ask when we've finished moving the furniture. I'm standing with my hands on my hips, still slightly out of breath from all the exertion, and instinctively I arch my back gently, my hand on my bump, to stretch it out. It's odd to see a room that looks like ours, with furniture in the same position as ours, but with such different pieces. Nothing of Anna and Rob's actually matches; there's no unifying theme. A lot of it looks like it might have come from second-hand shops or have been passed down from friends or family. It's not a problem, though. If Anna wants, I can easily pull it together with soft furnishings and accessories.

'It's awkward because it's such a long, thin room,' I say, 'but it works like this. If you want it even more streamlined and can stretch to it, a flat-screen TV fixed to the wall will save you floor space. We have one. It just means the room's less cluttered.' I look around for my coffee and take a sip, grimace and put it back down.

'Gone cold?' Anna asks. 'Can I get you anything else?'

'Some water would be great, thanks.' I flop onto the sofa, suddenly aware of how physically worn out I am. It's only half eleven – too early for lunch – but I don't want the day to end now. I'm looking forward to going out for lunch with her.

'Do you want me to help with anything else?' I ask when Anna returns with the water.

'Umm.' She frowns. 'I know. Could you help me decide where to put my pictures? I think they're in this box . . .' She opens a box and pulls out three or four framed prints. They're pretty nondescript and I'm kicking myself for being a snob about them when Anna sighs. She's holding one out at arm's length. It's a stylized picture of some colourful flowers that I know was from Ikea ten or more years ago.

'I don't know,' Anna says. 'They're a bit tired, aren't they? We've had them for years. They were mine before we got married. Maybe it's time for something new.'

'It's up to you.' I pause, aware that I mustn't come across as desperate. 'The sales are on at the moment . . .' I cock my head. 'If you fancy doing a bit of shopping, I'd be happy to come and help you choose?'

Anna smiles. 'Really? You wouldn't mind?'

'Absolutely! I love shopping. Even better when it's not my money! When do you want to go? This afternoon?' She looks taken aback and I suddenly think I've been too forward. 'Unless you have something planned?'

'No. I . . . no, that's fine.'

'Okay. Great!' Lunch! Shopping! 'So,' I rub my hands together. 'What about upstairs? Do you need any help there?'

She hesitates for a beat, which stretches, then she says, 'Sure. Come and have a look.'

I follow Anna up the narrow stairs. The master bedrooms aren't big in these houses but Anna and Rob's seems more spacious than ours. It takes me a minute to figure out why: our king-sized bed takes up most of the available floor space, but Anna's standard double leaves more carpet space. Apart from two small bedside tables, it's the only piece of furniture in the room.

'It's the same as mine,' I tell her. 'If you just turn the bed this way . . .' I mime it with my arms, 'then you'll open up this area, which means you get better access to the wardrobes and can use this area here. Shall we?'

Pushing and pulling, we move the bed and stand back, pleased with our work.

'It looks great. Thank you,' Anna says. She follows my eyes, which are looking at a photo on the bedside table. It's of her and the man I saw on Instagram.

'Is that Rob?' I ask.

She picks it up and hands it to me. Anna looks a lot younger and her hair's a few shades darker.

'That was when we first got together,' she says.

'Aww, you look good together.'

'I hope he likes the house,' Anna says, taking the picture back. 'He hasn't seen it yet. There's not a lot of storage space. I tried to get his stuff in here but it's a bit of a squash.' She opens the wardrobe door. 'I've had to give him a load of the hanging space for his shirts. Good job I don't like dresses!'

'I know,' I say. 'It's brutal.'

I step out onto the landing where there's another door. I put my hand on the knob. 'Is this the . . . ?' I raise my eyebrows, remembering the picture of the white cot she'd put on Instagram hashtagged '#wishlist'.

'Yes. But I'm not showing anyone.' She puts her hand on her bump. 'I don't want to jinx anything.'

'I get that. Completely. I was the same. Nothing until the baby's completely viable, right?'

She smiles at me. 'Exactly. Rob thinks I'm superstitious,' Anna says, 'but still.' We go down the stairs to the hallway, where we stand awkwardly for a moment, then she pulls her phone out of her pocket.

'Oh no,' she says, looking at the screen. 'I know we talked about lunch but some urgent work's come up. I'm not going to be able to make it after all.' She looks up at me with an apologetic smile. 'Why don't we postpone lunch to Monday? Do the shopping then? My treat.'

The empty day suddenly yawns ahead of me and there it is: the blackness that's been kept at bay all morning. It trickles coldly around my heart, trying to find a way in, but I push it back.

'Sure,' I say, forcing a smile. Then I have an idea. I look over Anna's shoulder back into the living room. 'Do you mind if I just take a few pictures? I'll have a think about what'll bring the room together so when we go shopping we don't make any mistakes. Would that be okay?'

Anna waves at the room. 'Help yourself.'

I take a couple of quick pictures of the living space, feeling a bit odd as I do so. Her tone makes me feel as if I may have overstepped the mark by asking.

'Right, I'll have a think what we can do,' I say, slipping my phone back in the bag. 'See you on Monday.'

'Have a great weekend,' Anna says.

'You too.' Already I'm wondering what she's going to be doing all by herself over the weekend. She must be busy with work. I think of my phone with the images of her front room on it. Well, that makes two of us.

I KNOW WHERE YOU WENT
ON YOUR FIRST DATE

It couldn't have been more Disney if he'd tried. It couldn't have been more of a cliché; wouldn't surprise me if he flew over specially when he heard you were in New York.

The Rockerfeller Center, New York City, December.

'You are assured magical memories that you will cherish forever,' says the website. Ten out of ten for the perfect date. A public space, nothing too pushy, nothing presumptuous, a little fun, and the potential to go out for a drink afterwards, should it go well.

As if it won't go well.

'Meet me at the Rock,' he says. 'Dress warmly.'

And, of course you wonder if he's taking you skating. Why else would he want to meet at the Rockerfeller Center in the weeks before Christmas? Does he know you can skate? I doubt it, because he hasn't done his research, has he? Not like I have. He imagines you clinging to him; him holding you up as he sweeps you around the rink: manly, strong. Could there be a more perfect first date?

And I have to give it to you: you look adorable. Just the right note of sweet and vulnerable and sexy all wrapped up in black leggings and a longline twinset of cashmere sweaters in the palest of shell pinks, with a scarf and gloves, your cheeks rosy with cold and your hair flying. Yes, the rink's smaller than he thought, not as glamorous – not quite the setting he'd imagined from the movies – but it doesn't matter. The lights in the adjacent skyscrapers twinkle as dusk falls and he sweeps out onto the ice in the shadow of the enormous Christmas tree.

But you: you hang back. Of course you do. You watch as he demonstrates skating forwards, a wobbly turn, backwards, another turn, a bit of speed and then a show-off hockey stop that showers you in a spray of ice crystals.

'Come on!' he says as you stand beside the ice. 'Don't be scared! It's easier than you think. I'll look after you!'

And then you step onto the ice, not at all like Bambi: like an Olympic figure-skating champion. You laugh, and then you're off around the rink, fast, graceful, confident, your hair flying out behind you while he picks his jaw up off the ice. You do a high-speed turn, your hair whooshing into your face, then you look back at him and laugh again as you launch into a leap, a spin, and then a beautifully executed salchow. I know you do it again because he gets a photo this time. It's there, on Instagram: your silhouette in mid-air looking every inch the ice princess. You're so proud of that picture, aren't you? You roll it out regularly for Instagram's #throwbackthursday. Eight times, so far.

'I *love* skating!' you call, and he ploughs over towards you, conscious only now of how unrefined his own moves are. But it doesn't matter. He's made you happy. 'I've always wanted to skate here!' you say, catching his hand and squeezing it. 'It's a dream come true!'

But is that the moment that seals it? Is it as simple as him booking two general-admission tickets to this tourist-trap of a rink?

I believe it is. By the end of the session, he knows he wants to marry you.

It's enough to make me puke.

9

It's a measure of how involved I am in creating the mood boards that I don't hear the car pull up outside the house. Neither do I hear the sound of Jake's key in the lock and the opening and closing of the front door. If the skin on the back of my neck does that animalistic prickle to warn me he's about to arrive home, I miss it – not even my famous sixth sense picks up the fact that my husband's home and quite likely shrugging off his jacket in the hallway. It's Saturday evening and I'm at the desk, lost in Pinterest images. I'm staring at the screen, click-clicking till my wrist aches as I gather images and send them to a printer that's constantly whirring into life with a rattle so alarming it makes me think, every time, that it's about to die. *Please don't die!*

The whole desk's under siege: I've got a little production line going. On the other side of the table from the computer, I gather the images together, cut them to size with a metal ruler and scalpel, and then I laminate them and move them to a piece of A1 foam board on which I'm collating the look I think will work best for Anna. It's a strong, eclectic style, which I hope she'll like because I've used the colours that I know she likes – the red of the sofa as well as the blue of the sweatshirt she was wearing – and I've used some rich yellow to lift it. It's a triadic colour scheme that looks global, and I think it really works as the yellow pulls in all the random items and makes the whole room look more styled.

I've also got a smaller board on the go with an image of my own living/dining room at the centre – the images surrounding that are all in calming blues and whites. I can't imagine it's Anna's taste, really, but I want to show her what could be done should she wish to invest in more of a change. But the main thing, I think as I tap my lip with my finger and switch a couple of images around on the triadic mood board, is that Anna's pleased with what I've done. I really want to impress her; I want her to think I'm an expert; to give her a reason to look up to me, to respect me and, of course, to want to spend more time with me.

I swap the position of a couple of the images, step back to view my masterpiece, and nod to myself. Only now will I start fastening the images in place. I pick up my StudioTac then let out a yelp as Jake throws his keys onto the desk next to me and kisses the top of my head.

'Oh my god!' I fan my face, faking a faint. 'You nearly gave me a heart attack!'

'That's a nice welcome from my wife after a lonely week on the road,' Jake says. 'Sorry. I thought you'd heard me and were deliberately ignoring me . . . Unless you were giving your lover time to escape out the back?'

The question hangs a moment too long and irritation flares in me before I'm able to beat it back down. How dare he?

Jake holds his hands up. 'Sorry. Unfair. Let's start again. How was your day, sweet wife of mine?'

I take a deep breath in and out to clear any residual anger. 'Busy, dear husband,' I say. 'I was lost in . . .' I wave my hand at the table. 'I'm making a mood board for Anna.'

'Lipstick lady?' It takes me a minute to realize he means Sarah.

'No. This is my friend from the walking group.'

'Oh, good.' Jake loosens his tie, slips it off and hangs it over the back of a dining chair.

'She's really nice *and* she lives just around the corner. You'd like her.'

'I look forward to meeting her.' There's a pause, then Jakes finally asks how the baby is.

'Coming along nicely.' I pat my belly. 'How are you? Good week?'

'Awesome,' says Jake, rolling his eyes. 'Training idiots. God, you would think they would have to have some aptitude for or interest in the job before they were hired, wouldn't you? Come on, let's sit down. I'm parched.'

Jake gets a couple of cold drinks and pats the sofa next to him. I sit down so our bodies are touching.

'So what are you doing for this Anna woman?' Jake asks. 'Doing up her house?'

'Sort of. She's quite new in her house and has no idea about furnishings, so she asked me to help. Her husband works in the Middle East. Qatar, I think she said. Or somewhere like that. He hasn't even seen the house, and she wants it to be nice for him.'

Jake nods. 'Yes, I can imagine he doesn't make it home most nights.'

'You can say that again.'

'So you're doing her interior design for free – lucky girl.' There's an edge to his voice. It's just how he is: every minute of his time is charged to one client or another. He's not used to doing things for free.

I tut. 'I'm just trying to make friends. And maybe, if I'm good at it, it's something I could turn into a business.'

'Sure,' he says. 'I'm not knocking it.'

We sit in silence for a moment, then Jake says, 'Maybe we could have them over for dinner one night when the husband's back. What do you think?'

'Good idea. I've no idea when he's back, though. She made it sound like he's hardly ever home.'

'Oh well. Bear it in mind.'

'I will.' I close my eyes and sigh, thinking about the loneliness;

the talking to myself; the constant fight to stop the blackness from taking me over; and the wretched ways in which I'd tried to make friends when we first arrived. Jake doesn't know but I used to go to the Greek deli and buy things I'd never eat – tubs of olives and feta – just because the woman behind the counter seemed nice and I'd thought maybe we could become friends. The thought of it now makes me cringe. Had I really been so desperate? But as I sat there on the sofa that night, I sensed that things were changing. This was the beginning of a new chapter. I'd got a friend, and no way was I going to let her go.

10

'm at the station at bang on ten on Monday morning, ready to catch the train to Victoria with Anna. It's a blustery day and I sweep into the ticket hall, slightly out of breath from having had to walk into a strong headwind, my coat and scarf flying out behind me. I know at once, even before I've scanned all the people in the ticket office, that Anna isn't there. My heart shrinks with disappointment.

There are three sets of people waiting, so I join the end of the line and start stressing immediately about whether or not I should buy Anna's ticket to save time, or wait to see if she actually turns up. It's not my best trait, but I get quite anal about tardiness. The first couple in the queue leaves the counter, putting their tickets and purses back in huge handbags, and we all shuffle forward. I want to believe the best of Anna, but it wouldn't be the first time she's postponed an arrangement we've had. In fact, when I think about it, which I try not to but feel I have to, Anna's delayed every single plan she's made with me: the packing day, the lunch, the shopping day. Not cancelled – delayed. *You're being too sensitive,* I tell myself, and shuffle another step closer to the ticket counter.

Too quickly it's my turn and, until the words actually come out of my mouth, I honestly don't know how many tickets I'm going to ask for.

'Two one-day travelcards, please,' I say and, right as I'm wondering if I've just made an expensive mistake, Anna bursts into the ticket hall and rushes up to me, pulling her wallet out of her bag as she reaches the counter.

'How much is it?' She whacks a twenty-pound note on the counter and I almost throw up with relief, not because of the money, but because Anna's actually turned up. I knew she would!

'Hey! Morning!' I say, then I do a double-take as I see what she's wearing. 'Oh my god!' I laugh. 'You've got my coat! I swear I didn't copy you!' I laugh to show I'm joking.

But Anna frowns as she looks at her coat and then at mine. The two couldn't be more different.

'Doh!' I say. 'I'm not wearing it! But I have it at home. I swear it's my favourite!'

Anna smiles and shrugs as she touches the sleeve of her coat. 'I love it, too.'

'Like minds!' We smile brightly at each other. 'Right, ready for a day of shopping?'

'Can't wait,' says Anna. Her cheeks are pink and her hair windswept. She looks pretty and fun and full of life, and I'm so pleased to be standing here with her in this moment. So proud to be her friend.

We pass through the ticket barriers and onto the platform. 'I've got something to show you,' I say. I'm so full of the joy of giving and sharing, I feel like it's Christmas Day and I'm about to give a child something really cute and fluffy like a kitten. Anna looks quizzically at me as I get out my phone and click on Photos, then I turn it towards her so she can see the screen.

'Look. It's a mood board I did for you. What do you think?'

'Oh my god. You did this for me?' She takes the phone.

I nod. 'It was too big to carry up to London so I photographed it for you. I'll send it to you so it's on your phone, too.'

'Oh wow.' Anna's enlarging the image and looking at all the different pictures. 'Oh my god, the style looks so . . . "done". It looks amazing. And you think this would be possible to do in my living room?'

I nod again, feeling like Croydon's answer to Kelly Hoppen. 'You have a lot of those colours there already. It's just a matter of getting a few more bits – some cushions, throws et cetera – and some accessories. Easy-peasy. I thought we could start in John Lewis, have a mooch in Zara Home, and maybe pop down to Habitat and Heal's after, if you've got the energy. What do you think?'

'Sounds great,' says Anna. She closes the photo then clicks on another. 'Ooh, is this another one? What's this? Do you mind?'

'Oh that? That's one I did using the colours Jake and I have in our house,' I say. 'I don't know if it's your style . . . We go for a sort of New England look. Coastal, I guess.'

I watch, secretly pleased she's found the other mood board until I remember with a jolt the collage I made of her pregnancy pictures, which suddenly now seems inappropriate. I pretty much snatch my phone back, click it closed and drop it into my bag. She doesn't seem to notice anything peculiar.

'Oh my god, it's gorgeous,' she says, smiling as if she's just seen a holy vision. 'Do you think I could do that?'

'You like it?'

'Yes! I love it! If I had to describe how I want my house to look, that would be it! Can we do the blue one? Please?'

Honestly? I'm surprised. From what she already owns, I didn't have her down as a New England type – but who am I to argue? I'm chuffed to bits she likes my style.

'Sure,' I say. 'It'll mean buying a few more bits, and perhaps covering your sofa and painting some of your wooden pieces, but we can do it. Sure.'

'Thank you, thank you, thank you!' says Anna.

'Look, here's the train now,' I say, looking down the track so Anna doesn't see how much I'm smiling.

* * *

It's nearly five o'clock by the time we get back to Croydon. I don't know about Anna, but I'm exhausted. We're laden down with bags of all shapes, weights and sizes, and my steps, as we head towards Anna's, get slower and slower. The wind's still blowing and it takes all my energy to walk against it with the bags bumping against my legs as if they're on a sadistic mission to trip me up.

'Look at us hunched into the wind like a couple of old ladies,' I say. 'Wow, London's exhausting. That really took it out of me.'

'This wind really doesn't help.'

'At least it's not raining.' I imagine trying to hold up an umbrella as well as carrying so much stuff. 'That would be awful!'

'Dreadful.' She pauses. 'Soon we'll be pushing prams everywhere.'

'I can't even imagine.'

We struggle on in silence until we reach Anna's house.

'Finally!' says Anna, dropping her bags and searching for her keys. 'Can I get you a cup of tea before you head home?'

'Thanks. Just what the doctor ordered.' I follow Anna into her house. The musty smell's still there but I've got a plan. I rummage in one of the bags and pull out an elegantly boxed reed diffuser.

'Ta da!' I say, presenting it to Anna. 'Sorry it's not wrapped, but "happy new home"! Just a little house-warming gift.'

'Oh wow,' says Anna. 'Thank you.'

'I thought you could put it here in the hall, then it'll be the first thing your guests smell when they come in.'

'Great idea,' says Anna. 'I love it. Thank you so much.' But she doesn't unwrap it; she simply puts it down on the hall table and heads into the kitchen to make the tea. I look at it for a moment, then I open it and set it up.

I go through to the kitchen where Anna is putting on the kettle.

'Do you mind if I sit?' I ask as I pull out a dining chair and collapse onto it with a sigh. I slip off my shoes and circle my ankles, then I roll my shoulders in small circles, trying to release some of the tension from all that bag-carrying.

'Make yourself at home,' she says. 'Sugar? Sorry, I've forgotten.'

'No thanks. I'm sweet enough. Oh, by the way,' I say, suddenly remembering, 'Jake and I were wondering if you'd would like to come for dinner one evening when Rob's back in town. What do you think? It was actually Jake's idea!' I laugh, unsure why I want him to get the credit for this.

'That's kind of you, and we'd love to,' Anna says as she pours the water into two mugs, 'but I don't know when Rob's next back. He often can't confirm until a day or so beforehand.'

'Sure. Or maybe you could come on your own? We won't bite.'

'That would be great,' Anna says. 'Maybe a better plan, actually. Rob's usually really tired when he comes back. He often just wants to relax at home, to be honest. Boring old fart that he is.' She smiles. 'Right. Have you got the energy to open some of these bags? I'm dying to see what everything looks like.'

It takes a good hour to arrange things – an hour in which I feel a bit like a magician waving my wand over the house. Anna's face lights up as her living room transforms in front of her eyes. I take a few pictures of my handiwork.

'Right, we just need to get some pictures in those frames and get them up on that wall,' I say as we stand back to survey the room, 'and, if you painted that bookcase white or even a combination of white and maybe a pale, chalky blue, it would make a world of difference. It would come up a treat with some Annie Sloan paint, and it's not difficult to do.'

'I wouldn't know where to start.'

I smile. 'I'm happy to help. Painting furniture's my therapy!'

'You're amazing. It's incredible what a difference you've made,' Anna says, and I seize the chance.

'Would you mind if I put some pictures online? It's the first "project" I've done and it might help me drum up some business if

I decide to do this professionally.' Anna opens her mouth but I interrupt. 'I could tag you, if you like? Or not.'

'Oh, I . . .' Anna begins, then she shrugs. 'Be my guest. As long as I'm not in them.'

'Why not?'

'You never know who's out there,' she says, then laughs. 'I'm not paranoid, I'm just . . .' she frowns as she searches for a word, 'wary.'

She tells me the name of her account, and I type it in as if I don't know it, then click follow. 'Perfect. Done. I'll tag you when I upload them.'

Anna leads me to the door then turns to me. 'Thank you so much.'

'It's a pleasure. So, are you up for the walking group on Wednesday?'

'Yes, sure. See you there.'

'You will do!'

'If Simon doesn't get to you first!' Anna waves from the door. 'Safe journey!'

We both laugh and I'm still smiling to myself as I set off, thinking back over the day. Anna's a good shopping companion, openminded and willing to go along with whatever I suggested; never shy of paying for things, either. I've been shopping with friends who, when it comes to actually making the decision, never actually buy anything – and where's the fun in that?

Later, when everything's happened – a lot later, when the police have bowed out, the dust has settled and life has moved on as it inevitably does – I remember this day with Anna. I remember how happy I was.

I KNOW WHAT YOUR FAVOURITE RESTAURANT IS

Wahaca.

A Mexican chain, where 'the food is fast, fresh and feisty'.

You may deny it – if asked, you'd probably name some fancy place where all the celebs go – but the trail's there, isn't it? Six check-ins in two months. Instagrammed: crispy prawn tacos. Instagrammed: Mexican feast. Instagrammed: *huitlacoche empanadas*. Instagrammed: *ancho* chicken tacos #fresh #streetfood #market-food #lovemexico #clean #authentic. Nom fucking nom.

Oh, you think you're such a foodie. The phrase 'street food' falls out of your mouth like diarrhoea. To listen to you, anyone would think you're the first person to have discovered authentic Mexican food; that you've single-handedly pioneered Wahaca's success; that it's entirely down to you that *Time Out*'s called it London's 'trendiest chain for chatting and chowing down'. You spout off about 'fresh' and 'honest' ingredients to anyone who'll listen. It's like you think you're Deliciously fucking Ella.

But what do you actually do to earn the label of foodie? Did you know the best chefs before they became famous? Do you travel the world seeking them out; do you go to places just to immerse yourself in the food culture? Have you ever travelled rough from Hanoi to Saigon, living hand to mouth and eating the best *op la*, *pho*, and *bun rieu*? That's street food for you, princess. That's being a foodie.

Oh no. You think all you need to do is check-in every time you eat out, and Instagram your food from above, and you think that makes you part of the in-crowd, don't you? One check-in at the Wimbledon branch. Two in Covent Garden – could it be more 'cringe'? Three check-ins on the South Bank.

That's your favourite, isn't it? Those containers in their bright colours overlooking the laconic sludge of the Thames. 'It's so authentic,' you bleat, but you're not lying: your favourite thing in the world is to eat there then walk along the South Bank, watching the street artists, listening to the buskers, watching the boats and pretending you're some kind of trendy London type. It makes me want to puke. Can I tell you something, sweetie-pie? You're no foodie: you're boring. You're pathetic. The only food you are is *fucking vanilla*.

11

Long before I reach the walking group's meeting point, I see her straight blonde hair and bright blue coat sticking out among the sea of browns and olives that ebbs and flows around her. On Instagram, she's posted a collage of shots she took on our shopping trip '#new friends' and I'm on top of the world. I sneak up behind her.

'Do you come here often, young lady?' I say in my creepiest voice. She spins around defensively, almost as if she's going to strike out, then her face softens as she realizes it's me.

'Hey. Morning! No sign of lover-boy today so it looks like you're stuck with me.'

'Oh, I suppose I'll survive!' I say, rolling my eyes to hide how pleased I am that I'll get her to myself.

A few minutes later we set off. The others fall into groups and we tag along near the back of the raggle-taggle string. Anna takes a quick picture of a squirrel that's unusually close to the path.

'Instagram!' she sings, slipping her phone back into her pocket.

'So, how's Rob?' I say, taking deep breaths of the fresh air. It's cold and damp, not really the blue-sky day I'd hoped for, and there's a heavy scent of petrol fumes in the air, but at least it's not raining.

'Fine, I guess. I haven't spoken to him,' says Anna.

I tilt my head. 'Really?'

'It's difficult with the time difference and everything . . .' She shrugs. 'We message. Talk once a week.'

'I guess you're more used to being apart than I am. I'm on the phone with Jake most nights.'

I don't point out that it's him who calls me, and that I suspect it's only to prove that he's not out with a woman. Not that a phone call proves anything, of course, but he doesn't seem to see it that way.

'How long have you guys been married?' Anna asks.

I kick a pile of brown leaves, sending them flying into the air.

'You should never do that,' Anna says. 'There might be hedge-hogs under it.'

I look to see if she's being serious, then apologize, thrown off-balance that I might have upset her.

'No worries,' she says. 'Don't do it again. So, how long have you been married?'

'Two. And together for one before that.'

'Not so long then.'

'How about you and Rob?'

'Seven years married. And you know what they say about that.' Anna rolls her eyes.

'Seven-year itch?' I ask, and she takes a deep breath and lets it out slowly. It surprises me. Young couple, pregnant wife – I'd assumed, I suppose, that their marriage was a garden of roses. But I, of all people, should know that's not necessarily true.

'It's difficult keeping things alive when we're apart so much,' Anna says carefully. 'I only see him for a few nights every four to six weeks. Sometimes it feels as if he spends more time on aero-planes than he does with me. It's a joke I even got pregnant. And now . . .' she exhales. 'Now, I guess I'll be pretty much raising this baby alone.'

'But he'll come home for the birth, won't he? Stick around a bit?'

She shrugs. 'You'd hope so, wouldn't you?' We walk a few steps while I digest this, then Anna speaks again. 'God knows what he gets up to when he's away.' She looks away from me, across the park.

'Surely not a lot? It's Qatar, isn't it?' I'm really out of my depth now but, from what little I've heard about Middle Eastern countries, I imagine Rob's living in some sort of compound with other male members of staff. Segregated from the women. Or is that Saudi Arabia? I'm ashamed how little I know, but it can't be like California, can it, where temptation-in-a-bikini is all around.

Anna sighs. 'I think it's pretty relaxed in the big hotels. They can get alcohol and stuff. There are clubs and bars, and pretty, young cabin crew a-plenty.' She shuts her eyes. 'I just try not to think about it. So how do you and Jake keep it alive while he's away?' she says.

I laugh, thrown off guard by the question. 'I'm hardly the right person to ask.'

'Oh, come on! I need some tips.'

I go to kick another pile of leaves and remember I mustn't. 'I just try to keep him interested, that's all. So he doesn't look elsewhere. But, you know . . . with the baby . . .'

'It's safe, isn't it?'

'Yeah. Course it is. It's just . . .'

Anna smiles. 'I know exactly what you mean. The most important thing is to get the baby to full term, right? After what you've been through.'

'Yes!'

'And surely he understands that? I mean – it's his precious son and heir, right?'

'Exactly. Yes, of course.'

We smile, understanding each other perfectly.

'But before that. What did you do to keep him interested?' she asks. 'You've got to have some tricks up your sleeve, right?'

I suck my teeth. 'Well, we'd talk on the phone . . .'

'Like . . . dirty talk?' She's peering at me, her curiosity naked.

'Sometimes. And I'd send him pictures. Nothing that'd be worth hacking my iCloud for. Just a bit of a tease.'

'To keep him interested?'

'Yeah. You know how it is . . . handsome man; travels a lot . . .' I exhale, plastering over the wound of Jake's infidelity in my head; thinking further back to a time before I'd caught him cheating. 'I dunno. I might buy some fancy new underwear when he was coming home after a longer trip. Not every trip, just now and then. And he likes a bit of role play, so – wow, this goes back to before we were married, I don't think we've done it in ages – god, I'm embarrassed to say, but I'd get some dress-up costumes. We used to be quite playful.' I laugh, self-conscious now, and sneak a sideways look at Anna. 'It sounds seedy, doesn't it? It was just a bit of fun.'

'It's not seedy, and I didn't mean to embarrass you. I hope you didn't mind me asking, but who else can you ask but your girlfriends?'

I shake my head. 'It's fine. You don't do any of that, I take it?'

'Rob's not the sort. He's more your wham-bam-thank-you-ma'am type. You know, straight-up, no frills. If I put on fancy underwear he'd think I'd got a boyfriend coming over.'

I can't imagine lovely Anna with someone who sounds, frankly, so dull. 'How did you two meet?'

'Long story. Boring story. Not-telling-you story.'

I pout to disguise my hurt. 'Really?'

'It's not worth the breath. But let's just say I was vulnerable at the point at which he came into my life and I think that's got something to do with the fact we got together. He was what I needed at the time. Manly. Protective.' She looks off into the distance and I remember the picture of him in her house; how much taller than her he is.

'Sounds intriguing, not boring.'

Anna sighs. 'It's a story for another day.'

We walk in silence for a while. It hurts that she doesn't want to tell me after everything I've just told her. It's like three steps forward, one step back but I don't want to push too hard.

'So have you made any other friends?' she says.

'Well, funny you should mention that,' I say, 'but I've been invited to join a book club.'

'Wow, I used to be in a book club in Bristol.' She laughs to herself. 'Fun times. Who's running that?'

Even as she's speaking, my mind's running at high speed. Sarah said I could bring a friend, and Anna's within walking distance.

'Would you be interested?' I ask. 'I mean, I'd have to check, but it's run by a woman in my street. It'd be awesome to have you there – if you're a reader, I mean. Don't join if you don't like reading. What do you think?'

'Really?' We're walking quite fast and Anna's face, as she turns to me, is flushed. 'I'd love that. Thank you!'

And, for the first time since I arrived in London, I feel I'm doing something useful – making friend connections – and it fills me with happiness, which is probably why, when footsteps run up behind us and I turn to see that it's Simon, I give him a huge smile.

'Hello, Taylor,' he says, falling into step with us. 'I thought that was you. Very distinctive walk you've got. And you're Anna, aren't you?'

Anna nods and gives him what I realize is clearly a fake smile and he smiles back then looks away.

'How's your dad?' I ask.

He smiles again and I notice a couple of hairs sticking out of his nose. They quiver with every breath. He pushes his glasses back up his nose. 'He had a much better week, thank you for asking.'

'Good. And what about you? How was your week?'

He gives me another smile and shrugs. '*Comme ci, comme ça.* It is what it is.'

'How long have you been caring for him?' I ask.

'It's been a year since I moved in to Father's place. I had to. It was too difficult otherwise. I couldn't be everywhere at once.'

'There's no one else who can help?' I realize what a daft question that is as it comes out of my mouth. Anna, who's remained silent throughout this exchange, gives me a sideways look.

'I don't have any siblings,' says Simon. 'It's okay. I don't mind. It can just be a bit intense sometimes, which is why I enjoy coming to this group – getting outside, seeing other people, feeling like I have a normal life . . . Otherwise I tend to live my life vicariously through social media.' He gives a nervous laugh.

'Don't knock it,' I say. 'Saved my life. When I moved here. I didn't know anyone. If it wasn't for social media, I think I'd have been dragged away by the men in white coats by now. My husband likes to joke that my best friends are Twitter and Instagram.'

'Lol,' he says with an ironic smile. 'You are quite prolific.'

I do a double-take. 'What?'

He taps the side of his nose with one finger. 'Oh yes, I've checked you out already. I liked a couple of your posts. On Instagram, and Twitter.'

'Really?'

'Hmm. You won't have known it was me: my account's a load of random letters and numbers.' He waggles his eyebrows at me. 'I don't like to give anything away.'

'Weeeird,' Anna says *sotte voce*, then, more loudly, 'Well, if you don't mind, I'll leave you two to it.'

'No!' I blurt, desperate to keep her with me. But Anna holds her hands up.

'It's fine. Don't let me stop you. I need to get back anyway, so I'll call it a day here. Lots of work. Let me know about book club.' And, with that, she wheels around and is gone.

12

Every story has its linchpins; those moments around which the story turns. And, if this story starts the day I join the walking group, it takes another turn when I join book club, because this is where I meet Caroline Hughes-Smith. Anna knocks on my door that night, and we walk down the road to Sarah's together.

'You look nice,' she says as I shrug on my coat.

'Oh please,' I say. 'It's hard to dress a hippo.'

'Don't be daft. You look amazing. I only hope I look as good as you when I get to your stage. You must be getting excited now the end's in sight?'

'Yeah.' I sigh. It's difficult to put into words what I'm feeling about the impending birth of my first child. I remember viewing becoming a mother almost as you might view changing species, so alien is the concept. You hear stories, of course, but I simply can't imagine what it's going to be like. 'Exciting but also terrifying,' I say. 'I don't know about you, but I can't believe I'm going to have this little person to look after 24/7 – and not entirely sure there's any point in me actually joining this book club, given I'll probably be too knackered to read anything except parent manuals for the next five years.'

'Oh, come on, it won't be that bad. At least you'll have Jake there.'

'True,' I say. 'Right, this is Sarah's house.'

'What's she like? Do you know anything about her?'

'Only what I've seen on Facebook. She looks like a bit of a party animal – her photos are all high heels and cocktails.'

'You're friends?' Anna asks.

'No – but her account is wide open so I had a quick look.'

Anna tuts. 'What are you like?'

'She's a neighbour! I needed to make sure she wasn't a psycho!'

We drop our voices as we walk up the path. Sarah's house isn't one of the Victorian terraces that Anna and I have, but a post-war semi – one of a few tacked onto the lower end of the street. I ring the doorbell and Sarah opens at once. The hallway behind her is lit with a lamp and the warm glow is inviting, as is Sarah's smile.

'Come on in,' she says. 'Caro's already here.'

Sarah waves us into a lounge-diner where a woman's already sitting at the dining table flicking through a book. I recognize her from Sarah's Facebook. She looks up when Anna and I walk in.

'Hi,' I say brightly. 'I'm Taylor. Nice to meet you.'

'Likewise,' she says smoothly, standing up and holding out her hand. 'Caroline.'

She's wearing a silk shirt and necklace over elegant black trousers; her hair is loose and thick and her face glowing. Discreet diamonds glitter on her fingers and at her wrist. Although I'm fit and generally doing all right in pregnancy, I immediately feel inferior in my maternity jeans and smock top. It's a feeling I quickly get used to whenever I see Caroline. In terms of looks, she's as far from me as it's physically possible to be. Her flamingo to my hippo.

'You look nothing like you do on the internet,' Caroline says, and that wrong-foots me. 'Oh, don't look like that,' she says, shaking her head so her hair cascades over her shoulders. 'Everyone does it.' She snorts a laugh. 'Anyone who says they don't is a liar.'

I look pointedly at Anna and bite my lip. She gives me a tiny eye roll, then turns to Caroline.

'Hello, I'm Anna,' she says, then there's a pause that Caroline makes no move to fill, so I take a step towards her. 'What are you reading?'

'Oh, just flicking through Sarah's books,' she says. 'She has . . . interesting taste.' She raises an eyebrow on the word interesting and I see she's holding a book with a saccharine chick-lit cover. She looks me up and down. 'When are you due?'

'February.'

'Okaay,' she says, looking at my bump and nodding. 'Wow.'

I want to tell her Anna's pregnant too, as it's not immediately obvious, but I don't feel it's my news to tell, so I bite my lip and wait for her to notice.

'Right,' says Sarah, coming back into the room. 'Have you all met? I thought we could play a little game to introduce ourselves. Can you each just say a sentence about you; plus tell us two things no one else knows about you.' She giggles. 'That could be fun, right?'

Anna, Caroline and I smile brightly at Sarah. I wonder if we're all thinking, 'Do we really have to?' We all take our seats on the sofa and easy chairs and look expectantly at Sarah.

'Okay, I'll begin,' she says. 'I'm Sarah. Obviously.' She laughs. 'Divorced. Marketing manager. FMCG stuff. Won't bore you with it. Two kids. Who live largely with their dad.' She looks at each of us, her eyes sliding from one to the other, trying to latch, trying to find some grip with someone. 'Right, two things no one knows about me . . . hmm. . . . Okay. I've never been to Spain. Can you believe it? Not even Ibiza! Though that might change now I'm single, ha ha. And – oh, this is a good one: I'd love to have another baby. No idea how, but I'd really love to.' She looks down for a minute, then back up again with a smile. 'So that's me. Ta-da!' She does jazz hands and Caroline starts slow-clapping. Unsure of what to do, Anna and I both give a little clap, too.

'Thank you,' I say, which sounds a bit odd, but I don't know what else to say.

'Right,' says Sarah. 'Who's next? Shall we do it in the order you got here, just to be democratic about it? So . . . Caroline?'

Caroline leans back on the sofa and pouts a little as she thinks, her head tilted. We all wait, then she speaks slowly, pronouncing her words deliberately and precisely, in a manner that I come to realize is very much her signature.

'Well, I'm Caroline, obviously. Hughes-Smith,' she drawls. 'I'm an architect, currently on sabbatical. Right. Two things no one knows about me.' She frowns and I'm honestly surprised to see she hasn't had Botox. 'There are so many things no one knows about me. And that's how I'd like them to stay. Does that count as one?'

'Are you telling us you're secretive?' says Sarah, looking at Anna and me with a laugh.

'If that counts, then yes,' says Caroline. 'One: I'm secretive. Two: I've been someone's mistress.' She holds both her hands up, diamonds sparkling, to prevent us from voicing the questions that spring to mind. 'You didn't ask for explanations. Just facts. That's your fact. Take it or leave it. I'm not explaining anything, other than to say I was rather good at it, even if I do say so myself.' She looks away rather theatrically and Sarah raises an eyebrow.

'Ooh, a lady of mystery. Thank you, Caroline. Right, who's going first out of you two? I think Taylor stepped over the threshold before you, Anna, so let's go with her.'

I breathe in deeply, trying to shake off the dislike I feel for Caroline for stealing someone else's husband. I don't know the circumstances. I mustn't judge.

'Okay,' I say. 'I'm Taylor. I'm from California, moved to Croydon a few months ago. I used to be cabin crew. Currently not working and . . . I can't really say I'm pregnant, can I, because I guess you all can see that. Umm. Okay – number one: it's a boy.'

'Objection!' Caroline holds her hand up. 'Presumably your husband knows that?' I nod. 'Well,' she says, 'then it doesn't count because Sarah said it had to be things that no one else knows about you.'

I'm about to say that presumably her lover knew she was his mistress, but Caroline barges on.

'Come on: two genuine things. Chop-chop!' She claps her hands together.

'Umm. Okay.' I decide to let it go. 'I've never, ever watched *Mary Poppins*,' I look at Caroline, 'and no, my husband doesn't know that. And . . . I joined a walking group here in Croydon only so I could meet people.' I bite my lip to look coy. 'I actually hate social groups! Present company excluded, of course.'

Anna widens her eyes at me so I nod at her and mouth, 'it's true', realizing too late that I should have kept that quiet.

'Right,' says Sarah. 'Your turn,' and we all look at Anna. She wrings her hands together.

'Umm. I'm Anna. Currently working as an indexer. I'm twenty weeks pregnant and my husband works in Qatar but she,' she nods at me, 'knows all that, so . . .'

'Congratulations!' says Sarah. 'Almost outnumbered by pregnant women.' She looks at Caroline. 'All the more wine for us.' She laughs. 'Anyway, sorry. Carry on.'

Anna bites her lip. 'Okay. Here's something no one knows.' She looks at me. 'The baby wasn't planned.'

I try to look inscrutable but inside me fireworks are exploding: she knows I know that! I'm so happy she's made me complicit in her little lie. She's finally trusted me. I close my eyes and breath in deeply. At last.

'And,' Anna continues, 'umm, when I first saw Taylor at the walking group, I thought she was Emma Stone.'

Now I shrink back on my chair, my hand on my breastbone.

'Get outta here!' I laugh, swatting the air. I've never had that before. Reese Witherspoon, sometimes, though I don't really have her chin, but not Emma Stone.

'No, really!' says Anna. 'Remember when she was blonde for *Spiderman*?' She shakes her head. 'It's something about her cheeks and lips. And eyes. Do you guys see it?'

Sarah cocks her head, 'Yeah, maybe now you mention it.'

'Nope,' says Caroline. 'Sorry.'

Sarah rubs her hands together. 'Right, thank you, ladies. Maybe we'll get to the bottom of all those intriguing leads as we get to know each other but, for now, I suppose we should get started. I hope you ladies are hungry because I went a bit crazy at the deli.' She looks at me. 'It's all right for you two, you're eating for two! But some of us have weight to lose.' She puts her hands on her hips and jiggles them like a belly-dancer.

'Eating for two is a fallacy,' says Caroline. 'All these women who stuff themselves under the excuse of being pregnant live to regret it, trust me.'

'Agreed there's not much need in the first trimester but don't they say you need more calories in the third trimester?' I say mildly. It's not really a question.

'A few,' Caroline shrugs. 'Four hundred maybe? Not a lot. A modest tuna sandwich. Not a baker's dozen of jam doughnuts as most women seem to believe.' She pauses. 'February? So have you done your birth plan?'

'I'm not doing one,' I say. 'I just want the baby out safely, however the midwife deems fit.' I pause and look at Anna for support, but no one speaks so I carry on. 'I'd rather avoid a C-section unless it's absolutely necessary. But all that stuff about music and candles? I don't see the point. My doctor says babies make their own plans.'

Caroline rolls her eyes. 'One of those, eh? Good luck with that. But, if you want my advice, I'd say have an idea in your mind of what you want before you go into labour.' She smiles at me; a big smile that doesn't reach her eyes. 'You can't go wrong then.'

I smile back at her, echoing her big fake smile. 'You're absolutely right. I hadn't thought of it like that. Thank you.'

Anna shoots me a look and I imagine the laugh we're going to have about this later. I thought we'd escaped all this by avoiding the mummy-to-be coffee mornings.

'So, how many children do you have?' I ask Caroline.

She looks down then back at me almost with a challenge in her eyes. 'None.'

'Oh, I just . . .'

'Anyway,' says Sarah, 'How do we all want to proceed? Would you like to jump into discussing particular books, or just plan how we're going to operate?'

* * *

I don't recall how it comes out, but out it does come, that it's my birthday in a couple of weeks. By then, Sarah and Caroline have finished one bottle of wine and are halfway down the next. Anna and I are stone-cold sober.

'So what are you doing for your birthday?' Caroline asks. 'I don't suppose it's much fun being that big. There's not a lot you can do.'

'No idea. I'll probably go out for dinner with Jake,' I say, surprised that she called me big. My bump's neat; everyone tells me that.

'Oh, you've got to do something!' Sarah says. She looks at the other two. 'By the way, have you met her husband? He's gorgeous! He's got eyes like . . .' she slits her eyes and taps her nails on the table. '. . . Keanu Reeves! All dark and brooding.' She turns back to me. 'I can imagine why you might want to keep him to yourself, but it's your birthday!'

'Jake?' says Caroline narrowing her eyes. 'Not Jake Watson?'

'Yes!' I raise my eyebrows at her. 'Do you know him?'

She nods. 'Dark hair, dark eyes? Grew up around here?'

I nod. 'Yes, that's why we moved here.'

'Oh, fuck me sideways,' says Caroline. 'I used to go to school with him.' She laughs. 'Jake The Rake!'

'No! Surely not!' I'm laughing, but all the while trying to imagine-not-imagine my husband with this glamorous gazelle of a girl. Did he date her? Would he find her attractive now? I flick my wrist to stop myself going down that mental rabbit-hole.

'Oh my god, it was a hundred years ago,' Caroline says. 'Not that I look old enough, obviously. We were at primary school together.'

'That's amazing!' Primary's good. They can't have dated.

Caroline looks at me appraisingly now, nodding a little, as if assessing the type of woman that Jake The Rake finally married, and I'm thinking I can't wait to ask Jake if Caroline was a bitch at school.

'All very interesting,' Sarah says, 'but, if you two have finished, as I was saying: you need to go out for your birthday.'

I swivel back to face her. 'I hardly know anyone.'

'You know us!' Sarah bangs the table, her voice too loud. 'We should all do something together. Husbands, too. What do you all think?' She taps her knife against her glass. 'Ting, ting, ting. All those in favour of doing something for Taylor's birthday, raise your hands.'

She flings her own hand up in the air at the same time as Anna, then Caroline raises hers to the height of her shoulder, a small smile gracing the corners of her mouth. Sarah turns to me.

'Right, that's unanimous. Where shall we go? Dinner some-where fun? What do we all like? Italian, Indian, Chinese, Mexi-can? Greek?'

'Ooh, I love Mexican,' Anna says.

'Me too!' I say. 'Oh my god, did you ever go to Chronic Tacos when you lived in the States? I still dream about that place.'

'Yeah, there was one in Fort Myers I used to go to every time I was in Florida. And one in Tampa. I loved it. So authentic! But have you tried Wahaca here? It's just as good. Better, even.'

'I have! I love it!'

'There's a brilliant one on the South Bank. It's made from ship-ping containers!' Anna says.

Sarah gives a dramatic shudder. 'I love the tacos. They're so moreish.'

Caroline rolls her eyes. 'Oh for fuck's sake, listen to you all sounding like a flock of foodies. It's not a competition to find the most authentic street food: it's her birthday. We should go some-where nice, not some half-baked food truck.'

I put my hand up tentatively. 'One more thing: could we make it a lunch? I'm not keen on going into town late at night these days.'

Sarah holds her hands up. 'Okay, okay. Leave it with me. I'll come up with something. And don't worry, it won't be anything completely crazy. Just something nice. I promise.'

I KNOW YOU HAVE
A 'SPECIAL PLACE'

I mean, who apart from a five-year-old has a 'special place'? And, if that's not sickening enough, where exactly is your special place? Shall I say it, or will you?

Disneyland. Yes. You heard.

Have you any idea how that sounds to a normal adult?

So, it's your first holiday together. He suggests Florida, wanting to impress you with a fancy art-deco hotel in Miami Beach, and you fling your arms around him, batting your stupid eyelash extensions and say, 'Disneyland! Oh, please, please, pretty please?' and he has no choice but to oblige you.

The most revolting thing is, he doesn't mind.

Let me say that one more time: Disneyland.

Yeah, yeah: you went there as a child and you want to share it with him. I know your type, all cuddly jumpers, teddy bears and wholesome memories – makes my stomach turn just thinking about it. And him, he always was such a sucker. He hates roller-coasters but he does them for you, doesn't he? Splash Mountain and Space Mountain? You get on that stupid log flume and you ride up that cranky old mountain through all those stupid forest animals singing and, all the way along, he can't admit how much he hates it and how petrified he is because you're wriggling in your seat, telling him you were practically born on that ride; that you first rode it when you were, like, still in the womb. And then you come out at the top and there it is, the fifty-foot drop, and your hands are in the air and he can't scream, not in terror, because he wants to look like he's enjoying it so he squeezes his arm tight around you and you think he's being all manly and protective.

Did he tell you about his fear of heights?

Didn't think so.

You don't buy the photo; he rushes you past the booth so you don't catch sight of the terror on his face as you tip over the edge.

And then, when he thinks it's over, you shake the splash out of your hair and jump up and down on the spot, pulling him across the park towards Tomorrowland like a kid wanting candy from its mum, and the realization dawns on him that there's only one reason why you're doing that.

Space Mountain. The King-Lord-President of the Disneyland rides.

And what can he do, what can he say? 'I hate heights, I feel claustrophobic in the dark, the lights trigger my migraines, please don't make me go on this?'

Ha ha ha.

'Sure thing, honey,' he says in a phoney American accent that makes you laugh, and you have no fucking clue. He lets you lead him by the hand to Space Mountain but all the while he's hoping the queue'll be too long and you'll give up but you've pre-booked, haven't you? You've used a Fast Pass to get in without queuing. He'd know that, too, if he checked your Instagram.

I wish I'd seen his face.

And when it's all over, the three minutes of hell in the dark, he gets out and maybe it's the adrenaline, maybe it's the relief, but he gets down on one knee and he only asks you to marry him.

Fuck you. Fuck fucking Disneyland.

13

Jake's asleep on the sofa when I get back from book club. I look at him, his legs stretched out in front of him; his head lolled sideways, a little line of dribble trailing to the sofa cushion, and I smile to myself. Keanu Reeves? I always thought Keanu had eyes that hold secrets – dark secrets at that. A year ago I wouldn't have said that he and Jake had similar eyes – I'd have said Jake's were mischievous – but it's funny how quickly mischievous eyes can turn into secretive eyes. When I first saw Jake, I didn't even really fancy him – there never was that spark, that jolt of attraction. I'd thought he looked a shade too close to boring – too neat, clean and ironed, like a mummy's boy, and 'reserved Englishman' wasn't my type. I've never told him that. It was actually Jake's voice that drew me to him. That and the length of his fingers; the slimness of his wrists. Silly things. Maybe I should have looked at the bigger things.

I step over to him now, lean down, balancing myself on the back of the sofa, and kiss his cheek. He jumps awake and I see the momentary confusion as he tries to work out where he is and why. I wonder if 'she' flashes through his mind.

'You're back.' He rubs his eyes. 'What time is it?'

'Just gone eleven.'

'Did you have a good time?'

'Yes. Book club was great, but you'll never believe who I met. Do you remember a girl called Caroline Mackenzie? You went to school with her?'

He squints his eyes for a moment, then a smile spreads slowly across his face. 'Oh my god. Cazza? Really?'

I snort. 'I don't think she'd like to be called Cazza these days. She's all silk and diamonds and "excuse-me-la-di-dah" like she's the Queen of England. Caroline Hughes-Smith now. Married to the honourable Mr Toby Hughes-Smith, as she went to great lengths to tell us.'

Jake's sitting up now, paying attention. 'Do you have a picture of her?'

'Hang on.' I do a quick search but her Facebook's locked and her profile picture is tiny. I enlarge Sarah's cover photo – the one with her in it – and hand it to Jake. He peers at the screen.

He raises one eyebrow. 'Wow. Cazza. Looking good.'

I beat down my irritation. 'What was she like at school?'

Jake laughs to himself. 'One of a kind, that's what she was.' He shakes his head, still smiling in a way that I don't like, and gives me back my phone. 'Wow.'

'Well, these days she's the world's number-one expert on pregnancy and birth, even though she's never had kids.' I can't keep the bitchiness out of my voice.

'Oh dear,' says Jake. 'Rattled your cage, did she?'

I tut. 'No. Anyway, how was your day?'

'Fine. Usual.' Jake drags himself up off the sofa and holds his hand out to me. 'Come on. Let's get to bed. It's late.'

May god forgive me, but I don't tell him about Keanu's eyes.

14

The day after book club, I'm just checking Instagram – Anna's posted a pile of books with '#books #amreading #bookclub' – when a WhatsApp pops up from her. I laugh to myself: how quickly my life's become all Anna-Anna-Anna. The message is a picture of an envelope and a baby's rattle. I'm about to text 'how sweet!' when another message arrives: 'When can I call you?'

'Oh my god, I don't know what to do!' Anna says on the phone a moment later. 'You saw the rattle?'

'Yes – it's nice. Cute.'

'Someone put it through my door last night.'

'And . . . ?' Although I'm up, my brain's not fully awake and I'm not connecting the dots.

'In the middle of the night. Like 4 a.m.'

'Oh,' I say. 'Who's it from? Does it say?'

'No, that's the point!' Anna cries. 'Don't you see? Let me spell it out: someone put an anonymous package through my door at 4 a.m. last night. Oh god, I heard the letterbox. I can't tell you how terrified I was. I lay in bed, frozen, like, waiting for whoever it was to break in. I couldn't breathe I was so scared.'

'Oh no, you should have called me. Not that I could have done anything, but . . .'

'Your phone was off,' Anna says flatly.

'Ah. Yes. I turn it off at night. So then what did you do?'

'I couldn't sleep – I kept waiting for someone to break a window, so I took a shoe – a high-heeled one – and I went downstairs. Oh my god, I was so scared. And there was that envelope on the doormat.' She pauses. 'I looked at it for ages, I mean, it could have been anything.'

'But you opened it in the end?'

Anna tuts.

'And it was just the rattle?'

'Isn't that bad enough?'

'No note I'm guessing?'

'It just said in thick black marker: "for the baby".'

'Okaaay . . .'

'Oh, never mind. Sorry to have bothered you,' Anna says sharply and I feel bad for not taking her seriously.

'I'm sorry. You've really no idea who it's from? No other clues anywhere?'

'No!' Anna's voice is both exasperated and panicky.

'Do you want me to come over?' I ask.

I hear her breathe in and out slowly, as if she's trying to calm herself.

'It's probably just from some well-meaning stranger,' I say. 'I mean, people have seen you walking about town . . .' I break off, realizing that her bump, especially under her coat, is not that obvious.

'What sane person would be putting rattles through anyone's door at 4 a.m.?' she asks.

'Maybe they were coming back from a night out?' but even I can see that no one comes back from an all-nighter and puts a baby's rattle through a stranger's door.

'You're more obviously pregnant than I am,' Anna says. 'Why isn't it you? Not that I wish it was, but you know what I'm saying? There are hundreds of pregnant women in Croydon. Why me?'

'Has anything else like this happened before?'

Anna sighs.

'What?' I ask.

'I just . . .' she breaks off. 'I don't know. I'm probably just being paranoid, but I just get this feeling that . . . god, I sound mad . . . sometimes I just feel that I'm being watched.'

'Oh, I get that sometimes, too,' I say. 'It's not easy alone in a big city when your husband's away. But it's always nothing. Just my own paranoia. Anyway, no offence, but why would anyone want to watch you?'

'I don't know!' she snaps. 'I knew I shouldn't have said anything. I knew you'd think I'm imagining it.'

'No, no! Not at all,' I say. 'But it's a funny time, you know, with our hormones up the creek, and you alone with Rob overseas. It's not easy. I know that.'

Anna sniffs. 'Thanks.'

But all the while, I'm thinking about Simon from the walking group. The only person I know who I can imagine doing something like that is him, and that would be because he was shy, not for any malicious reasons. Though I would have thought he'd have been more likely to put something through my door than Anna's. He hasn't shown a lot of interest in talking to Anna, to be fair.

'Maybe I should call the police,' Anna says.

'What?' I can't hide my surprise. 'Really?'

'It's not normal to put anonymous packages through people's doors at 4 a.m.,' Anna says. 'What if it's something else next time?'

'Oh, come on!' I say, losing patience now. 'That's a bit extreme, don't you think? Whoever did this probably meant well. Or maybe it was just kids having a laugh. What do you call it? ASBOs or something, who stole their baby brother's rattle and put it through the door of the pregnant woman. And, to be fair, what exactly would the police do? It's not as if gifting someone a rattle's a crime.'

'Maybe they could watch the house? Drive past a few more times?'

'Wouldn't that be nice?' I say. 'But I doubt they have the

resources. Can you do anything to add more security to your house? Do you have an alarm?'

'I do. There's an alarm, and I have those extra bolts I had put in.'

'Okay.' Job done, I'm thinking.

Anna sighs. 'Okay, well, thanks.'

We hang up and I can't help feeling she's somehow disappointed in me; that my response wasn't what she was hoping for. But I ask you: if someone puts a gift for your baby through your front door, would you go running to the police? Course you wouldn't. To this day I feel I gave her the right advice.

15

'm just deconstructing my conversation with Anna in my head and making my coffee when my phone rings again. It's an unknown number and I hesitate for a moment before picking up, but it's only Sarah.

'Taylor! It was *so* good to see you last night,' she says. 'But I felt we didn't get a chance to chat, just the two of us. Do you fancy lunch today? God, I'm not the sharpest this morning . . . I could do with a good slap-up lunch to clear the cobwebs. What do you say, neighbour?' Then she laughs. 'In fact, I'm not taking no for an answer. I'll see you at the Italian on the corner at 12.30.'

And who am I to argue?

'Oh my god,' she says, slumping into a chair opposite me at the restaurant after giving me a hug and a perfumey kiss. 'I'm *hanging* today.'

I laugh. 'You certainly were a generous hostess.'

'I should drink more water,' she says. 'I never learn. I wonder how Caro is.'

I shrug. 'The benefits of being pregnant. It was a fun night. Thank you.'

'Oh, you're welcome. Do you think it went okay? Do you think everyone enjoyed it?'

'It was great, and I like the book we chose. I can't wait to get into it.' In fact I've brought it with me in case Sarah was late. I've been dabbling in the first chapter, reluctant to start it when I haven't got time to give it much attention, yet desperate to begin so I finish before the baby comes.

'It got good reviews,' Sarah says. 'The book bloggers like it, and that's always a good sign. Anyway, what are you having?'

'I was thinking about the lasagne. Can't beat a good lasagne.' My mouth's watering already.

'Mmm,' Sarah nods. 'And it's very good here. But I need something creamy. Ah, bingo.' She puts the menu down and taps it. 'Carbonara, with fettucine. That'll hit the spot.'

'Jake always has that,' I say. 'He says it's good.'

Sarah waves over a waitress and, after we've ordered our food, she asks for a large glass of wine.

'You don't mind, do you? Hair of the dog,' she says, winking at me. 'Thanks for bringing Anna last night. You two are sweet together, what with your matching bumps. She seems nice.' She laughs. 'God, if either of you ever change your mind about having your babies, I'll be there like a shot with the adoption papers!'

I give a little laugh and fiddle with the napkin. 'I doubt that's likely to happen.'

'Shame,' Sarah says with a smile.

'So, what did you think about Caroline's confession?' I say, keen to move the conversation on. 'The mistress thing? I wasn't sure what to make of that.'

'I know! Who knew.' Sarah raises her eyebrows. 'What a dark horse. I was dying to ask but she clearly didn't want to say. Don't you worry. I'll do some digging.' She rubs her hands together and cackles. 'I love a bit of sleuthing!'

'Have you met her husband?' I ask. 'Do you think she's cheating on him?'

Sarah shakes her head. 'Honestly, I've no idea. Maybe it was before she was married. If you were cheating on your husband, you wouldn't simply announce it to people you've just met, would

you? Not unless you're some sort of a narcissist or drama queen.'
She pauses and I suspect we're both weighing up the chances of
that. 'Honestly,' Sarah says, 'she'd be absolutely freakin' pterodac-
tyl nuts to cheat on Toby. He's loaded. Hedge funds.' She takes a
sip of her wine and inhales between her teeth. 'But you never really
know what goes on in someone else's marriage, do you?'

'So, how do you know each other, anyway?' I ask.

'Oh, we met in Waterstones.' Sarah laughs. 'Yes, really! We were
both looking for the same book. It was *The Night Manager*. The
shop only had one copy, so I said to her, "Why don't you buy it and
I'll buy it off you when you're done?" So we had to stay in touch.
Nuts, isn't it?'

'How funny,' I say, because what I can actually picture is Caroline looking Sarah up and down in the shop and telling her to
'eff off'.

'So, haven't you got work today?' I ask Sarah.

'Oh. I do the company social media once a week from home.
I'm allowed to go out for lunch!'

'I see. Of course.'

'Ooh, would you look at that.' Sarah nods towards the door,
where two men in business suits have come in. A waitress shows
them to a table. Sarah nods appraisingly. 'Not bad. Got to keep an
eye out these days.'

'Wedding ring,' I say, 'at least on the one I can see.'

Sarah laughs. 'Doesn't stop them. Watch this,' she says.

She gets up, then sashays past the table the men are sitting at. I
watch as both of them follow her with their eyes. She goes up to
the counter and looks for a minute at the desserts under the glass,
then sashays back past them, hips swinging. She's a little overweight
but has good curves. The men both look again, and exchange a
word or two.

'Typical,' I say when she sits back down. 'But it's quite a leap
from looking to cheating.'

'Well, as you're happily married, I'll just leave it there,' Sarah says, raising an eyebrow. She takes a sip of wine. 'At least, you think you're happily married . . .' She laughs then realizes what she's implied. 'Oh my god, I'm so sorry. That was out of order.'

I shake my head. 'It's okay.'

Sarah sighs and fiddles with her cutlery. 'You know, it's not so easy being single at my age. Despite everything, I do miss being married. Don't fuck yours up.'

'I'm trying not to. But it does take two to get it right.'

'And it only takes one to fuck it up,' she says bitterly, 'unless the other's prepared to turn a blind eye.' She sighs again. 'Anyway, we're not here to dissect your marriage. My problem now is I'm forty-two and single. I have two tweenage boys, and I want another baby before it's too late. If I don't find someone, it's going to have to be the sperm bank. It's not ideal, but I want the baby more than the husband.'

'Oh, well . . . I . . .' What I want to say is that I'm not smug, sitting there with everything that she wants: a baby and a marriage. I want to say that my marriage has been shattered and I don't know if we can get it back together; that I'm so grateful for the pregnancy; that I'd rather be back home in California; and that the reason I'm here in Croydon is because I want things to work out with Jake; I don't want us to be another divorce statistic. But I can't find the words. It seems too deep for Tuesday lunchtime in an Italian restaurant full of businessmen.

'Oh, ignore me,' Sarah says as the waitress brings over our food. Sarah asks for Parmesan cheese, black pepper and another glass of wine. 'I can get quite maudlin about the whole thing.' She smiles at me. 'You have such a lovely time ahead of you with the baby. It'll be tiring, obviously, but – oh my god – the first smile! And then those gummy little smiles before they get their teeth. The teeny-tiny fingers curled around yours.' She sighs. 'The baby smell. Oh my god, I could bottle that.' She smiles at me again. 'Even the night-time feeds. Are you going to breast-feed?' I nod. 'Oh, even the night feeds with the baby curled up against you in bed, all snuggly and warm and you drifting off to sleep. It's going to be amazing. And ignore anyone who tells you otherwise.'

She continues to talk about babies while we eat, pausing the conversation once to lean over and take a half-drunk glass of wine from the table next to us after the people leave.

'Oh, the look on your face!' she says. 'It was a Chablis! I heard them order. The most expensive one on the menu. So wrong to leave it.' She pours the wine into her own empty glass and puts the empty one back on the table waiting to be cleared. 'No one's going to be any the wiser. Didn't you ever do that when you were younger? God, I got through college nabbing other people's abandoned drinks. Mine-sweeping.' She laughs, lost in her memories.

I shake my head. 'I must have missed that bit.'

By the time we finish lunch, Sarah's more than a little inebriated. She's talking loudly and holds onto my arm as we exit the restaurant, teetering slightly in the high-heeled boots she's wearing with her jeans.

'Come back to mine for a coffee,' she says as we make our way unsteadily along the pavement. 'Unless you have something planned? What are you up to these days? Washing all the baby clothes? Oh they're so cute, aren't they? They're so tiny . . . the little babygrows. Aww! I never kept mine. I thought I was done with kids but you never can tell what life has in store for you, can you? So will you come back for a coffee?'

'Sure,' I say. 'Just a quick one.'

So I end up in Sarah's house again, less than twenty-four hours since I last was there. She flops onto the sofa, pulling off her boots, and I head to the kitchen to make some coffee in the hope that it might sober her up a little. In the sink is the detritus from book club, still unwashed. The wine glasses, cheese plates and knives not even soaking but just as we dumped them when we left last night. I find two mugs, and some instant coffee and the teabags, and make us each a drink. When I go back to the living room, Sarah's got a scrapbook open on her knees.

'Aw, look what I found. You made me all broody. Come and look.' She pats the sofa next to her so I sit down and she pushes half the album onto my knees so we can look at it together. She turns the pages back to the start.

'This is Archie the day he was born. Look! Look at that little bundle! . . . And here he is four hours old . . . Aww, this is when he first properly opened his eyes and I saw for the first time what colour they were.' She sighs. 'Oh, such precious days. I'm so jealous of you, you know.'

'He's very sweet.'

'I bet you can't wait to meet your own little bundle, can you?'

'No. I can't wait to see what he looks like. Whether he'll look more like me or Jake – or neither of us.'

'It's such a magical time. You're very lucky.'

'I know.'

Sarah takes my hand and looks me in the eye. 'Just enjoy it. That's all. It goes by in a flash. Before you know it, he'll be sprouting hair and getting spots and next thing you know, your baby will be gone.'

'Okay,' I say, and then I extricate myself, leaving Sarah to her memories. I walk back home slowly, thinking about her. I like her, but there's something slightly desperate about her; something clingy, something grasping, and I can't put my finger on exactly what it is.

I KNOW WHERE YOU
HONEYMOONED

I hardly need to say it was your choice, do I? You bring up the topic and him, he's so obedient, so well trained, he just stares at you, drinking in your stupid face, imagining you actually being his wife and he goes along with whatever you suggest. If you'd said Iraq, he'd have said 'how about Basra?' That's the ridiculous thing: his pathos I can almost understand, because he's a fool for you – but yours? You have the whole world to choose from, and you pick Mexico. Who do you think you are? Jennifer fucking Aniston?

But of course it wasn't ever going to be the tourist strip of Cancun, was it? With its all-inclusive hotels and its package tourists, knees-to-nose on their tin-can charters. Oh no. This is *you* we're talking about. Princess fucking you. It has to be something self-righteous, something squeaky clean and lentil-eating; something different and 'look at me, I'm so right on'. So you choose an ecoresort. A cabana on the sand in an 'I'm-so-amazing' eco-resort.

At least it's not Disney, I give you that.

And so, the morning after the wedding, you fly out to your Mexican eco-beach cabana that looks like it should cost ten bucks a night but probably costs a hundred times that and you think it's perfect with its white four-poster beds, its hardwood floors and its rough-painted turquoise walls that remind you of the Caribbean that's right outside your hut. It's so charming, you think. Not that he cares because all he intends to do the entire week is fuck you anyway. In that white four-poster bed. On the beach. In a hammock at two in the morning, when you think no one can see.

I'm right, aren't I?

But you have a list. A list of things you want to do and see. The biosphere. The cenotes. Tulum. Coba. Chichen Itza. You can't go to Yucatan and not see Chichen Itza, can you? So you book a private tour, and when you get there he realizes you don't just want to look at it: you want to climb it. You want a honeymoon selfie of the two of you at the top of the pyramid. 'Oh no,' he says, 'I don't have a head for heights, and just look at the ambulance parked down there – surely it's not safe, I don't want anything to happen to you on our honeymoon,' but there's nothing like you on a mission for a selfie. You've already kissed his nose and are twenty steps up and he has no choice but to follow you, heart hammering as his feet are longer than the crumbling steps are wide, and all the while he's thinking 'this shouldn't be allowed, there should be rules against this, it's way too dangerous, I can't believe I'm going to die here.'

Oh, hear me laugh.

He nearly gives up halfway when the sun's beating down on him and the mosquitoes are circling like vultures, but he can't give up because you're already at the top. 'Come on!' you shout, and he remembers that stupid fish in that Disney movie. 'Just keep climbing,' he says out loud. 'Just keep climbing. Don't look down,' and he sticks close to the chain that's there to hold onto and he makes it to the top where he nearly passes out but you're there, skipping about the top of the pyramid where the ledge is at least a bit wider than the steps, and he finally manages to look out at the view and he's got to hand it to you, it really is amazing. It looks like the entire world is coated in dark green forest as far as the eye can see. But you don't let him stop for long, he barely gets his breath because you need to get that selfie so you lean out over the edge and try to drag him with you so your heads are together cantilevered over the steep, steep drop where the ambulance below is the size of an ant – no, a baby ant – and you're laughing, teasing him without a care in the world. 'Come on, it'll be worth it when it's on Facebook,' you say, and, somehow, you get the photo with half of you and all of him in it and once you've applied a filter or FaceTuned it or whatever crap you do to your picture, no one will know how terrified he really was.

And that night, when he's safely back down and you've had a couple of drinks, he's full of the sense of having survived; he's so full of hot lifeblood that he thinks, when he fucks you, that you're going to get pregnant. He convinces both of you that you're going to get a honeymoon baby; you're drunk as skunks on the idea.

It doesn't happen, does it?

Oh yes, I know that, too.

16

Anna goes away on a course for work a couple of days after book club and I miss her more than I care to believe. I check her Instagram several times a day but all she posts is an arty shot of a notebook and pen with a pair of glasses on top '#workinghard #backintheclassroom' and her WhatsApp status just says 'Busy' so it's not till the following walking group that I get a chance to dissect the book club evening properly with her. Only, on the day, she calls me to say she won't be coming and I feel as if my backbone's snapped: all the life goes out of me and I slump against the wall.

'I'm so sorry,' she says. 'I was really looking forward to it.'

'You and me both. It's not about the rattle, is it? You're not . . .' I want to say 'scared' but I also don't want to sound like I'm belittling her worries.

She pauses for a fraction too long. 'No. I've got a bit of a cold, you know how it is. Could do with resting up. I don't want it to get worse.'

I don't entirely believe her, but: 'Oh I'm sorry to hear that,' I say. 'Let me know if you need anything.'

'Thanks. I'm all right at the mo,' she says. 'I've got stuff. I'll see you next week, anyway. Oh, is there any news about your birthday? Have you heard from Sarah?'

'Oh. No. I had lunch with her the other day, but she didn't say anything.'

'You had lunch with her?'

'Yes, she called me after book club and wouldn't take no for an answer.'

'Oh . . .' says Anna. 'Where did you go?'

'That Italian on the corner? With the blue front?'

'Oh yes. I know it. Very nice. Maybe she was trying to impress you. Do you get the feeling she doesn't have many friends?'

I pinch the bridge of my nose: it could be me she's talking about. 'Anyway,' I say. 'For what it's worth, she got drunk and talked non-stop about babies. Think I took one for the team, there.'

This seems to please Anna. 'I wonder if she even remembers she volunteered to arrange something,' she says. 'She was quite tipsy at book club as well, wasn't she?'

'Yeah. What did you make of Caroline?'

'Drunk on her own amazingness,' she says. 'Though she didn't seem to like me, did she?'

I rewind in my head. 'Really?'

'She didn't say hello to me. Pointedly ignored me. You must have seen that? It was the first time we'd ever met. I mean, it's just good manners to say hello, isn't it?'

I'm beginning to think Anna's a bit paranoid, and I don't have a lot of patience for that. I can't stand drama queens.

'Don't read anything into it,' I say lightly. 'She can't have anything against you if you've never met before.'

'Hmph,' Anna snorts. 'Anyway – weird that she went to school with your husband.'

'Isn't it?'

'Did he remember her?'

'Yeah,' I say slowly, still not entirely sure what he'd thought of her. 'He remembered her name.'

'Wow. I hardly know anyone I went to school with. Anyway,

look I'm sorry about walking. Have a good time. Simon will be pleased to get you alone.'

I tut. 'He's harmless enough.'

'So you keep saying.' I can almost hear Anna raising her eyebrows down the phone line.

She was right, though: when I got to the park, Simon was there.

* * *

'No Anna today?' he asks with a smile that tells me it's good news to him, and I shake my head. 'Her loss, my gain,' he says. 'So, how was your week?' and so I tell him a bit about book club, and how Caroline was at school with Jake, and he tells me a bit about his week, until the group starts to move off.

'Shall we?' Simon says, and we fall into step together.

'So what other things do you get up to? Other than walking and reading?' Simon asks as we walk along. I notice that he closes his eyes and takes a deep breath before he speaks, and that the muscle at the side of his eye twitches. He keeps pushing his glasses up his nose with his index finger and it makes him look like he's nervous, so I explain that I'm not just new to the area but new to the country, too, and still finding my feet. I know I can come across as super-confident even when I'm not. It's part of the flight-attendant thing. Fake it till you make it and all that.

'How about you?' I ask.

'I don't get out a lot,' Simon says. 'I wasn't joking when I said I live my life on social media. It's basically my window to the outside world.'

'What did you do before your dad . . . you know?' I don't really know how to say it because I don't know if he was always housebound, or if something happened to make him so.

'Back in the day, I used to be a forensic accountant, you know, going into big companies and going through the accounts with a toothcomb, looking for discrepancies, fraud and so on. I have an eye for detail. But a few years ago I retrained as an ethical hacker.' He whistles the first notes of the *X Files* theme tune and widens his eyes at me.

Despite myself, I laugh. 'Did you say "hacker"?'

'An ethical hacker. No, it's not illegal. Basically, I'm hired by companies to probe their networks and computer systems to find any weaknesses and hopefully prevent data theft and fraud.'

'So you're paid to hack into companies' websites?'

'Yes, in a nutshell.'

'How on earth did you get into that?'

Simon pushes his glasses up his nose again. 'Well, I was always good with computers. I speak their language. I was always fascinated by that sort of thing. So I looked into careers in IT and this,' he shrugs, 'well, it was right up my street. And business is booming in that sector. It's really up and coming. So I trained and got my qualifications – and the rest is history, really.'

'Are you telling me there are qualifications you can do in hacking?'

'Ethical hacking, yes. I'm officially a CEH: a Certified Ethical Hacker. Qualified hackers have to agree to uphold the code of ethics and never "engage" with unlawful hackers.'

'Wow. That's incredible.'

Simon smiles. 'So, basically, I spend my days at the computer, trying to penetrate my clients' websites and networks, testing their security systems et cetera.' The hairs on my arms stand on end when he says the word 'penetrate'. It sounds sexual coming from his mouth and I wonder if he chose it deliberately. 'I love it because you have to try and think how the "black hat" hackers might think,' he continues. 'You have to imagine what tricks they might use, and outsmart them.' His eyes gleam as he talks. 'I love trying to second-guess them. It's like a game to me – and, as long as I have the right equipment, I can work from home. Once I have the brief, it doesn't really matter where I'm based, so I can be there for Father. What about you? Do you work?'

'I used to be cabin crew. But I'm thinking of retraining as an interior designer.'

'Is that your passion?' Simon asks.

'Yes. Yes, I really love it. I get a kick out of pulling a look together; finding the right accessories and so on . . .' I tail off, realizing how shallow I sound. We walk in silence for a minute.

'So will your book club be reading the classics?' Simon asks apropos of nothing. 'Jane Austen, Thomas Hardy, D. H. Lawrence et cetera?'

'Oh, I don't know. I don't think so. The focus seems to be more on what you can pick up in the "new releases" each month. Though I love the classics. Jane Austen in particular. She's so English. Obviously, I've read a lot of the American classics, too: *Little Women*, *Huckleberry Finn*, *To Kill A Mockingbird* . . .'

'Oh, okay,' he says. 'Of course you have. I should have guessed that.' He looks as if he's going to say something else then doesn't.

'Yeah,' I say. 'I love classics. Don't get me wrong. I love contemporary fiction, too, but the classics are classics for a reason – right?'

Simon takes a deep breath. 'Yes. Yes, of course. Umm, it's just that I'm going to an arthouse screening of *The Great Gatsby*, and I wondered if you fancied coming with me? It's at a little cinema not so far away. I was going to go on my own, but if it's your kind of thing, maybe you fancy coming with me . . . obviously not a date or anything because you're . . .' He waves his hand at my belly, presumably to indicate that he gets that I'm off bounds for being pregnant and married. 'Nothing like that. I'm not one of those men who loves pregnant women.' He whacks his forehead. 'Oh god, that sounded terrible. Nothing like that. Just – if you fancied it?'

And I've no idea why but, somehow, I find myself saying, 'Yes, that sounds brilliant, I'd love to, thanks,' and all I can think, as Simon beams back at me like all his birthdays have come at once, is 'what have I done?'

Anna will have a field day.

17

Jake walks into the house that evening looking at his phone. With him comes the smell of winter, the wind and his office, clinging to his clothes.

'Who's Sarah?' he asks, leaning in to kiss me.

'She's the one you met in the doorway the other night? The one who runs the book club. Why?'

'Oh yeah . . . I remember. Lipstick, right?' He rubs his cheek where her lips had touched him and taps something into his phone. 'She messaged me. Wants to meet up tonight,' he says, and the old hurt stampedes through me like a herd of wild horses. How did she get his number? Why didn't she ask me the other day? Has she been in touch with him behind my back? Is he hiding something? I know he's good at deceit: we've been there.

'So you don't mind if I go, do you?' Jake says. 'It's to talk about your birthday. Apparently she's planning The Birthday Surprise.' He injects the capital letters into his voice; says the words in the voice of a game-show host. 'Anyway, how are you? How was your day?'

It's a good question. I've spent every moment since I left the park this morning, fretting about agreeing to go to the cinema with Simon. But I don't have his number, and neither do I know where he lives. The thought of the arrangement makes me uneasy.

But it's just catching a movie with an acquaintance, isn't it? I've nothing to be worried about.

'Oh, fine, thanks,' I say. 'Went walking.'

'Great. See your friend Anna?' Jake's perched on the arm of the sofa, distracted with his phone.

'She wasn't there so I chatted to that Simon guy.'

He loosens his tie and flexes his neck, disinterested in what I'm saying. I'm about to tell him about the film when his phone buzzes. He opens the message.

'Okay. It's Sarah. I've said yes and she's walking down to get me at eight. It's dinner apparently.' He looks at me and we stare at each other for a moment.

'We're planning your birthday . . .' Jake says firmly.

'Sure,' I say, moving it on. 'But, look.' I point at my belly. 'Nothing wild, please. My idea of a good night out right now is a warm bath, a book and bed. Please don't sign me up for a bar crawl, strippers, anything involving me having to watch everyone else get drunk, in fact anything that doesn't involve a quiet dinner and an early night.'

Jake rolls his eyes. 'You're a whole bag of fun. Maybe we'll just let you leave early and carry on without you.' But then he comes over and hugs me, and I try to imagine a life when I haven't got a human being sitting in my stomach and might look forward to nights out again.

* * *

The doorbell rings bang on eight. Jake's been upstairs getting ready and I hear his feet thunder down the stairs. He lets Sarah in, and I hear the smacky sound of air kisses, then they're standing in the living-room doorway in a cloud of perfume.

'Hi,' says Sarah. 'Don't get up. You don't mind me borrowing your husband tonight, do you?' She gives a laugh two shades dirtier than white. 'Got a few ideas I want to go through with him.'

After our lunch the other day, what I want to say is: 'Just behave yourself – he's spoken for,' but what comes out of my mouth is, 'Don't go to too much trouble. I'm really not up for much.'

'Oh, come on!' Sarah says. 'It's your last birthday before you become a mum! It's a cause for celebration. End of an era and all that.'

I shrug. 'I'll still be me.'

Sarah laughs and nods. 'Course you will. Anyway,' she turns to Jake, 'are you ready? We have a booking for 8.30 so we better get going.'

'Where are you going?' I ask.

'The Italian, so we can have a few bevvies and walk back. Do you like Italian food?'

My heart skips a beat: the Italian I went to with Sarah may be a bistro by day but by night it's another creature altogether: all candles, cosy lighting and romance.

'Love it,' says Jake patting his tummy. 'Especially a good carbonara. Right, will you be all right?' he asks me.

'Fine.'

'Okay, we won't be late.' Jake kisses the top of my head.

'I'll get him home before midnight. Joking!' Sarah calls, and then the door opens and shuts and they're gone, leaving nothing but a scented cloud of their two fragrances mingling: his and hers.

* * *

I call Anna later that evening when I'm slumped on the sofa watching-not-watching something on television. All I've had for dinner is a bowl of homemade soup, a compromise between the wolf of my hunger and the physical sensation that there's absolutely no space left inside me for food. I imagine the soup sliding its way around my organs and the baby, filling what small spaces it can find. Sometimes I feel as if the baby's so big his arms might start poking out of my ears.

'How are you?' I ask.

'Much better, thanks.'

'Any more weird deliveries?'

'No, but . . . oh, it's nothing.' Pause. 'How was walking?'

I shift myself back on the sofa, easing into a more comfortable position. Anna clearly wants me to quiz her but I don't have the patience.

'I walked with Simon,' I say.

'Surprise, surprise. What's your husband got to say about that? Another man muscling in on his pregnant wife.'

I half laugh, half frown at the living room. 'Don't be daft!'

'Jake's not the jealous type, then?'

'He trusts me.'

'But?'

I suppose I walked into that one. 'But nothing.'

'You don't always trust him?' Anna prompts.

'Nothing,' I say.

'Oh my god, something's happened? He's done something, hasn't he?'

'No, no, no. It's all a long time ago and we don't talk about it. All right?'

There's an awkward pause and I wonder if she's going to question me further.

'Okay,' Anna says lightly. 'Any news on your birthday plans?'

'Actually, yes,' I say. 'I should know later tonight. Jake's out with Sarah right now, discussing it. They've gone for dinner.'

The pause is infinitesimal but definitely there. 'Dinner?'

'Yes. The Italian place.'

'Lovely,' says Anna, then, 'I wonder what they'll come up with.'

* * *

I have every intention of waiting up for Jake to get back but, by the time my head's fallen down and snapped up twice in front of the television, I decide to go up to bed. It's 10.30 and I can't imagine Jake will be much longer – still, I've already been asleep when I hear the sound of his key finding the lock; maybe it's half eleven.

The door opens and I hear a giggle and the sound of shushing. The door shuts very quietly, then footsteps move towards the living room. Water squeals in the pipes as the tap's run: Jake must be making them a coffee. I doze off again so I've no idea how much later it is when I hear murmured voices in the hall below.

'Good night.' It's Jake, then something I don't catch that ends with 'fun'.

'Night,' Sarah says, then there's a silence for one, two, three long seconds – three seconds in which I'm plummeted straight back into the day I picked up Jake's phone in the States and learned what he was up to. You imagine that finding out your partner's cheating will be all drama, shouting and fireworks, but sometimes it's the silences – the things that are missing – that tell you more than the words. I lie absolutely still, holding my breath, waiting for the door to open, then finally there's a scuffle of feet, and it's Jake who speaks, his half-whispered voice cheerier than usual, carrying straight up the stairs to where my bedroom door is ajar.

'Night then.' There's a rustle of clothing, then a giggle that's stifled as soon as it starts. The front door opens and then Jake speaks again.

'Bye now,' he says quietly. 'Will you be all right getting home?'

Sarah says something I don't catch, then laughs, another of her low, dirty laughs. Outside the window, her heels clack down the path. The door clicks shut, Jake shoots the bolt as quietly as he can, and I know he's pulling the door tightly in to ease the passage of the bolt, which gets stiff when the door's swollen with damp, and I wait, still holding my breath. Jake's footsteps go to the kitchen and again the pipes squeal, then I hear the click of the light switch and the tread of his foot on the creaky bottom stair. I lie there, full to the brim with baby, and pretend to be asleep.

They kissed. I'd put my life on it.

18

After a fractured night of dreams, which I spent chasing Jake and Sarah around a department store, catching sight of them kissing behind various displays, I know I can't keep my suspicions to myself. The moment Jake's eyes open, I ask him.

'How did you and Sarah get on last night?'

'Not bad,' he says, his voice croaky from whisky and wine.

'Sounds like you had fun when you rolled in drunk. Did you kiss her?'

Jake shoots up onto one elbow. 'No!'

I raise my eyebrows at him.

'Is that what you think? What makes you think that?'

I just look at him, every cell of my body screaming *past behaviour.*

'Oh, come on!' he says. 'Look, I learned my lesson, okay? You're pregnant. I'm not going to do it again. You have to understand that.'

'But . . .' I start but then realize there's no point. He's a good liar. We both know that. He'll deny it until I work myself into a hole. I flop back onto my pillow and speak to the ceiling.

'If you do it one more time, I'm leaving. You know that, don't you? I'm taking the baby and going straight back to the States. Okay?'

'I didn't kiss her, I swear.'

'Fine.'

* * *

I slobbed about the house in an XL t-shirt and leggings after he'd gone to work. I did a bit of cleaning, I guess – a bit of vacuuming and a bit of dusting, punctuated with lengthy bouts of sitting down drinking tea and checking social media – but I couldn't settle to anything much. I was discombobulated – I love that word – after my talk with Jake and it was that kind of day: bright but windy; one of those days when the dramatic appearance and disappearance of the sun threw unexpected light and shade across the room, changing the mood from minute to minute. Perhaps it was because of that that I was unable to settle to anything much; perhaps it was my bad night's sleep, or just the unpleasant taste left in my mouth by Jake's night out with Sarah. I didn't need that at this point in my life. That's what I was thinking when the doorbell rang.

We didn't have a peephole back then but, even so, I didn't use the chain Jake had installed. I cringe now, thinking about it but then, as a California girl, I couldn't find it in myself to be as security-conscious as I ought to have been. I was smiling as I opened the door – I remember that.

And it was only Simon. Standing there on the doorstep in his green anorak, the collar of a pink shirt peeking out the top, and his pink skin so freshly shaved it looked somehow naked. I felt completely wrong-footed to see him on my doorstep with no warning. I remember that, too.

'Taylor! Oh, I'm so glad I got the right house,' Simon says as if it's the most natural thing in the world for him to knock at my door. 'I wasn't sure I remembered it right.'

Had I told him where I lived? Maybe there was a discussion about which street it was when I was telling him about Sarah and the book club but, if there was, it's slipped my mind – it wouldn't be the first time.

'What can I do for you?' I ask.

He pushes his glasses up his nose and then holds up a paper gift bag. 'Delivery,' he says. 'I got a little something for the baby,' and I think immediately of Anna's rattle.

'Oh,' I say. 'Well, thank you.' I take the bag then hesitate.

'Can I come in?' he asks, leaning in towards the door and looking past me into the house.

'Oh . . . sure . . .'

Simon follows me inside and we stand in the living room. Without thinking what I'm doing, I put the dining table between us, suddenly aware that I'm alone at home, pregnant and vulnerable, and that, now he's in my home, I don't know Simon so terribly well. He's a tall man and he seems very big in my space. I place the bag on the table.

'Shall I open it now?'

Simon shrugs, his shoulders moving up and down in the jacket. I imagine him in the shop, choosing that particular coat, that particular shade of green. 'If you like. It's just little. A token.'

'Thank you.'

Inside the bag are two wrapped gifts. I unwrap the first, telling myself to look happy no matter what it is.

'Ah!' I say. It's a wooden alphabet jigsaw, of the sort you have to fit the letters into their cut-out spaces. It's brightly coloured and I can picture a toddler having heaps of fun with it. 'Thank you. It's lovely.'

'Do you like it?'

'Yes. But you didn't have to.'

'Oh, but when I saw it I realized it would look perfect in your nursery.'

I freeze and his voice fades.

'Instagram,' he says with a shrug. 'Sorry. It was one of the pictures I liked. Remember I was telling you? You have a beautiful home, by the way.'

I give him a weak smile, glad the table is still between us.

'I was going to get a rattle,' Simon says. 'That's more conventional for newborns, isn't it, but I thought you probably had one already.' He pauses. 'Anyway, he or she probably won't use this for a year or so, but you got to start 'em young on the reading, haven't you?' He nods at the other package. 'That one's for you and Jake.'

I really don't like the sound of Jake's name in his mouth. I open up the parcel. It's a copy of *Go The F**k To Sleep*. I can't say the word out loud in front of him so I flick through the pages.

'I'm hoping for a good sleeper, of course,' I say, 'but you never know . . . I'll probably get an insomniac.'

'From what I hear, it'll be tough for the first few weeks,' Simon says quite seriously, 'but I don't need to tell you that.'

'First few months even, maybe.'

'It is what it is,' he says. 'Think positive.'

I gather together the wrapping paper. 'Thank you. Really. It's very thoughtful of you . . .' I wait, but Simon shows no sign of leaving. 'Would you like a coffee or something?'

'I'd love one, thank you. If it's no trouble,' he says, unzipping his jacket.

'It's fine.' I look at my watch. 'I've got something in half an hour,' I lie, 'but I've got time for a quick one.'

I make our coffees then we go, somewhat awkwardly, into the living room. Simon sinks onto the sofa so I perch on a dining chair.

'Are you sure you don't want to sit here?' he asks, patting the cushion next to him, his fingers stroking the fabric, and I imagine sitting there next to him, our bodies touching at shoulder, hip and thigh, and stifle a shiver. 'You'd be more comfortable,' he says.

'No, I'm fine here, thank you. It's easier for me to get up.' I laugh and take a noisy sip of coffee even though it's still far too hot and it burns my lips.

'Is the nursery upstairs?' Simon asks. Then he rolls his eyes. 'Sorry. I guess it is.'

'Yes, it is.' I look up, as if I can see through the ceiling to the small room where the blue and white cot is waiting; the tiny sleep-suits all washed and ready, just in case the baby comes early; my hospital bag packed.

'Good,' says Simon. 'Very good.' There's another awkward pause and I take a sip of coffee, then Simon speaks again. 'I never had kids.'

I tilt my head at him. 'There's still time. It's easier for guys.'

He sighs a deep sigh, then pushes his glasses up his nose again. 'Came close once. When I was married. My wife was pregnant.' While I rejig my idea of him to include being divorced, he pauses and shakes his head to himself. 'Got everything ready: the nursery, the toys, the clothes, everything. Went to all the appointments, the scans and the classes. It was a boy.'

Dread twists in my stomach 'What happened?' I can't bear stillborn stories, not at this stage. The thought of having to deliver a dead baby is too horrific to countenance. I've seen those pictures in the papers, the pictures of mums holding their dead babies, and they make me sob great big, unbidden, uncontrollable sobs that explode out of my mouth.

'He wasn't mine,' Simon says and I bite my lip to hide my relief that I don't have to picture a dead baby; a mother destroyed. 'A couple of months before she was due, she told me she was leaving. Must have been about your stage, actually. Had another nursery set up in her lover's house. Took her stuff and left.' He looks down at his hands and I see he's struggling to compose his face. He's rubbing and twisting the bare skin of his finger where a wedding ring would have encircled it. 'I managed to sell most of the stuff; gave some bits to charity.' He looks up, his lips a straight line. 'At least the bitch was honest about it. Could have been worse. Kid could have grown up with the wrong father, and what kind of a fuck-up would that have been?'

He looks at me defiantly and I see suppressed anger still there.

'I'm so sorry,' I say.

'Thank you. Time helps. He's three now, and I . . . well, I have Father to take care of. That's enough for me.' He takes a deep breath. 'No use fretting about things you can't change.'

'Did you just take her word for it that the baby wasn't yours?' I ask and realize, as the words come out, that I might be opening up an issue he doesn't wish to dwell upon.

'You mean did I do a paternity test? No. There was no need.'

'Really? I think I would have done, if I were you.'

Simon laughs. 'That's because you're American! No, I trusted her. She should know.'

I stop myself from blurting out what I want to say, which is: *you trusted a woman who cheated on you?*

'Have you ever seen the baby? The child?' I ask.

'Once.' He shakes his head. 'I'm sure he wasn't mine, if that's what you mean.'

'Okay. All right.' I sigh. 'I'm sorry.'

'It's okay.' We both take sips of coffee. 'So,' says Simon, 'about the film. Are you still up for it? I thought we could fix a date. I do have to plan ahead a bit just to make sure, you know, that there's cover for Father.'

'Of course.' I take a deep breath and exhale slowly: this is my chance to cancel, but I feel bad for Simon, especially after what he's just told me.

'Tell you what,' I say. 'My book club was also talking about seeing that film. Mind if they tag along with us?'

'Sure,' he says. 'I'd love to meet your book club.'

'I'm not sure if they have a rule against men but I'm sure they won't mind for one evening.'

'Oh, there are rules, are there?' He raises his eyebrows. 'One of "those" book clubs . . .'

'Every book club has rules,' I say. 'I just don't know what our rules are. Not sure they've been documented yet. It's a very new book club.'

'Well, thank you for inviting me,' says Simon. 'Let me know

when you decide to go, and I'll try and get cover. It'll be nice to get out.'

I'm standing up and the baby suddenly moves, causing me to breathe deeply and press my hands against my belly.

'You okay?' Simon stands up.

'Yes,' I grimace. 'There's not a lot of space for acrobatics these days. Uh.' I feel as if it's squashing the breath out of my lungs. How my own organs still fit in my abdomen, I've no idea. 'Uh! There's the foot.'

Simon is staring at my belly. He steps a little closer.

'Oof!' I say, exhaling and touching the bit where the baby's foot is pressing outwards. It's a spot just below my bottom rib. Simon holds his hand out then snatches it back as if remembering it's not his to touch. There's longing in his eyes, and in my mind I see Anna holding her hands out in Costa that day, cackling 'Can I have a feel?'

'Would you mind if I ... There's nothing weird about it. I just ... I miss that feeling of life, right there, waiting to be born,' Simon says.

I breathe in and out slowly while trying to think. What harm will it do?

'Okay,' I say and, as Simon places his hand on the side of my belly, I feel the surprising warmth of his hand through my t-shirt. 'Keep it there.'

We wait, motionless, a strange pair – him with his hand on my belly, and me with arms out to the sides, giving him space to feel. We're so close I can smell the coffee on his breath and see the fine lines on his forehead and around his eyes. The only sound in the room is that of our breathing, and then the baby's foot presses outwards again, a strange lump moving across my skin.

'There!' I say. 'Did you feel that?'

'Yes.' His hand presses a little harder. 'Hello, little one,' he says. He takes his hand off and looks at my face. 'It's incredible to think there's new life in there. Look after it.'

'I will,' I say, and it sounds like a wedding vow. The moment breaks and suddenly I feel dirty for letting him touch me. I usher him to the door.

'Well, thanks for the gifts,' I say brightly as I practically push him onto the street.

He pauses on the threshold. 'Oh, and about the film? You'll be in touch?'

'I will.'

'Okay. Bye now.'

I shut the door firmly behind him and lean against it. What in god's name just happened?

I KNOW HE CAN'T
AFFORD THE BABY

Not that you know anything about it. Listen to me laughing: of course you don't know. Have you ever seen his payslip? The bank statement?

Didn't think so.

You don't know the half of it; you've never given a moment's thought to where the money comes from. You live like there's an endless pot of cash under your pretty little arse, but I can tell you that, although it's filled regularly, that pot's pretty empty. I can hear the sound of it being scraped from here. Houses, sweetheart, houses in London and new cars and babies don't come cheap. And then there's you fannying about the shops, buying new vases and throws and fake fucking flowers and whatever other crap you stuff into that house.

And don't forget the private health insurance he needs you to have because you want to pop out the baby somewhere where it won't have to make its scrawling appearance on a trolley in the corridor; somewhere that won't kick you out ten minutes after you've birthed the placenta. But private health insurance doesn't come cheap when you're pregnant, does it? And I haven't even got started on all the baby stuff – the pram and the cot and the clothes and the toys – and then, there it is, sitting there like the elephant in the room: the shiny new car.

Yes, the one you made him buy. Oh, I know you Instagrammed that picture of it on the forecourt with that stupid bow on the bonnet: #gratitude #luckygirl. I know you told everyone it was a surprise, but don't forget I know you. I know how you operate.

It was you who bought the car magazines, wasn't it? It was you who showed him the reviews, then suddenly he's back for the weekend and it's all 'guess what, darling?' and before he can blink you're in the showroom and out on a test drive and you're batting those stupid eyelashes and saying, 'Oh, I love it. I'd feel so safe in a new car,' and he has no choice: he hugs you and that's it, you've suckered him hook, line and sinker.

But he can't afford it. I already told you that.

And that's the crux of it. Black and white. Each month he worries how he's going to make the payment; worries he's going to tell you he's got to give it back or – worse – have it taken away; declare himself bankrupt. The embarrassment. The shame.

Oh you think I'm lying now, don't you? I can hear you arguing: 'He earns a good salary; he's good with money; blah, blah, fucking blah,' and I have to hand it to you: you're right. He could manage the payments, if only he didn't have a little secret. A dirty secret. It's not difficult to find out.

Online gambling.

So what do you want me to tell you? It starts innocently enough. He's got a couple of beers in one evening, and an ad pops up on his phone and he thinks, 'What the hell?' He has a bit of a flutter; wins a couple of hundred quid, and suddenly he sees how his money problems could be solved.

I know you're shaking your head.

I am too.

But it's an addiction, isn't it? Right up there with drugs and alcohol. Oh, I wish I could see it, the day he admits to you that he's gambled away your life savings.

And he knows that pay-day loans aren't the answer. He does. But still he Googles them; still he clicks through from the ads, working out ways to keep the car; keep the cash flowing; keep you from finding out. And, all the while, all the time he's borrowing from Jack to pay Jill, he's thinking one thing. He doesn't want to think it but I know he is. It's tormenting him. He's up at night, chewing the skin around his nails, thinking the thought that makes him sick to his stomach.

It'd all be okay if we weren't having the baby.

You've no idea, have you? But that's exactly what he's thinking.

19

The cinema foyer smells of stale popcorn. We're here for an early-evening screening; it's a funny time, when most people will surely be sitting down to their evening meal. Outside, a steady rain's falling – it really is a night to be huddled up in the warm, not venturing out. I wasn't hungry when I left home but now my stomach rumbles and I glance over at the food counters: bright-pink hot dogs, greasy-looking, yellow nachos, over-salted or tooth-grindingly sweet popcorn – maybe a box of Maltesers is the best of a bad bunch. Immediately my mouth salivas up at the thought of my teeth sinking through the layer of soft milk chocolate to the crunch of the honeycomb inside.

I flick through Instagram and see Anna's reposted the picture she took of the muffin in Costa: 'From muffins to movies with my new friend,' she's written, with an emoji with hearts in the eyes, '#newfriend #arthouse'. I double-tap to like.

'Hey.' Simon appears from the side. He bobs his head down towards me and skims his cheek against mine. He's in his dark green jacket and jeans, and I get a waft of carbolic soap. For some reason the smell of any chemical cleaning agent actually makes my mouth water at this point of the pregnancy. I fantasize sometimes about eating sponges frothing with soap. I have to swallow.

'Glad I'm not the first,' says Simon. 'How are you?'

'Good thanks.'

I put my hands on the side of my bump, subconsciously echoing the position where his own had been the other day. I pull myself up tall and straight to best fill my lungs with air. 'Good as can be.'

'I'm sure you're perfectly justified in hibernating at this point,' says Simon. 'Aren't you supposed to be nesting? Cleaning the house, if not lying on the sofa eating chocolate?'

'Funny you mention the chocolate,' I say. 'I was just eyeing up the Maltesers.'

'Ooh, I love a Malteser or two,' says Simon, rubbing his hands together. We both look towards the counter. 'Back in a jiffy,' he says, heading off that way, and I see Sarah and Caroline at the door and give them a wave.

'Hi,' Sarah says as she comes closer, looking me up and down. 'How are you? Blooming, by the looks of it!'

'Still not popped? Are you eating curry and having lots of sex?' says Caroline, undoing her coat and shaking out her hair. She always speaks slowly, almost drawling the words as if she's the Duchess of Somewhere Fancy. 'You should try, or you'll end up the size of a house.' She waggles her finger at me. 'Remember, every extra day's an extra stretch mark!'

Anna appears from behind, her hair all over the place, raindrops on her coat. She's wearing 'my' Zara coat again and I feel a pang of longing for my own one, which no longer does up.

'Hello, hello, hello,' she says, nodding at us each in turn. 'Sorry I'm late. I came straight from a meeting.'

Out of the corner of my eye, I see Simon heading towards us with two boxes of Maltesers and a big smile on his face. I hold both hands up to stop the chatter.

'Ladies, I just have to tell you I've invited someone else. I hope you don't mind. It's . . .'

'Your weekday husband?' says Anna. 'How did I guess? Oh, speak of the devil. Hello, Simon. Joining us for book club, are you?'

I don't mention that the film was his idea. Simon gives a small

smile and passes me a box of Maltesers. It feels like an intimacy –
and that, by taking them, I'm complicit in allowing it to exist. Am
I encouraging him?

'Taylor was kind enough to invite me to join you tonight,' he
says. 'I've always wanted to see this film. I hope you don't mind. I
can always sit in a different row if you want to be left alone.'

'Don't be ridiculous,' I say. 'Let me introduce you. This is
Sarah, who started the book club and lives a few doors down from
me. This is Caroline, her friend, and you know Anna from walking, right? It's only a small book club.'

Simon nods his head politely at both of them and then there's
an awkward pause I feel I should fill as the common link between
all these people. I open my mouth to say something but Sarah beats
me to it.

'So, Taylor,' she says, rubbing her hands together, 'does your
husband know you're out with a man tonight?'

I laugh. 'Of course.'

'I suppose it's only fair since I had yours to myself the other
night.' She laughs to herself and wiggles her shoulders in a way
that jiggles her breasts. 'Hubba, hubba!'

'Really?' says Caroline, one eyebrow raised, looking between
Sarah and me. 'You let her out with Jake Watson?'

I tut. 'It wasn't like that.'

'I should hope not,' says Anna, 'with you pregnant.'

'You'd be surprised how many men play around when their
wives are pregnant,' says Caroline as if she's God announcing the
creation of the universe. 'Just look at all these footballers. It's up to
the wives to keep them interested, I say. So many give up trying.
Become complacent.' She sniffs and tosses her hair. She's beautiful
and graceful to look at, and she dresses with that certain British
something. I want to like her, I really do, but she's not making it
easy.

'Those WAGs are hardly complacent,' says Anna. 'They work
full-time on their appearance. Have armies of chefs, personal

trainers and beauticians, I'm sure.' She looks at Sarah. 'So did you decide what we're doing for Taylor's birthday, or were you too busy shaking your booty at her husband?' She gives Sarah a fierce look and I bite my lip to stop myself smiling. I can handle myself very well but it's really, really nice to have someone else fight my corner. Reminds me of my cabin-crew days: girls, together forever.

'Yes. We did. I'll message you.' She looks at Simon. 'Do you want to come, too? It won't be anything major, just dinner at mine. And I'm on orders from her husband not to keep her out too late.'

Simon shrugs. 'Thank you. But I'm sure you ladies don't need me there.'

'Well, the invitation's there,' says Sarah. 'God knows we could do with some male company.'

'Right,' says Caroline. 'Taylor, did you say you have the tickets? How much do we owe you?'

I rummage about in my bag. 'I've got them here. It's okay – pay me later. No rush.'

'Thanks for booking,' Sarah says. 'It's good one of us is organized.'

'No trouble,' I say. 'No trouble at all.'

And then, heavily pregnant, I went and sat next to Simon in the dark for the best part of ninety minutes. Is that weird?

20

ooking back, I try to understand how Simon won his place in this story. Everyone could see at the time that he'd got a crush on me. Anna clearly didn't like him and, although I could see with my own eyes that he was a bit off-grid, I just couldn't bring myself to be mean. I don't know if I can blame it on hormones, but he had a vulnerability that I couldn't ignore, and I guess it aroused some sort of mothering instinct in me. I kept telling myself that Simon had been deeply hurt by his ex-wife, and that he was committed to caring for his dad – that's a good thing, isn't it? On top of that, he didn't get out much, and his job involved interacting with nothing but computers, so he probably wasn't the most socially competent person. I've always liked to champion the underdog.

These are the things I told myself at the time; these are the reasons why I allowed Simon into my social circle. Maybe I'm talking rubbish but, looking back, I have no other explanation for why I didn't just tell him to get lost.

And it wasn't as if I fancied him in any way: Jake and Simon were chalk and cheese. To Jake's raffish good looks and easy charm, Simon was awkward; a geek. If Jake was the captain of the rugby team, Simon was the librarian, the head prefect, the IT expert who wouldn't sweep you off your feet at the prom, but could likely hack the school mainframe. He placed little store by fashion or grooming – not that he looked unkempt – but I imagined he'd not be fussed about the brand of his shampoo or his soap; not go out of his way to buy the latest cut of jeans or shirt; be bemused in the face of my own yearning for handbags and shoes that cost more than a two-week holiday in the sun.

But then, I found myself wondering, would a man like Simon be more reliable, more honest, than a Jake? Maybe that was it. Maybe that's what I was searching for. Honesty and integrity. Were they the qualities I saw in Simon? He was persistent, too. Somehow, he wormed his way into my life at this late stage of my pregnancy – and, before I knew it, there was something in the timbre of his voice that visited me in my dreams. I never told Anna that. I liked his self-deprecating sense of humour, too, and those ridiculous specs that he was forever pushing up his nose; and I found it funny the way he said 'et cetera' all the time. Am I making excuses if I say I was lonely? Neglected? In need of male attention? I understood that Jake needed to travel, but that didn't mean that I liked it.

And then there was the question of what had happened that night between Jake and Sarah. Yes, he'd denied it, but I also knew what I'd heard. Giggle-giggle-silence-two-three-four. I'd put it in a box and sealed the lid but, deep down, I knew exactly what had happened and I didn't like it one bit. It's possible, then, that there was a bit of revenge in the mix – a bit of tit-for-tat. I suppose I was ripe for the picking. I suppose it was inevitable that, if Simon asked me out, I'd go.

* * *

He invites me to Wahaca, the one on the South Bank – the one made from coloured shipping containers that Anna had said she liked. It's as if he was at book club that night and overheard the discussion. And for a moment it seems odd, but I've told him, I think, about how it's where Jake took me for our first date-night in London. If he were interested in me 'that way', he'd be put off by that, wouldn't he?

'How about a Mexican meal before the baby comes?' he asks. 'One last *empanada*?' He tries to put on the accent and sing the word while miming playing the guitar, and the result is so ridiculous coming from such an English-looking and -sounding man that I can't not laugh, but it's done the trick: now my mouth's watering at the thought of the smells and tastes of all those delicious dishes, and somehow, in all the laughter, it's agreed that we're going. I don't recall him specifying that it would be dinner, and I don't recall actually saying yes.

But Wahaca is casual. It could be worse, I tell myself as I pull on my maternity jeans and a sweater. We could be going to the Italian Jake and I each went to with Sarah, with its romantic lighting. If Simon had asked me there for dinner, I might be worried, but this is more of a canteen. It's safer.

We take the train up to London together. It makes sense, and I'm glad to be with Simon as we battle the rush-hour crowds, the pushing and jostling, the steps and escalators. He's a quiet person to travel with but it doesn't bother me. We talk a little about the plans he's made for his dad's care while he's out with me, but mainly he looks out of the window, so I do the same, enjoying the buzz I always get as I head towards central London. At Victoria, we cram onto the tube for a few stops, clattering around the green line without saying much, and then we're walking over the river, its swirling mass making me slightly giddy, and then there we are: suddenly in front of the restaurant.

'You want to take a walk by the river first, or later?' Simon asks, nodding to the embankment that fringes this busy stretch of river, home to street artists, joggers, walkers, commuters and tourists. It's a cold evening, but dry, the black water of the Thames reflecting the city's lights back at us.

'Oh, you're cruel,' I say. 'You bring a hungry pregnant woman to food and expect her to wait?'

'It was a question!' Simon says, hands up like a surrender. 'Sorry! Eat it is!'

He's never been to a Wahaca before; never eaten Mexican aside from Tex-Mex tacos in some food court, somewhere.

'Don't worry,' I say, leading him inside and taking a seat at one of the colourful tables. 'I'll order for you.' And perhaps I get carried away – perhaps, as my dad would say, my eyes are bigger than my ginormous belly, because I order way too much food.

'Are you sure about all this?' Simon asks as I name dish after dish. 'I hope there are some *empanadas* there. I've always wanted to try one.' And so I add those, too, and then, when the busyness of ordering's subsided, I start talking to disguise the uneasiness that's crept up on me. This is not a date, but suddenly it feels like one. I wonder if the baby can feel my nerves; can somehow sense that mamma's with a man who's not his papa.

'Stop,' Simon says, putting his hand on top of mine on the table and taking an exaggerated deep breath, closing his eyes and lifting his face with the inhale, then looking at me as he exhales slowly. 'Just take a moment to breathe in and breathe out, and just "be" in the moment.'

'What?' My hand is stiff under his.

'You're talking a mile a minute. I can barely keep up. You're like a bee, buzzing from one thing to another. Worse than a bee. A bee on a sugar high.'

I look at him and feel a blush rising. I pull my hand away. 'Sorry.'

The guacamole arrives and Simon pauses before taking some. 'Do you want to Instagram it?'

'No, it's okay. That's more Anna. I swear she can't eat anything without Instagramming it first.'

'I've noticed.' Simon dips a chip and puts the whole thing in his mouth, leaving a smear of guacamole on the corner of his mouth. I watch as he licks it off, his tongue sliding around his lips.

'Mmm,' he says. 'I don't usually like avocados. Horrible slimy things, like the bogeys of giants . . .'

'Bleurgh!' I pretend to gag. 'Thanks for that delightful image. I can't un-see that now!'

'But this is delicious, absolutely delicious. The chilli and the whatever else it is in there completely changes it.' He dips in another tortilla chip and takes a big scoop. 'I see why you like this place.'

We take our time eating, as if waiting a little will allow our bodies to create more space in which to cram the extra food. But even I have to concede defeat. I ask the waitress if she can pack the remains for us to take away.

'It's such a waste,' I say to Simon, worried he might think me cheap. 'My parents always had this thing about not wasting food. Does your dad like Mexican food? It might be a treat for him.'

Simon looks down. 'Father's on a very bland diet these days. It'd probably make him sick.' He sighs. 'Anyway . . .' He sticks his abdomen out, puts his hands on either side of it and gives it a rub. 'I see how you must feel. It's like I have a baby in there myself. But that was decidedly the best food I've ever eaten. Thank you for introducing me.'

'You're welcome.'

Without discussing it, we find ourselves meandering down towards the river, and then ambling along, watching the boats plying up and down: brightly lit dinner cruises, RIBs, water buses and glass-covered catamarans. On the opposite bank, blue lights are strung along like bunting; in the distance, the dome of St Paul's is lit up white: the sight of that and the old-fashioned black lampposts under which we're walking makes me feel as if we're in a movie. I rub my hands together and flex my fingers, then blow into my cupped hands.

'Here,' says Simon, and he takes my left hand in both of his, gives it a rub, then places it inside his jacket pocket along with his own. All the while he does this, he continues to walk, as if it's no big deal for him to be holding my hand inside his jacket pocket and, because he acts like it's no big deal, I feel I can't pull away without making an issue of it. Simon's hips bump my side until we fall into step and I walk along, my left arm stiff, wrestling with myself: I know he likes me, so am I encouraging him? Or am I being a prude for reading more into this than he probably means?

'Have you ever been on one of those?' Simon nods his head to a RIB, cleaving through the water. 'Water taxis. Fastest way to get around London, but cost a fortune. Four hundred quid I think, per hour.'

'And people pay that?'

'Stressed-out bankers maybe. Or tourists. I guess you get the whole boat for that price. If you clubbed together . . .'

We come to a halt and turn to face the river.

'How's your other hand?' Simon asks and he simultaneously takes it in his and places both our hands in his other pocket and, in that moment before I realize a line's been crossed, he lurches his head towards me and presses his mouth onto mine. I wrench away but not before I've felt the softness of his lips; the teeniest bit of wetness from his saliva. I step back, my hand over my mouth. Simon stares at me, aghast, both hands raised in apology.

'I'm so sorry! I . . . I shouldn't have . . . I just . . .' He shakes his head. 'I'm sorry. No excuse.'

We stare at each other.

'It's fine,' I say finally. 'Forgotten already. But don't try it again or I'll chop your balls off.'

We sit in silence on the train.

21

'So how are you feeling?' Anna asks as she eases her car into a gap on the main road the next day. She's taking me for a day at a spa as a thank-you for the help I gave her with her house. It's still early and the traffic's all stop-go. Anna's car is warm and snug after the chill of the air outside, but it's so stuffy I can barely breath. I wonder if she'll be able to tell by looking at me that something happened with Simon. I feel strangely guilty. Complicit even, as if it was me who kissed him.

'Oh . . . I'm okay, thanks.' I undo my scarf, then struggle to undo my coat under the seatbelt.

'Are you too hot?' Anna puts her hand to the dial. 'It's a bit warm, isn't it? Your built-in heater's bigger than mine!' She gives a little laugh and turns the heating down a couple of clicks. It's still not enough but I don't think anything bar opening the windows to let in the icy air would cool me enough today.

'Thanks.' I sigh. 'Oh, all right. Tired. I think the "blooming" stage has bloomed and gone.' I sigh, realizing I sound ungrateful. 'No, it's great, it really is. I just didn't sleep much last night, that's all.' I flash her a smile but she's focusing on the traffic.

'Me neither,' she says.

'What kept you up?'

'Oh . . . I'd gone to bed early but the phone rang a couple of times in the night.'

'Oh?' I imagine the shrill ring of the phone; Anna jolting awake, alone in the darkness, her heart pounding.

'Wrong numbers.'

'Did you speak to them?'

'One wanted a massage, the other didn't say anything. But after that I couldn't get back to sleep.'

'Someone called you wanting a massage?'

Anna indicates to turn off the main road and sighs. 'I've had a few calls like that lately. I think my number must have been printed in an ad somewhere by accident. It can't be a coincidence, can it? So many men calling for massage?'

'Oh no! That's terrible. How can you find out? Have you asked them who they're trying to call?'

'They hang up the moment they realize they got the wrong number. Some don't speak good English. Others are just embarrassed.'

'Oh god, that's awful. I hope it stops soon. The last thing you need is Tom, Dick and Harry calling you up for happy finishes!'

Anna gives a small laugh without much mirth. 'You and me both. Anyway, how come you couldn't sleep?'

I take a deep breath. 'I went out for a bite with Simon,' I say as casually as I can. 'And I think the food was a bit rich. Either that or I just ate too much.'

'I see,' says Anna. I steal a peep at her to try and read her face, but she's looking ahead, out of the windscreen. 'Where?'

'Wahaca?' I say, inflecting my voice upwards though I'm not sure why.

'On the South Bank?' Anna asks, still focusing on the road.

I nod. 'Easiest, I guess.'

Anna's silent for a moment.

'Well, I hope he behaved himself,' she says, and there's something off in her tone. 'Honestly, Taylor. You're so trusting. You barely know the guy. You should have told me what you were doing, just in case.'

'You're right. I should have done,' I say, and I mean it. It's been ages since I've had a friend who cared enough to watch out for me. 'Anyway, how are you aside from tired? Feels like I haven't seen you in ages.'

'I'm great.' Anna smiles. 'Desperately looking forward to a massage.'

'That makes two of us.'

* * *

And we're not disappointed. The massage is blissful. Anna's done her homework and the spa has special massage beds with big holes in them for pregnant bellies, and ridiculous-looking holes for boobs, so we can lie face-down. I hadn't been expecting that and it's a wonderful surprise. I take my time getting up afterwards and practically glide down the corridor to the relaxation area where the therapist settles me on a teak lounger and pours me a cup of steaming-hot ginger tea. I lie back and close my eyes. Why don't I do this more often? I used to do it all the time when I worked. Between flights, I was in and out of spas for massages, facials, mani-cures – you name it, I had it. But these days . . . I'd kind of thought the Brits didn't really have that spa culture, but maybe I'm wrong. Maybe they do and I just haven't uncovered it. I feel as if Anna has shown me a luxurious new side to living in the UK.

'Hey.' Anna pads into the room in her spa slippers and settles into the lounger next to mine. 'How was it?'

As she talks, she takes a snap of the teapot, then arranges her slippers by the lounger for another photo.

'Mmm,' I say. 'Awesome.'

'Good. I'm glad.' Anna looks up from her phone. 'I've booked us each an application of make-up and a blow-dry later, so we leave looking good.' She shudders. 'I hate leaving spas all greasy-faced and covered in oil. Ick.'

'Me too! Thank you so much. You really didn't need to do all this. It's too much.'

Anna gives a self-deprecating laugh. 'No. Thank *you* for your help with the house.'

It's my turn to laugh. 'Seems like a win-win situation to me: I get to spend your money doing something I love, then you thank me by buying me a massage!'

'Are you always so positive?'

'Yep. It's in my DNA.'

Anna uploads her pictures then we lie side by side on our loungers in silence for a bit, just absorbing the niceness of where we are.

'We won't be able to do this much longer,' Anna says. 'Once the babies come.'

'No. Speaking of which, I meant to ask . . .' I wince to show I hope I'm not treading on her toes. 'You said it was a story for another day, and I hope you don't mind me asking, but how did you and Rob get together? You never did tell me.'

Anna sighs and gives her head a little shake. 'It's a long and not very nice story. Although . . .' she looks over at me, 'it could possibly help you understand what's going on in my head at the moment.'

'I'm here all day,' I say.

She takes a deep breath. 'Okay. Well, if you really want to hear it?'

I nod.

'Well, don't blame me if it upsets you. It is upsetting. All right?'

'Okay.' I pull my dressing gown closer around myself despite the warmth of the heating.

'So I had this friend, Louise,' Anna says and I note the past tense. 'This is about her, really.' She looks at me to check I'm still interested and I nod for her to go on. 'We were really close: flatmates. We'd known each other since school. We got on really well – shared everything. We never fought like some women do when they live together. She was like my sister, actually, only better.'

'Okaaay,' I say, imagining Anna coming home and finding Louise in bed with her fiancé. That old chestnut.

'Well, one night she'd gone out and I'd stayed home. We usually kept tabs on each other; made sure we were safely home, but that night I'd fallen asleep. She was later than usual. It was 2 a.m. when I heard footsteps creeping up the stairs, and I didn't think anything of it.'

'No,' I say. 'Why would you?'

'Exactly. I just thought, "Great, Lou's home," put my ear plugs in and went back to sleep.'

'Okay.'

Anna runs her hand through her hair and shuts her eyes. 'Oh god. To this day, I go over and over the sound of those footsteps on the stairs. They haunt me. How was I to know?'

'What happened?' My heart's suddenly running in my chest; I can feel it pulsing. I put a hand on it and press.

Anna shakes her head, then bites her lip. 'They think he'd been watching her in the club where she was dancing.' My eyes go wide. 'Maybe he took a fancy to her,' Anna says, 'or maybe she did something to annoy him, we'll never know, but, for whatever reason, this man followed Lou home. Somehow he got into the house and went up to her bedroom. Oh god! When I think about it . . . It was across the landing from mine. My door wasn't locked.' Anna's voice breaks and she puts her hand over her eyes. Seeing how distressed she is, I lean over and touch her arm.

'It's okay. You don't have to tell me . . .'

'It's fine.' She swallows and wipes her eyes. 'I found her in the morning. She was on the floor. I thought she was asleep and then I saw . . .'

Anna stops talking and I wait but her eyes are closed. Then she opens them and gives herself a shake. 'Gagged, raped and stabbed.' Anna speaks so quietly I cock my head towards hers to hear over the thrum of the distant traffic. 'Left for dead. I hadn't heard a thing.'

The breath goes out of my lungs. 'Oh my god. That's horrific. I'm so sorry. I can't imagine.'

'I know,' Anna says dully. 'She was barely alive but she survived. Went through counselling, but we drifted apart. It was as if I reminded her of what had happened. She moved away, and I never really got over it. It's why I was so scared when that rattle came through my door. It brought it all back. I felt I was being watched.'

'And now the phone calls.' I speak my thoughts before I think them, and regret the words as soon as they come out.

'Exactly,' Anna says. 'I'm the first to admit I'm probably more paranoid than most people, but . . .' She shudders. 'I can't help putting two and two together sometimes and getting five.'

'Oh god, I'd be paranoid too, if I'd been through that.'

Anna gives me a small smile. 'I thought it might explain a few things.'

We lie in silence for a minute or two while images play in my mind of Anna waking up, going downstairs, waiting for her friend to wake up, then calling her, getting no response and finally knocking on the door. Waiting for her friend to invite her in, then tentatively pushing the door open to find – oh god, I just can't imagine how awful it must have been.

'It was then that I met Rob,' Anna says. 'I used to hang out with a few people – you know just go to the pub or the movies et cetera – and he turned up at the pub with us one night; he knew one of the guys.' She closes her eyes and laughs to herself. 'Yeah, I fell for him straightaway. He's a big man. He made me feel safe. It helped that he swept me off my feet. He took me on really fancy dates and helped me forget. And that's it, really. The right man at the right time.'

'Oh my god.' I really want to give Anna a hug but short of climbing onto her lounger, I can't. 'I'm so sorry.'

She breathes in deeply and lets it out slowly. 'So that's how I met Rob. The irony is I got together with him because he made me feel safe – and now he lives on the other side of the world. Fat lot of good that turned out to be.'

She fixes a smile on her face. 'So now I've told you that, tell me something happy. Is Jake excited about the baby?'

I nod. 'Yeah. Totally.'

'That's good. When I told Rob, you'd have thought I'd asked him to climb Everest in flip-flops and a bikini. He went all pale and quiet.'

I laugh. 'I guess they all take the news differently.'

'But was getting pregnant his idea or yours?'

'Well . . .' I have to think about this. 'Yes . . . we both wanted it. When it happened the first time, we were both over the moon.' I pause. 'After that . . . if I'm honest, when it became hard work, he went off the idea a bit. I think there was a while when he was wondering if it was worth all the effort, but I wanted a baby more than ever. It's like it was this thing that everyone in the world had but was out of my reach. I used to do those fertility-test kit things and lie in wait for him on fertile days.'

'Oh my god. That's crazy. But he's pleased now?'

'Yes.'

'That's great.' Anna nods to herself. 'Sometimes I think we're lucky our husbands aren't here all the time. Do you ever think that? You hear about so many couples who fall apart during the pregnancy; who start fighting. There's so much to organize, so many decisions to make, I suppose . . . and the financial worries, and the hormones . . . I mean, when it comes to us, I'm the boss of an executive committee of one. I make the decisions on my own and he rubber-stamps the big ones – like the car – when he's home. There's no fighting. I don't have multiple personalities!'

We're still laughing at that when the spa manager appears with two elegant glasses on a tray.

'Here we go, ladies.' She places them carefully on the table between our loungers. 'Cheers.'

I shake my head. 'Oh, these aren't ours. We didn't order them.'

'They're part of the package.'

'It's fine,' Anna says, motioning the manager to leave them. 'Thank you.' She turns back to me. 'A glass of prosecco each was included but I asked them to bring elderflower pressé instead. I hope you don't mind.'

'Course not.'

Anna leans forward, picks up a glass and hands it to me. 'Cheers,' she says and we clink the glasses together. I raise mine to my lips and let the cold liquid seep onto my tongue. It may not be prosecco, but it's good.

'Thank you. Absolutely wonderful day.'

'You're welcome.' Anna smiles.

'No, I mean for everything. For being my friend. For letting me into your life.'

'It works both ways,' says Anna. 'Don't forget I was new here too. I didn't have many friends either. So I should be thanking you.'

'You had work, at least.'

Anna sighs. 'Remotely. It's not as if I have colleagues to chat to every day.'

'I used to go to the deli just to talk to the lady behind the counter,' I say, and Anna laughs as if I'm joking. 'No, really. Ridiculous, isn't it? The longest conversation I'd have all day when Jake was away would be about olives or the amount of hummus I wanted. I hate frickin' olives.'

'No!'

'And you know what I said about joining the walking group to meet people? I can't tell you how happy I was to spot you there. I was so jealous when you went to talk to that other woman – Polly? – and left me with Simon!'

'Oh, so you're blaming Simon on me now, are you?' Anna says. 'Charming.'

We sit in silence for a moment, both thinking, I imagine, about the walking club and the days before we met.

'So,' says Anna. 'Tell me again about Simon. How come you went out for dinner with him?'

I lick my finger and slide it around the rim of the glass to make it sing as I try to work out for myself why exactly I went out with Simon.

'Did you tell Jake?' Anna says. 'You didn't, did you?'

'No, but . . .'

'Oh, for god's sake, Taylor. You've got to wise up. You barely know the guy and you go out alone at night with him, in London, without telling anyone. Anything could have happened. Anything!' Her voice rises and I realize she's actually angry with me.

I sigh. 'I'm sorry. I . . .'

'Didn't think. You didn't think, did you? But – oh god – after what happened to Lou, I just can't even begin to . . .' She buries her head in her hands then looks up at me. 'I don't want to lose another friend. That's all. Please be careful.'

'Thank you. I will.'

Anna's quiet for a moment. 'So he behaved himself, then?'

'Of course. I mean, look at me!' I sweep my hand over my belly. 'I'm a baby elephant.'

'I'm not even going to try and guess what goes on in his mind,' Anna says. 'But let's look at the facts: meets you, fancies you, sees you're pregnant, *still* fancies you, asks you out, takes you out . . . hmm . . . He's after something. Trust me.'

I'm focusing on the glass. 'You're overthinking this. Understandably – I get that now. But I think he's just a bit lonely. Can you believe he'd never had Mexican food before?'

'Or that's what he told you.' Anna whacks her forehead. 'God, there's one born every day. Go on, tell me: you ordered for him.

He thought you were amazing for introducing him to it? This is so predictable.'

'It wasn't like that!'

'Okay, how was it then?'

I shake my head. 'It was fine. Nothing more, nothing less.'

'If you're sure,' Anna says doubtfully, giving me a long, hard look.

'Yep, all's good.' I take a deep breath and pick up my glass. 'So, as I was saying: cheers. To us. To friends. And thank you for looking out for me.'

'Yes, to friends,' says Anna. 'Cheers.'

I KNOW HOW YOU
PAID FOR COLLEGE

Oh yes, you'd like everyone to believe you came from a good
family; that money was never an issue, but that'd be a lie, wouldn't
it? And you know how I hate lies. You know they make my blood
boil; how they make anger swirl inside me like hurricane fucking
Katrina. Lies make me want to hurt you, slowly and carefully. I
want to watch your face as you register the pain, watch as the
agony increases, watch as you realize I've completely and utterly
destroyed your perfect little life.

But look, you're distracting me.

Let's talk about what really happened when you finished school.
About how your parents could barely scrape together enough
money for you to go to college in the first place. How your mum
wrung her hands, and your dad worked nights trying to make
enough to keep his princess happy. How you begged and pleaded
and said you'd get a job.

Oh, how fucking noble you were. As if you're the first kid to
pay her way through college. But for once you were as good as
your word, weren't you? You got a job. And what was it? What did
you tell everyone?

'I'm a dancer.'

Oh fucking la-di-dah. But shall we elaborate here, sweetie-pie?

What was it? Ballet? Contemporary? Or maybe you taught line-dancing at old peoples' homes? Aww, wouldn't that be sweet.

Dance, my arse. You were a stripper. A common-or-garden stripper.

And how dare you shake your head like that: I could have said hooker, couldn't I? Because we both know what went on in that lap-dance club, don't we? We both know that the skimpy under-wear with the nipple holes was the most clothing you wore all night. We both know that for thirty bucks you peeled off that excuse for a bra and pants and gyrated naked in the laps of strangers, sliding your pussy against their hard-ons, shoving your tits in their faces.

Thirty bucks a time, princess. Are you proud?

But that's not where it ended, is it? You forget I know about the back room. The room with the red velvet loungers and the one-way windows . . . the room where you made a hundred bucks a trick, two hundred or more . . . the room where men slipped you their cards and offered you four hundred for a home visit; a grand to meet them on their yachts.

Dirty little bitch, aren't you? And now you're going to be a mother. Oh, hear me laugh.

If I were you, sweetie-pie, I'd start paying me a bit more attention. Not that it'll change anything, but . . . I'd like to feel you'd made at least a bit of an effort.

22

Lying in bed on Saturday morning, with my eyes still shut, I can hear Jake pottering about downstairs. Long gone are the days when he'd reach for me first thing on waking. Now he tiptoes out of bed as quietly as he can, trying not to wake me. Is he being considerate – or avoiding me?

I squirm in the bed as if changing physical position can make my thoughts more comfortable, but the truth is I feel I don't know Jake any more. I said I'd forgiven him, and I believed I had, but the scars of infidelity can't be erased just like that. The mind may want to forget, but the soul cannot. And now Jake's distant again and my warning bells are ringing. This is what happened last time, this is how the affair started, so who is it this time? Sarah? Or someone else? I'm thinking all this, when the bedroom door swings open.

'Your breakfast, madam.'

Jake's standing at the door in his boxers and a t-shirt, with a tray in his hands. It's a week or so into January and the days have that flat, post-Christmas, post-New Year feel to them, and I can't believe how grey everything is, both figuratively and literally. It's going to be a long haul till spring.

I push my hair out of my eyes and wriggle into a sitting position, surprised. The baby shifts, too, causing me to adjust myself again.

'What's going on? It's not my birthday, is it?'

'I just wanted to make a fuss of you,' says Jake, and it's so out of character these days that fear twists in my stomach. A red neon sign flashes in my head: G U I L T Y. 'We'll soon be too busy with the baby,' Jake says. 'Here.'

I smooth the duvet over my lap and he places the tray carefully on it.

'Wow,' I say, looking at it. There's fresh orange juice, coffee, a croissant and marmalade, even scrambled eggs and smoked salmon on a bagel. Propped between the dishes there's a folded piece of paper. I pick it up.

'What's this?'

'Have a look.' Jake looks excited, so I open the paper and read: it's a hotel booking confirmation.

'Brighton?'

Jake nods. 'What do you think?'

'I . . . wonderful! But why?'

'I thought we could have a mini-break. A last fling before the baby comes and we're up to our eyes in nappies and night feeds. It's too late to fly anywhere so I thought how about a night in an hotel?' He does the silent 'h' thing. 'And this is by the sea . . .'

I cock my head. 'Well, this is a surprise. When?' I'm looking at the confirmation form. 'Today?' I look up at Jake.

'Yes, today! Why not?' Jake shrugs. 'I thought we could drive down after breakfast; potter about The Lanes; walk along the sea-front; grab some lunch before we check in? Get some sea air; eat some fish and chips. Take the chance to be just us again before the baby comes. What do you say?'

'Sure . . .' I'm warming to the idea. He's right – it would be lovely to get away for a night; get a change of scene.

'Sarah suggested it,' says Jake. 'She thought you'd like a "baby-moon".' He draws the inverted commas in the air with his fingers and I can see he's pleased with the word. 'Honestly, I wouldn't have thought of it myself.'

'Great. I'll remember to thank her.'

Jake ignores – or misses – my sarcasm. 'Have you ever been to Brighton?'

'Not really. Only once, and I didn't stay over.'

'Right, well, eat up and we can pack and get going.'

Jake goes off to get our overnight bags and I google the hotel. He's picked a three-star place on a side street off the main seafront. It looks okay and it's in a good location. I hope our room's one of the ones with a partial sea view rather than a view to the car park out the back. I scroll through the other hotels on the booking website then see one I've actually heard of: The Grand. I bring up its website.

'Oh wow.' I cup my hand over my mouth as I scroll through gorgeous room after gorgeous room.

'Did you look at The Grand?' I call to Jake. 'It looks gorgeous.'

'Yeah – no space.' His voice is muffled from the inside of the under-stairs cupboard. 'Some conference or something.'

'Oh, shame.'

Still, we're off to Brighton! I find an image of Brighton seafront and upload it to Instagram. #Babymoon

23

The hotel was dreadful. I've no other word for it. The reception was tatty, with a threadbare carpet and a teenage receptionist who'd clearly rather be Snapchatting her mates than doing her job. Having worked for so long in a service-industry role myself, this is my pet hate and guaranteed to make my blood pressure rise in seconds, so I'd turned away and browsed a rack of leaflets of things to do in Brighton, trying to shut out the sound of her nasally voice. She did nothing to make our check-in go smoothly, and I could hear in Jake's tone that even he was becoming exasperated as she made him fill out a long form while she looked on, snapping the gum that she was chewing. There was a largely unidentifiable smell of old food hanging in the air – a cross between stale grease, eggs and toast – but even then I was still hoping for the best; hoping that the room was going to be better.

It wasn't. After we'd creaked our way up a narrow staircase past rooms from which we could hear snippets of other peoples' lives – a television blaring, a couple arguing while a baby cried – Jake opened a small door and we stood on the threshold of the room, already pinned against the wall by a bed that took up the entire space. The 'en suite' bathroom turned out to be a toilet and a sink on a tiled area behind a shower curtain that looked as if you could catch something off it.

Jake and I look at each other.

'I'm sorry,' he says. 'It looked better in the pictures. Shall we just go home?'

I throw my handbag onto the bed and sigh. 'It's such a shame. I was so looking forward to being in Brighton.'

'We could come back next weekend?' Jake says.

'We're here now.'

Jake closes the door behind him and we sit next to each other on the bed, which sags beneath our weight. There's not even space for a chair in the room. The wallpaper is flowery, with damp patches; the view is of the brick wall of the next-door building.

'We could go to The Grand and see if they've had any last-minute cancellations?' I say.

Jake shuts his eyes then opens them slowly. 'We could do. Is that what you want?'

I nudge him playfully. 'Well, it is a lovely hotel . . . and this is supposed to be a romantic break . . . What do you think?' I smile and he doesn't say anything. 'In fact . . .' I get out my phone and open my booking app. 'Let me just have a look here . . . Oh wow, great! It's got space! They must have had some cancellations.'

I look hopefully at Jake.

'How much?' he asks.

'Various,' I say. 'Have a look.' I hand him my phone. 'Just look at the size of some of those rooms! They have a sitting area – a sofa – a balcony. And they face the sea!' I'm clasping my hands together, forefingers crossed by my temples in the hope that Jake will go for it. 'It'll really be a babymoon to remember.'

Jake scrolls through the pictures and prices.

'Okay,' he says finally. He taps the screen a few times, then pulls out his credit card. 'You really want this?' I nod. 'Okay. Done.'

So we get back in the car and drive around to The Grand. When we walk in, pulling our cabin bags behind us, I almost expect the doorman to push us right back out of the revolving door. Although the outside's not really what I expected, the inside is like walking into a palace. With its huge, expensive-looking rugs, incidental sofas, beautiful staircase and even a grand piano – oh my god, a grand piano! – it's homely and grand at the same time. It makes me feel as if we're entering the home of some very, very rich friends.

'Wow.' I say it quietly, not wanting to look like we don't belong in a place like this, but also needing to say something. 'I can't believe this is a hotel.'

Jake smiles. 'It's certainly very nice.'

He walks up to the reception desk to check us in while I wander about, looking at the furniture, the lamps and the flower arrangements before sitting on one of the settees. I'm so excited to be here, I upload a quick picture of the reception area to Instagram: #Brighton #thegrandbrighton #livingthedream

'Right. The room's ready,' says Jake, coming over. 'We can go up to it now. Let's hope it's better than the last one.' He holds out his arm for me to heave myself up. 'Shall we?'

* * *

Jake opens the door and stands back for me to enter first. If he hadn't, I might just have pushed my way past him.

'Oh my god!' I say, going straight to the window. There are three huge, floor-to-ceiling windows, through which I see the black of an intricate balcony rail and, beyond that, the irresistible sparkle of sun on the ocean. It's a cold day, but bright, and I cross the room, absorbing as I do so the tranquillity of the greys and whites, the pale settees, the white coffee tables and the lushness of the pillows and the throw on the bed, but my focus is on one thing only: the ocean. I hadn't realized how much I've missed it. I pull open the balcony door and step outside, breathing in the damp, slightly fishy smell of it. Seagulls wheel around us, their squawks ripping the air.

'Wow!' It's all I can say. I turn and wait for Jake to catch me up.

He slides his arms around me, pressing his warmth against me as we both look out at the sea, the strip of orange beach, the road below us and the pier.

'How does madam find the view?' Jake asks.

'It's perfect.'

'It's not sand, by the way. It's shingle. I don't want you to be disappointed when we get down there.'

'Really?'

'Sadly so. But it's not like we're going to be building sandcastles in this weather, is it?'

I breathe in deeply, pulling the cold air in through my nose and deep into my lungs, then breathe it out, imagining all the car fumes and city pollution being expelled from my body, and the baby responds with a flurry of cramped kicks. Without saying anything I take Jake's hand and place it on my belly so he can feel it too, remembering with a gush of shame the feel of Simon's hand in the same place.

'Weird,' says Jake, 'that this is perhaps the last time we'll stay in a hotel on our own without having to worry about childcare.' He pauses. 'Maybe the last time we stay in a nice hotel at all.'

I tut. 'I'm sure we'll do it again.'

'Once he's left home maybe.'

'Harsh,' I say and Jake laughs. 'Come on, let's go in. It's cold.'

24

While we were in Brighton, Jake made it his mission to take me out for fish and chips. Looking back it seems odd, but he was almost obsessed with the idea.

'I can't believe you've never been "down the chippy",' he says in the room that afternoon. He's standing by the window, looking down at the bustling seafront. We've been out for a walk and a bit of lunch but I tire easily and wanted to come back for a rest. I'm on the sofa with my feet up, flicking through the hotel information folder provided in the room. Jake's made us both tea, which I'm drinking with a packet of very English shortbread fingers.

I put the folder down on my lap and squint into the room – can he be right? 'I've had curry and chips,' I say. 'That's British, isn't it?'

'Not the same,' says Jake.

'Chips and cheese?' I say. 'Chip butty?'

'Nope. Right. I'm taking you to a greasy chip shop tonight. Nothing beats the real deal. Crispy batter, soggy chips in paper . . . salt, vinegar . . . mmm . . .'

'Sounds great,' I say, but then I turn to the restaurants page of the hotel folder and see that The Grand has its own seafood restaurant. I download the menu onto my phone.

'Darling,' I say. 'About the fish and chips. How would you feel about having them at the hotel restaurant? It's got . . .' I swallow the saliva that floods my mouth just reading the words, 'mussels, prawns, crab, market fish, lobster! A lobster burger! They've even got steak. Fillet steak. "Aged Aberdeen Black grain-fed beef which has been personally selected" . . .' I laugh. 'Do you think they interviewed the cows? "Madam, could you please come here? Please walk this way, walk that way, let me see your gait. What is your opinion of Brexit?"'

Jake laughs. 'Bet the prices match.'

I ignore him. 'Corn-fed chicken, surf 'n' turf . . . look!' I show him a picture of the inside of the restaurant. 'It's so glamorous.'

'Chips taste so much better out of paper from a chippy. Trust me.'

I stand still for a moment, looking at Jake. He's reading something on the iPad and he doesn't look up. I stand behind him and rub his shoulders, my fingers finding knots in his muscles.

'God, I wish I was still earning, then I'd treat us myself,' I say.

Jake twists around on the sofa so he's facing me. 'Do you really want to go?'

I pull a hopeful face.

'It's just I thought . . . the fish and chips would be more authentic,' he says. 'I tell you what. Why don't we get dressed up and have a drink in the bar here, then go out for fish and chips? We could get a takeaway and eat them on the pier. What do you think?'

'Okay, deal.' I smile, looking at the lights twinkling outside. 'Sure. Now let me see what I can wear so they don't think a whale's been beached at the bar.'

'Gives "beach bar" a whole new meaning,' Jake laughs.

I walk over to the wardrobe and survey what scant clothes I brought. I have one reasonably nice maternity dress. I loved it when I bought it four months ago, but I'm bored senseless with it now. It's plain and black. The words 'jazz it up with jewellery' are wearing very thin. Still, I've brought an interesting pendant that I hope takes the focus away from the plain dress and huge belly, and it's this that I'm wearing as Jake escorts me down to the bar and we walk straight into the elegant vision that is Caroline and a tall, thin man I can only assume is her husband, the famous Toby Hughes-Smith.

25

I plaster a smile on my face as quickly as I can.

'Caroline! What a surprise!'

She leans in and gives me an air kiss that doesn't touch my skin. There's an aura of expensive perfume wafting around her.

'I did wonder if we'd bump into you here,' she says. 'Have you met my husband, Toby?'

'Nice to meet you,' says Toby, shaking my hand and Jake's hand in turn. His skin is cool and dry, and makes me think of lizards. And then Caroline stands back and looks Jake up and down.

'And, well I never,' she says, her face coming truly alive. 'It really is Jake The Rake. Bloody hell.' She stares at him, taking it all in: the dark jeans and white shirt, the jacket he threw on in honour of the bar, the thick, dark hair and Keanu's eyes, and I stand there next to him, seeing how he and Caroline would make a beautiful couple, and knowing she won't find a single thing to criticize. Everyone likes Jake; he's easy on the eye and he's a people-person: it's a winning combination to any outsider, as I know from bitter experience. Toby, on the other hand, in his freshly ironed slacks, his blue shirt and herringbone jacket with the point of a hankie poking out of the top pocket, looks like he's never done anything fun in his life. I imagine he must be very wealthy.

Caroline's still staring at Jake as if she's seen an apparition. 'How many years has it been?' she asks.

'Twenty-something, I guess?' says Jake.

'No! Less than that,' says Caroline. 'We're not that old. We left school at eleven, so . . . oh . . . twenty-three.' She laughs. 'Who'da thunk?'

Everyone laughs and then there's an awkward pause.

'We were just about to have a quick drink before we head out for some fish and chips,' Jake says. 'Would you like to join us for a snifter?'

Caroline extends her arm and peers at a gold watch that hangs on her wrist. It's one of those ones with small diamonds floating inside the watch face.

'What time's the table booked for?' she asks Toby.

'Eight.'

They look at each other intensely for a moment as if they're having a silent conversation, then Caroline says, 'Yes, sure.' She does a little shrug, and we all head over to the restaurant. At the door, I can't help but stop and stare. It's an interior that draws a silent 'wow' from me: it's light and airy, all pale woods, big windows and ornately carved high ceilings. But, seemingly unimpressed, Caroline stalks straight over to the curved bar, picks up the drinks menu and peruses it, then puts it back down with a weary sigh.

'Oh god, I can't be fucked with this. Why don't we just have champagne? In honour of our reunion. Might as well get a bottle.' She clicks her fingers and a barman turns. 'Over here!'

Caroline places the order, specifying a sparkling, non-alcoholic cocktail for me, then insisting on a specific brand of champagne, questioning the vintage with the barman and double-checking how cold the bottle will be before we perch ourselves on the high chairs that hug the U-shaped bar in a line. Jake's on the far end, then Toby, Caroline and me. Caroline turns her back on her husband, and focuses her full attention on me while the barman opens the champagne and pours three glasses.

'So, what fun to bump into you!' she says, tilting her head and running her hand through her hair. Her teeth, against the pearly pink of her lipstick, are white. 'Without meaning to coin a phrase . . .' she pauses to laugh, 'do you come here often?'

'What do you think?' I laugh, thinking about the rubbish hotel Jake had actually booked. 'This is a treat. Jake wanted to take me away for one last fling before the baby comes.'

'Oh, how lovely,' Caroline sighs extravagantly and takes a deep glug of champagne. 'Mmm. This is good. You're really missing out.' She closes her eyes, perhaps in appreciation of the champagne, perhaps thinking about something altogether different. 'The Grand is gorgeous. It's my home away from home. We came here every weekend when the kitchen was being renovated.' She shudders. 'Worst job ever. So much dust. But babymoons are like gap years these days, don't you think? Never heard of them then, five minutes later, everyone's doing them. Friends of ours went to the Maldives. Heaven, they said it was. Utter heaven. Gorgeous little over-the-sea villa.' She laughs. 'It'll be some years till you can do that yourselves. Don't think they let kids in water villas, do they, in case they fall in? Still, the beach villas are nice, too. Have you been to the Maldives?' She snaps her gaze back to me and I shake my head. 'Oh, never mind. This is perfectly lovely, isn't it? I'm sure you'll have a super time.' I nod, and she waves her hand around the bar. 'We come here a fair bit. One of the perks of not having kids: romantic escapes.' She doesn't sound so happy; her words are out of kilter with the sentiment in her voice. 'So, you and Jake,' she says. 'Can't believe you're married to my old schoolmate.' She drinks more champagne and the waiter discreetly refills her glass.

'What was he like at school? Do you remember much?'

'What's he said about me? You must have asked him by now.'

'Oh . . .' I think about his sly smile. Was it admiration? 'Not a lot.'

Caroline pouts. 'Really?'

I nod. 'Really. You know what guys are like.'

She sighs. 'I don't remember so much either. It's funny how the memory goes. I remember odd scenes, and impressions. Jake was . . .' She sighs. 'How to put it? One of the "boy" boys.'

'Okay . . .'

'You know, attention span of a gnat. Bit of a reprobate, even then. Running about, causing trouble. Far too much testosterone! God, I can't believe you let him go out with Sarah! She's trouble in a short skirt.' She pouts thoughtfully. 'What else? He always seemed to have bashed-up knees – scabs or plasters hanging off, and a snotty nose. God, I remember green snot dangling out of his nose once. It went in and out as he breathed. He thought it was hilarious, though I think it traumatized me. Funny what you remember. What else? I don't know. We moved away for a few years and I lost touch with most of the kids from primary school so I never saw him again. Till now!' She pauses. 'He's obviously doing okay for himself if he's brought you here. Hats off to him. It's a good choice.'

'Yes, what a coincidence you're here too,' I say.

Caroline looks sideways at me. 'We booked long before I saw your post, if that's what you're implying.'

I stiffen. 'I didn't know you followed me.'

'Don't flatter yourself. Your name popped up as a suggestion and I clicked.' She shrugs. 'It's all out there for anyone to see. Anyway, no harm done.'

Caroline takes another drink; the barman lifts the bottle to pour again and indicates that it's empty. Caroline gives him a nod to get another bottle. 'It's nice to see old Jakey again.'

'What did you mean about Sarah?' I say. 'When you said she was trouble in a skirt?'

Caroline laughs. 'Nothing beyond what everyone can see: namely, that I'm not sure she has the same moral compass as the rest of us.' She examines her nails, then looks sideways at me. 'And I say that as someone who's committed her own quota of misdemeanours . . .' She lowers her voice to a whisper. 'Let's just say it takes one to know one.' She taps the side of her nose with her finger. 'Her business is her business as long as she keeps her hands off Tobes. Mind you,' she laughs, 'he wouldn't. I mean, really! The state of her.'

'I think she looks great,' I say, feeling disloyal for even having this much of the conversation.

Caroline rolls her eyes. 'Beauty's in the eye of the beholder, I suppose.' She pauses. 'And what is it you see in that Anna? She's a funny one.'

I recoil, hurt on Anna's behalf.

'She's really nice.'

Caroline snorts. 'I guess you're both up the duff. I suppose that's enough at this point. So, where are you off to for supper?'

'Oh, I don't know. Just somewhere quick and easy. Jake wants me to have an authentic "fish and chips" experience on the seafront.'

'Seagulls pinching your chips, you mean?' Caroline shudders. 'Dreadful birds. Can't stand them with their beaks and those enormous claws. Why don't you eat here? I'm sure they do a good fish and chips, and it's far more salubrious.'

'I'm happy going somewhere more casual,' I say, and Caroline looks at my dress.

'You don't look so bad. It must be so hard to dress at this stage. You know some women amaze me: the ones you can see from behind and not even know they're pregnant. Anna's a bit like that, don't you think? Though I suppose she's not as far along as you are.' She sighs. 'I hope Jake's not taking you to some dodgy street café. I wouldn't put up with that, if I were you.' She leans into the bar so she can shout past Toby and me. 'Hey, Jake The Rake! Where are you taking your wife for supper?'

'We'll find somewhere nice,' Jake says politely.

Caroline bangs the bar with her hand and I realize she's a little tipsy. 'Don't be taking her to any dodgy street café!' she says loudly. 'You don't want her getting food poisoning in her condition. Why not eat here? It's one of the best seafood restaurants in Brighton, for god's sake, and you're right here, in it!'

Jake shakes his head. 'No, it's . . .'

'Oh, come on!' says Caroline. 'We need to catch up! We haven't seen each other in a million years. Don't be such a spoilsport. Why don't you join us?'

'Caro,' says Toby quietly. It's practically the first word I've heard him say all night since he's been in deep discussion with Jake.

Caroline waves her hand. 'No, it's fine. I've known him forever. Why come here and not eat in? Tobes, can you change our booking to a table for four?'

And so it happens that we join the Hughes-Smiths for "supper". The bill, after Toby's eaten the king prawns and Caro's nibbled at the lobster and ordered two more bottles of champagne, could likely have fed a family of four for a month. Toby pays.

26

'D id you have fun?' I ask Jake as we get ready for bed back in the room. It was strange saying goodnight to the Hughes-Smiths in the muffled silence of a thickly carpeted hotel corridor; somehow it lent me the impression that Jake and I were staying at their own country house. I hate to say it, but Caroline did look quite at home.

'I'd have preferred fish and chips in paper on the pier, but hey. It is what it is.'

'Nice of Toby to pay, wasn't it?'

'Well, they invited us . . .'

'Yes, but still. They didn't have to get the bill.'

Jake tuts. 'I'm sure he can afford it.'

I take off my pendant and earrings, tie my hair back and start cleansing my face at the double sink.

'It was the champagne more than the food,' Jake says. 'Really got stung there.'

'Yeah, Caroline was knocking it back, wasn't she? It was a bit irresponsible to keep ordering when no one else was drinking it.'

'I don't think she noticed that it was just her. But you seemed to be getting on all right with her?'

'She was better than she was that night at book club. But there's still an edge to her like . . . I don't know. Maybe it's just her sense of humour but she . . .' I sigh. 'She swears a lot, doesn't she?' I splash water on my face. 'How was Toby?'

'Nice. Seemed like a solid bloke.'

'I wonder what they have in common. They're like chalk and cheese. He's so stuffy and she's so . . .' I wave my hand, lost for the right word to describe her arrogance, her confidence and her utter belief that she's the best person ever to walk the earth.

'I get the impression he's her rock,' Jake says. 'Perhaps he's what keeps her anchored,' and I get the image in my head of Caroline shaped like a balloon, tethered on a string to Toby the rock. Immediately I want to prick her and watch her shriek her way into the stratosphere.

'Poor guy,' I say. 'No wonder he looks so serious.'

Jake comes into the bathroom in his boxers and squeezes toothpaste onto his brush.

'Oh, come on. He seemed like a nice guy. I don't think they've had it as easy as you might imagine.'

'What, Tobes didn't get a seven-figure bonus last year?' I laugh at my joke.

Jake shakes his head while brushing his teeth. I have to wait till he's finished before he carries on. He spits, rinses his mouth, then says, 'I don't know. He hinted that something bad happened a year ago. That this was some sort of bad-iversary. Maybe that's why Caroline was drinking so much and he didn't stop her. I think there was more to it than what we saw, put it that way.'

'Oh really? Like what?'

'I don't know. I didn't like to ask.'

I tut. 'You're useless! Caroline didn't say anything of the sort, or I would have asked, for sure.'

'I know you would.'

'I wonder if that's why they were so keen for us to join them. It seemed a bit desperate, didn't it?'

'Who knows,' Jake says. 'Let's go to bed.' He gets into bed but I linger at the dressing table, fiddling with my lotions and thinking about what Caroline said about trusting Jake with Sarah. I know I should trust him but he's away so much. It's the perfect excuse, isn't it? He could have a whole separate family without me knowing. Or was Caroline just winding me up? She strikes me as a woman with her own issues and insecurities. Is she the sort who likes to upset others to make herself feel good?

Jake lets out a loud fake snore.

'All right, all right, I'm coming.' But before I turn off my phone, I take one more look at the selfie the four of us snapped in the bar before I join him: Caroline's smiling her beautiful, symmetrical smile right into the camera, but behind her eyes, now I think about it, is there a hint of something else?

YOU ABORTED HIS BABY

Oh, don't look so shocked. It's your dirty little secret, isn't it? The one that comes back to haunt you in the middle of the night. You didn't even tell him you were pregnant, did you, even though you'd been together a year? Just decided a baby wouldn't fit into your life at that point and got rid of it.

Who'd have thought you could be so cold-hearted? You, of all people.

And don't you go getting all self-righteous on me; judging me for finding out. You've no one to blame but yourself. You know your Instagram has 'location' switched on, don't you? All it takes for me to find out where you are is one click, and there it is, a pin in a map showing me how to find you.

I can't believe you wouldn't know that. No one's that naive, not even a fourth-grader.

And I'll be honest: sometimes I wonder if you leave it on for me; wonder if you're deliberately leaving clues for me – but then I have to pinch myself. Of course you're not. You genuinely are that fucking stupid.

So, I'm bored one day. You're quiet on social media for once. It's rare, but it's one of those days when you're not posting any-thing – no Tweets, no Instagram, nothing – so I decide to go for a drive; pay you a visit. And, honestly, there are worse things you can do in life than rifle through a few rubbish bins. I have latex gloves. I use them: it's not that disgusting. Food containers – ready meals for one; drinks cans (you really should recycle, though I suppose you have other things on your mind); used cotton-wool balls and tissues; coffee pods; and then there it is: the pill packet.

At first I'm not sure what it is. I don't take it. Oh no, I'm no amateur. I photograph it and I put it back. Exactly where I found it: under the lasagne box.

And then I google it. And you know those days you have when everything goes your way? Days that make you want to sing and dance? It's one of those days because what I find out is that that packet contained the abortion pill. For use at less than nine weeks. So how long do you think about it for? A fortnight? A week? A day? An hour? When you see those blue lines sitting on the toilet that morning, what are your thoughts? What drives you to the planned-parenthood clinic?

Oh, don't answer that: I know why you did it. You 'weren't ready'. Because, back then, you think there's a perfect time to have a child. You think you can take all the time in the world because getting pregnant is as easy as one, two, three. You think you can pop babies out like fucking McDonald's Drive-Thru orders, don't you?

I thought I knew you but this shocks me.

You don't deserve this baby.

You don't deserve it at all.

27

My birthday dinner was to take place the week after we'd been to Brighton, at Sarah's house. According to Jake, the two of them had talked through every possible restaurant option before agreeing over dessert that she would host the dinner at her house, on condition that she didn't have to cook herself.

'She's far too busy,' Jake had told me beforehand, in a way that pricked me like a heat rash. I knew I couldn't possibly compare my rather quiet life to that of a single working mum of two kids (even if they did live mostly with her ex), but that didn't make me feel better about the way he'd said it almost admiringly. The irony wasn't lost on me, either, that she got a night at a restaurant with Jake in order to decide that I wouldn't have a night out at a restaurant with him. So I suppose I start the day in the wrong frame of mind. The doorbell rings not long after Jake's left for work.

'Happy birthday to you! Squashed tomatoes and stew!' Anna sings as I open the door to a cloud of coloured balloons behind which I can just about make out enough of her to identify her.

'Aww, thank you. Come in.' I usher her into the living room where she hands me an envelope as well as the handful of balloon strings.

'Happy birthday!' she says. 'Here, let me. I thought we could . . .' She pulls out a dining chair and ties the balloons to the back of it.

'There, look: very festive. I'm sorry I didn't bring a banner – I bought one but completely forgot to bring it.'

'You can bring it tonight,' I say, opening the envelope. It's a voucher for an anti-ageing facial at the spa we went to, and a homemade voucher for one hour of babysitting from 'Aunty Anna'.

'Thank you so much!' I give her a hug. 'That's so thoughtful of you.'

'You're welcome,' she says. 'I thought that after the baby comes you might need a pick-me-up – or before. You don't need to use the vouchers concurrently.'

'It's so kind of you. Thank you. I'll do the same for you, of course, when you've had yours.'

'I'll hold you to that,' says Anna. She pauses, then takes a deep breath. 'Look, by the way, there's something I've got to tell you . . .'

She pulls an 'awkward' face, gritting her teeth and scrunching up her face as if she expects to be struck. I raise my eyebrows at her.

'What's up?'

'I can't make it tonight.'

'What? How come?' I stare at her, looking for spots on her skin or other signs of sickness. But she looks fine. Glowing, in fact.

'Rob's flying through London en route to the States,' she says. 'I'm so sorry. There's nothing I can do about it. He's booked the flights.' She rolls her eyes at me. 'He never thinks to ask if it suits me, just assumes I'm always available. He's arranged it so he's in a hotel overnight near Heathrow. It's date night. I might have to put out.' She laughs self-consciously. But I'm not laughing. Without her, my birthday evening falls as flat as the proverbial. 'You'll have a lovely time, though,' Anna continues, 'I'm sure Sarah's arranged a fab evening. I wish I could be there . . .'

'Why the States?' I walk into the kitchen and put the kettle on to hide the disappointment that I can feel pulling at my face, making my lip wobble.

'He's staking out a job in Texas,' Anna says. 'It'd be a promotion. More money. Better package.'

My stomach drops. 'Would you go too?' I say with my back to her. 'You've only just set up in London.'

'I miss the States. But it's early days. I can't stay for coffee, by the way, if that's what you're doing. Lots to arrange before tonight. He's about to board right now.'

'So you'd move back?' I say, switching the kettle back off and turning to face her.

'Let him get the job first, then we'll decide,' she says. 'Though we've lived in Texas before, so it'd be easy. Anyway, I imagine we'll talk about it when we see each other.' She laughs. 'But, look – sorry about tonight, but I knew you'd understand.'

'It's okay,' I say, trying to inject some sincerity into my voice. 'So when does he land? And leave again? How long do you have together?'

'Oh, he gets in about six in the evening, I think, and then leaves again around lunchtime tomorrow.'

'Lovely,' I say.

'Yep,' she says. 'He's planned it really well. We'll go out for dinner, then have breakfast tomorrow and off he'll go. I might tell him about the phone calls.'

'Oh! Are you still getting them?'

'Yeah.'

'I'd think about it, though,' I say. 'You don't want to worry him, especially when he's not here. There's so much I don't tell Jake when he's not here because I don't want him to worry.' I roll my eyes at Anna but she looks away. We move towards the front door. 'Anyway, thanks for coming over. And for the balloons and present.'

Anna faces me and puts her hands on my shoulders. 'Are you sure you're okay? You'll have a brilliant night. You'll have to tell me if Simon comes . . . and everything that Caroline gets up to.

And I want pictures. Especially of what Sarah wears. My guess is it's going to be up to here!' She draws a line on her upper thighs.

'Yeah, will do,' I say. 'You have a great time. Enjoy "date night".' I can't keep the sarcasm from coating the words but Anna's already halfway down the front path.

'Bye then.' She waves as she lets herself through the front gate. 'Have fun! Don't do anything I wouldn't do!'

I close the door then slump onto the sofa. Fancy cancelling on the day. Of course I get it that Rob's flying through, but of all the luck. If only he'd spoken to her, he could have flown the next day. I run my hand through my hair. For god's sake, why me? My last birthday without a baby; my first birthday in London; my new friends . . . except the most important one.

I grab the iPad and open a search page. 'Qatar to London flight timetable', I type into the search box. Sure enough, there's a flight listed that gets in at 5.55 p.m. Hope flares for a moment: maybe she could come for a drink at Sarah's first, then go to the airport. It'll take him a while to get through at Heathrow, for sure, and she's got all night and tomorrow morning. Can't she divide herself between both of us? I pick up the phone to call Anna then stop myself.

Instead, I click through to flight-tracking and find the flight. Anna's right, it's just taken off and is heading towards Iran.

'Huh, Rob,' I say nastily, jabbing at the little plane icon on the screen. 'You have no idea what you've just done. That's no way to treat your wife's best buddy, is it now?'

28

So I admit I go to my birthday dinner in bad grace. I'm glad I go, though, because I learn something there. I learn that I'm not imagining it: Sarah really does fancy Jake. Not just a little bit, but really, really, might-do-something-about-it fancies him.

She's ordered in something impressive from Cook for us to eat, and when we get there she's making cocktails in the kitchen. Jake hands her the flowers he's picked up from a trendy florist in London. I've already clocked how nice they are.

'Thank you. Virgin mojitos for the birthday girl!' Sarah says, giving me an air kiss and pointing to a small jug and a glass next to it. 'Help yourself. I didn't want you to feel left out. Hello, darling,' she says to Jake, going over and offering her cheek for a kiss. She's wearing a dress that does a very good job at hiding any extra weight she might be carrying around her middle. It skims all the right places, and the way the pattern's designed makes it even more flattering. Despite Anna's prediction, it falls nicely above the knee, showing us all that she has legs like a racehorse. Once again, I'm a blob in the ubiquitous black maternity dress, and that doesn't help my mood, either. I still remember the way Caroline looked at me in the restaurant at The Grand and said 'You don't look *so* bad.'

Even as I stand there in Sarah's kitchen with my little jug of virgin mojitos, I wish we weren't here. I wish Jake and I were in a restaurant on our own, just the two of us. Or, better still, just at home, me in my pyjamas with a take-out and a movie. Jake's leaving again in the morning and I really don't want to share what little time I have him with Sarah, friend or no friend.

'So did you have a good time in Brighton on your dirty little weekend with the Hughes-Smiths?' Sarah asks us. 'Lovely picture you posted . . .' Her smile doesn't reach her eyes and I realize that she's jealous; that she suspects that the four of us planned to go down without her.

'I couldn't believe it when we bumped into them there,' I say. 'Very random.'

'Bit of a coincidence, eh!' Sarah says, narrowing her eyes as she tastes the cocktail. 'Of all the hotels in the country and you both end up there; in the same bar at the same time! Mmm, that's delicious, even if I do say so myself.'

'It was a bit like that,' I say with a shrug. 'Is everyone here now?'

'Ah. Anna called. She can't make it. Apparently Rob's on a flying visit so she's off for some rumpy-pumpy.' Sarah shimmies her hips. 'Anyway, I bet you already knew that, given you two barely even breathe without tagging each other on social media. But yes, the Hughes-Smiths are in the lounge. Anyway, be a dear, why don't you take this through while I borrow your husband for a minute?' She puts the jug and a stack of glasses on a tray and holds it out to me. 'Are you okay carrying it? It's not too heavy.'

'It's okay,' says Jake. 'I'll take it.' Does he flash her a look, like, 'not now', or am I imagining it?

So he picks up the tray and we both go through to the cream-coloured living room. There's a party-like feel to the evening: Ed Sheeran playing in the background, the scent of perfume and aftershave filling the air, and everyone dressed up. It reminds me, for some reason, of Christmas gatherings back home. Suddenly, I feel a million miles away from everyone I hold dear – except for Jake, of course: my parents, my friends, all the aunts and uncles and cousins who are part of the fabric of who I am. Six weeks ago, I didn't know Sarah, Anna or the Hughes-Smiths. The ground almost wobbles beneath me and I hold onto Jake's elbow for support. I could really have done with Anna here.

'Hello, stranger,' says Caroline, coming over to Jake and me and giving me an extravagant air kiss. 'Twice in two weeks: what a treat. Brighton was super, wasn't it? Just perfect. We had such a lovely time.' She looks at Sarah, almost as if she's goading her. 'We'll have to make sure that doesn't happen again, or you'll start to think Jake and I are hiding something!' She tinkles a laugh and raises an eyebrow.

Her words fall into a well of silence but then the doorbell goes and, a moment later, the living-room door opens and I can't actually believe that Simon's come. I go to the mantelpiece and examine the framed pictures Sarah has on there. Loads of her with two boys who I presume are her sons.

'This is Simon,' Sarah says, leading him into the room. 'Jake, this is who your wife spends her time with when she tells you she's out walking. Ha!'

Jake laughs. 'Pleased to meet you, mate,' he says, shaking his hand, and I just know what he's thinking: You? Have a chance with my wife? Yeah right!

I go over to shake Simon's hand but he leans in and kisses my cheek, giving me a waft of the strange soap he uses that takes me straight back to that night on the Embankment.

'Hello, Taylor,' he says. 'Happy birthday. Looking radiant, as usual.'

I give him half a smile.

'Right, everyone – I feel I should have a gong!' says Sarah, tinging her nail on her cocktail glass.

'Dong, dong, dong!' calls Jake.

'Thank you. Right – if you wouldn't mind, could I please ask you to take your seats? I've done a plan – look for your name, and no cheating!' She looks at Caroline when she says this, and I just know that she's going to be next to Jake, and I'm going to be tucked away down the far end of the table. And guess what? I'm absolutely right.

29

I learn some other things that evening, aside from the fact that Sarah fancies my husband. I learn that Toby's an absolute gentleman. As predicted, Jake's at the head of the table, with Sarah and Caroline next to him, and I'm down the far end, at the other head with Simon and Toby on my left and right.

I won't bore you with the details of what we speak about. It's enough to say that the other end of the table's far more raucous than our end. Several times, we stop our own conversation to look quizzically at Sarah and Jake to see what they're laughing at so riotously. For a while, Caroline tries to talk to Jake, but Sarah's not having any of it, so she gives up and starts a spirited talk with Simon about the state of the NHS while Toby tries to engage me with a series of open-ended questions about the pregnancy, my answers to which get interrupted every time Jake or Sarah laugh and we all turn to see what was so funny. I curse Anna in my head for not coming: it irks me to be the only sober one in a group of people getting steadily drunk, and perhaps that's why Toby lays the drinks mat carefully over the top of his wine glass after one glass of red, and smiles conspiratorially at me.

What I will say, though, is that as I sit there, eating my way through roasted salmon and potatoes and green beans, I watch Sarah lay a hand on Jake's arm. Then I watch him reciprocate as he makes a joke. And then I watch her start to touch him almost every time she addresses him – which is all the time. She touches his arm, then his hand, and gives him a playful punch on the shoulder. It's as if the conversation they're having is 20 per cent verbal and 80 per cent tactile and, all the while, Jake's refilling her glass and her smile's getting bigger and brighter. At one point, to my utter disbelief, she takes his hand and traces the lines on his palm with her blood-red nail, so she can 'read his fortune'.

'You're going to become a father soon,' she says, biting her lip, and I'm honestly embarrassed for her. She looks dreamily at Jake. 'You're going to be a wonderful father. I can just see it.'

I give Toby a very slight eye roll and he shakes his head almost imperceptibly. Simon's looking down, checking something on his multifunction watch, clearly embarrassed too. We can all see how drunk Sarah's getting and how, with each sip of wine, she loses a little more self-restraint.

It's Simon who finally breaks it up. He stands rather suddenly, as if he's simply had enough, and starts clearing the plates. Jake jumps up to help, while Sarah leans back in her chair and beams at us all.

'What a brilliant evening! We should start a dinner club so we can do this every month,' she says.

'What a wonderful idea,' Caroline says smoothly. 'I can't think of anything more fun,' and, for once, I welcome her sarcasm.

'Definitely, let's plan it! Let's make it happen, guys!' Sarah says. She stands up, staggers slightly, and steadies herself on Jake, then slides her arm around his waist and squeezes him against her.

'Tell you what, Taylor, if anything ever happens to you, you don't need to worry: I'll look after this one and the baby. They're the perfect package!' Nobody answers. 'Oops!' she garbles, disentangling herself. 'Right. I'm off to get the you-know-what!' She lurches out of the room, Jake following with a stack of plates. I refold my napkin and look around the table.

'That was lovely, wasn't it?' says Toby. 'The salmon was delicious.'

'The joy of buying in,' says Caroline. 'You can't really go wrong.'

'She's very busy . . .' I say without much conviction.

'Flirting with your husband,' says Caroline.

No one replies.

'Oh, come on! You'd have to be sitting under the fucking table to miss it,' says Caroline smoothly, refilling her own wine glass. 'Mind you, maybe not even then. Could have been worse under there.' She laughs a rich, throaty laugh that implies way more than her words.

'She's just drunk,' says Toby. 'She doesn't mean anything by it. Ignore it, Taylor. You have bigger things on your plate.' He touches my hand, then withdraws it again.

'Exactly,' says Simon, 'but even so.'

'For fuck's sake, what are they doing out there?' Caroline asks as I realize it's gone very quiet in the kitchen, but then we hear giggles, the door opens and Jake comes in carrying a cake alight with candles, Sarah in his wake clutching a gas lighter. Her lipstick's long gone. Jake places the cake carefully on the table and Sarah starts to sing 'Happy Birthday' while pretending to conduct us. Jake and Simon join in; Toby mumbles the words, and Caroline just shakes her head.

When we leave, as soon as possible after the cake, Simon catches my eye, then, in a flash when no one's looking, he winks. I look away.

I KNOW YOUR HUSBAND'S GOING TO MISS THE BIRTH

I don't need to be a clairvoyant to predict this. I don't need a crystal ball or a pack of tarot cards to know that, when push literally comes to shove, he won't be in that birthing room with you. I'd put money on it.

How can I be so sure? Any fool can see. It's not rocket science, sweetie-pie. Do you remember that book *He's Just Not That Into You*? The one that was made into that film with Jennifer Aniston and Ben Affleck? Yeah, I didn't watch it either, but maybe you should. There's a lot to be said for the title. Have you ever sat and thought about what it actually means?

Yeah, yeah, he'll make a little effort – he'll be there when you buy the pram and the cot and all that crap, but his heart's not in it. You can tell a lot about a man by his behaviour – not that you ever want to see it. He hardly ever wants to be with you. Have you noticed that? I guess not. Your head's too far into those baby magazines, but if you look you'll see he's given you so many red flags in the last six months even I can see him waving them like he's drowning. But you – you refuse to see them.

I get that people miss things all the time. Buses. Trains. Even planes. But missing the birth of your first child? Oh, stop making excuses. Yeah, first babies are usually late. Yeah, first labours are notoriously long – but still that's no excuse. If he really wanted to be there, he'd be there.

So, yeah, in my 'humble' opinion, as they say online, the baby thing? He's just not that into it.

You'll have to trust me on that.

30

It doesn't take me long to lay into Jake after my birthday dinner. I don't mean to shout at him. I really intend to leave the conversation until we're both fresh in the morning, but the front door is barely closed behind us – Jake's bending down to shoot that tricky bolt – when the words fly out of my mouth.

'What in god's name was that all about?' My voice shakes with anger.

'What?' Jake says, straightening up and looking at me. He looks genuinely surprised, and that makes me even angrier.

'"What?" What were you playing at tonight?' I ask, my voice dangerously calm.

'What do you mean?'

I raise my eyebrows at him and watch as understanding creeps across his face.

'Sarah?' he asks. 'Oh god.' He shrugs. 'She was drunk. It was nothing. You know that.'

'I don't know anything,' I say. 'As far as I know, you kissed her and now she's all over you. So, tell me.'

I march down the living room to the kitchen and slam the kettle under the tap, whack it back on the counter and practically punch the button on. Then I turn to face where Jake's standing in the living room.

'Well? I'm waiting?'

Jake shakes his head. 'I . . . I'm sorry.' He gives a quizzical little shrug, which incenses me further.

'Sorry for what exactly? Sorry you flirted with her? Sorry you ignored the entire table all night? Sorry you humiliated me on my birthday? Which one are you sorry for exactly?'

'Oh Tay. Is that how you saw it?'

'That's not how I saw it!' I shout. 'That's how the whole frickin' dinner party saw it. That's how it was. You haven't changed at all. Once a cheat, always a cheat, isn't that what they say?' I burst into tears, and wipe angrily at them.

Jake pales. Since we agreed to move on, his affair has always been the elephant in the room: there, but never mentioned. This is a first. He takes a step towards me.

'No, no, no. Tay, I told you you could trust me and I meant it. There's nothing there – you have to trust me. I didn't kiss her. I told you that. She's a flirt but it doesn't mean anything. Oh shit, shit, shit.'

'Ask everyone else. They think you were practically jumping her in the kitchen. What was it? You had one kiss and wanted another? Or am I way behind here?'

Jake paces up and down, rubbing his neck. 'Oh god. Tay, don't be daft. This is all in your head. No one else thought anything. It's just your hormones talking. Let's get you a glass of water and sit you down. Come on.' He holds out a hand to me.

I leap back. 'Don't you touch me! Get away from me. You stink of her. What were you doing in the kitchen with her? What? Actually, don't answer that, I don't want to know. Are you having an affair with her? Just tell me!'

'There's no affair,' Jake says but I shove past him and head for the front door, where I squat down and start shoving the bolt Jake's just fastened, only it's so stiff that, balanced on my haunches, I struggle. I focus all my anger on the bolt and finally it rams back into the socket.

'What are you doing?' Jake's behind me.

'What does it look like?' I stand up, steadying myself from the head-rush for a second, then unlock the door. 'I can't stand to be in the same house as you.'

Jake grabs my arm and holds me by the bicep. 'Don't be ridiculous! Where are you going at this time of night?'

'Anywhere!' I try to shake Jake off my arm. 'Get off me.'

'Oh, over to Simon's, is it?' Jake snarls. His face is so close I can smell the coffee still on his breath. 'Yeah, that's right. I saw him looking at you all night. You think I didn't notice? I should be asking *you* what's going on with *him*.'

'Don't be ridiculous! I'm the faithful one, remember? The one who didn't break the marriage vows!' We glare at each other. I wrench him off my arm, lurch for the front door and pull it open. 'Leave me alone! Let me go!'

I stumble out onto the front path, the cold shocking me, but I'm too angry to go back; too angry to lose face. I storm down the path, wondering as I do where I'll go. Anna's not home, and I won't go to Sarah's. Caroline's? I don't even have my purse.

'Taylor!' Jake covers the path in three strides, then yanks me away from the front gate and kicks it shut with his foot. I try to push him off but I can't. We stand there locked in a struggle.

'Look at yourself,' I sneer. 'Fighting a pregnant woman.'

Jake drops his hands. 'I'm not fighting you. I'm trying to protect you. You can't go out there on your own at this time.' His voice sounds broken. I don't say anything. My heart's still pounding but I know I'm beaten.

'Come on. Let's go inside,' Jake says and, reluctantly, I let him lead me back into the house by the elbow, then flop down onto the stairs, my head in my hands.

'I'm sorry,' Jake says. 'I don't know what happened. She was just so . . .' he shrugs.

'All over you?' I say.

'Yes.'

'Everyone noticed. *Everyone*. I've never been so humiliated in all my life. Or maybe once.'

Jake closes his eyes.

'I introduce you to my friends and you make a fool of me. How do you think that feels? And me having your baby in a matter of weeks. *Weeks*, Jake. In weeks, we'll be parents. Is this how parents behave? Is this what our son deserves to be born into?'

'I'm sorry,' says Jake again, and I realize that all my anger's gone. There's no fight left in me. I'm empty, and I'm extremely tired.

'You're sleeping down here tonight,' I say. 'I don't want you in my bed.' I stand up. 'I'll throw down your things.'

And that's how my birthday ends.

31

Looking back, it's interesting to see how my friends reacted to the debacle that was my birthday. Caroline's the first to get in touch the next day, not long after Jake's left for a night in Tewkesbury. She sends me a WhatsApp.

'Well done for getting through it. See you at book club. If you're still coming . . .'

Sarah also sends a message. 'Thanks so much for the flowers. They're beautiful. Ouch, my head!'

Anna calls me towards midday. I presume after she's packed Rob off on his flight. 'How did it go?' she asks.

'It was . . .' I begin, but then I choke up. I struggle to speak.

'What . . . ?' she prompts, but I can't make a sound.

'Tay? What happened? Are you crying?'

'No,' I gulp. 'I'm fine. It's just . . .' I reach for a tissue and blow my nose, badly, with one hand.

'What? What happened?' Anna asks.

'Oh god. Nothing. Just – can we talk about something else?'

'Was it Sarah?' she asks. 'Oh my god, it was! What did she do?'

'We had a fight. I don't want to talk about it.'

'Who? You and Sarah?' Anna's voice is incredulous.

'No. Me and Jake.'

'Hey, come on! I'm sure it's not that bad,' Anna says. 'Let me guess: Sarah was out of order and what? Did he go along with it?'

I make a sound that I hope she'll take as agreement.

Anna's silent for a minute, perhaps weighing up how much further to push me.

'Well, look,' she says eventually. 'I'm taking you shopping tomorrow, okay? No excuses. I know you don't have anything on, and retail therapy is exactly what you need. So don't try and argue your way out of this one.'

We chat a little more then hang up. I may have convinced Anna that I'm fine, but the truth is I haven't convinced myself. I'm thrown not just by Jake's actions, but by the violence of my own reaction; by the row itself. After we got through his infidelity, we agreed – on the advice of a marriage guidance counsellor – that we'd move on, that I wouldn't throw it back at him, and that's precisely what I just did. I also can't get the look on his face as he shouted at me out of my head; the sight of his hand in Sarah's as she traced his palm with her nail. How did it start with the other woman, I wonder? Was it like that?

After I finish talking to Anna, I sit on the sofa for a good few minutes, mulling everything over. What's happening to my marriage? And why suddenly now, when it should be rock solid – when it should be the strongest it will ever be? How are Jake and I going to get through having a baby together? Before I know it, a tear's rolling down my cheek, then another, and another, and I give in to them. I get up and get the tissue box then I sit there, sobbing and blowing my nose into tissue after tissue, until all of the stress, the jealousy, the frustration, the anger and the guilt have come out. And just as my sobs are subsiding and the relentless silence of the house is starting to embarrass me for my outburst, as if even the walls are shocked by what loss of control they just witnessed, the doorbell rings. I pad over with my hands on my back and open it a crack. Simon's there, jiggling up and down on the spot, holding a flimsy plastic carrier bag.

'Hey,' he says. 'I've only got an hour but I wanted to come by and see if you're okay.'

'I'm okay.' My voice is thick with snot, my face is blotchy and my eyes are red.

'You're not fine at all,' Simon says. He edges closer. 'Can I come in? I've actually got something to show you.' He holds up the plastic bag.

I look away, unable to make the decision. He reaches for my hand, then pulls away without touching me.

'Taylor. I don't know what you're upset about, and I hope it isn't about what happened that night after the Mexican because I told you it won't happen again. You can trust me. I promise. But I don't want to leave you like this. If I can't come in, will you come out with me? For a coffee? You shouldn't be on your own. Think of the baby – stress hormones can't be good for him.'

I open the door wider. 'Okay. Just for a coffee, all right?'

'Thank you.' Simon follows me to the kitchen.

'So, there's something I need to show you,' Simon says. 'Do you remember you mentioned Anna was getting strange phone calls from wrong numbers? Well, I did a bit of digging and look at this.' He holds up the plastic bag.

'What is it?'

Simon pulls out a business card and hands it to me. On it, there's a picture of a woman in a basque and suspenders, her eyes blocked out by a thin black strip. 'Home massage. Personal services,' says the card.

'That's Anna's phone number,' I say.

Simon nods. 'I hope you don't mind. I took the liberty of checking and then looked around. It wasn't difficult. I found a few tucked into a bus shelter. So I looked at other bus shelters nearby and bingo! I took as many as I could.' He holds out the bag.

'Well, that explains it. But why?'

'It might just be a typo. Very annoying but nothing more. I guess we just wait for them to notice they're not getting any calls and double-check the number. Or I suppose you could take them to the police . . .' His voice trails off. 'Will you give them to Anna? You'll probably see her before I do.' Then he looks at me. 'Are you okay?'

I put the bag on the dining table. 'Poor Anna. She's so paranoid someone's watching her.'

'Really? But I'm more concerned about what's been bothering you,' Simon says. 'If you don't mind me saying, you looked upset when I arrived.'

'Oh, you know. This and that. Husband flirting with friend in front of everyone being the most obvious.' I give a little laugh.

Simon looks down. 'I didn't like to say. I hoped you hadn't noticed.'

'It wasn't just me, was it? I wasn't being oversensitive?'

'Well, you know him best. Do you think he meant anything by it?'

I stare at the kettle, then sigh.

'You wouldn't be human if it didn't hurt,' Simon says. 'You're vulnerable right now, and you have every right to feel how you do. But try to look at the big picture. Do you suspect him of cheating?'

I purse my lips. 'He's got form.' The words are out before I realize what I've done: I've let the genie out of the bottle. I'd planned never to tell anyone in London about what Jake did – not to let it follow us across the Atlantic and sully our new life – but here it is, out there in the air and in Simon's ears.

'What?' Simon looks genuinely shocked.

I shake my head. 'It was in the States. It's over.'

Simon's searching my face, trying, I imagine, to read my mood; see if it's worth asking more.

'Okay,' he says slowly. 'Have there been any signs that he's cheating?'

I laugh bitterly. 'He's never here, remember? Always on the

road. For all I know he could have another house up north and a whole extra family and I would be the last to know.'

'But at least it wouldn't be with Sarah. Think positive!'

There's a sparkle in his eyes.

'True.' I pour the coffees, add the milk, hand him a cup. We both move to the living room. I take a dining chair and he sits on the sofa.

'Seriously, he'd be mad to cheat on you,' Simon says. I look at him and he holds my eyes for a second before I look away. The rest of it is left unsaid: *I would never cheat on you.* And, somehow, I believe it.

'How's your dad?' I ask.

'Okay. We've a new carer who comes a few hours a day. They get on well. It means I can get out a bit more.'

'That's great.'

'Yeah. It is.'

We sit in silence for a minute, then Simon says, 'I saw the photos of your nursery. I really like what you've done. It looks amazing. I'd love to see it in the flesh, so to speak.'

I remember that he set one up for the child he thought was his, then had it snatched away.

'Sure.'

At the bottom of the stairs, I tell him to go first. 'Turn left at the top.'

By the time I get up there, he's gently pushing open the door. 'Wow,' he breathes. 'It's perfect.'

It's a tiny room but I've done the walls in pale taupe with wide-striped curtains in navy and white. The cot and changing table are white, and I've also managed to squeeze in a navy-blue armchair. On the walls, I've hung bunting in red, white and blue. It's plain, but clean and crisp. We go in, and Simon turns to me.

'I love it.'

'Thanks.'

Suddenly I want to show him everything. I go to the wardrobe and take out a tiny newborn onesie from the pile.

'Look! See how tiny they are?'

Simon looks between me and the onesie. 'That looks like it might fit already. Think you might have a rugby player in there.'

'Oh god, I hope not!'

I put the onesie back in the cupboard and we troop back downstairs. Simon stands awkwardly in the hallway and looks at his watch. I loiter on the bottom stair, not least because there's nowhere else for me to go with him blocking the door.

'Well, I hate to say it, but I need to get going. How are you feeling now?'

'Better. Thank you.'

He steps closer and puts his hand on my arm. With me on the step, we're the same height.

'Good,' he says. 'Look, if you're feeling bad and Jake's not around, just call me. Don't sit here crying. It's not good for either of you. Will you do that?'

'Okay.'

He looks at my belly. 'And you be good for Mummy, too, okay? Take care, Taylor.' He opens the door and is gone.

32

Anna holds good on the plan to take me out shopping. She arrives at my house with a baby-shopping checklist she's found online.

'It's not just about the big things,' she says. 'Do you have a mild washing detergent for the baby clothes? Muslin squares? Nappy bags? Night-time sanitary pads?' I nod at most of these. 'What about for you, though?' she asks. 'Don't forget that "happy mummy equals happy baby".' She says it in a sing-song voice. 'We need to make time for ourselves as well as the babies. We mustn't lose ourselves in being someone's mummy, okay? It's important. Do you have a good eye cream? A concealer? Dry shampoo? We're going to need them.'

'You've really thought this through, haven't you?'

'Oh yes. Any excuse to go to Boots.' She grins and I roll my eyes.

'All right. But, hang on – before we go, I've got something to show you.'

I take a card out of the bag Simon brought and hand it to her with a flourish. I'm so proud we've got to the bottom of it and I wish I could take the credit myself.

'Here's the answer to your mystery calls! Ta-da!'

Anna examines the card with a frown. 'That's my number. Where did you get this?'

'I didn't. Simon did. He found them tucked into bus shelters around town. Look . . .' I pick up the bag. 'He got as many as he could.'

I'm expecting her to be happy about this but she's looking more worried than she did before.

'Simon found them?'

'Yes!'

She closes her eyes and breathes out slowly and loudly through her mouth. 'This doesn't solve anything. It just makes me think he printed them himself.'

'What?'

'Maybe he had the cards printed to get other people to harass me. Maybe he orchestrated the whole thing.'

'What? Why would he do that?'

'I don't know!' Anna snaps. 'I don't know how he thinks, but all I can think of is that since I joined the walking group I haven't felt safe. I don't know what it is. I don't know why, but I know something's not right.' She shakes her head. 'I can't tell you what he wants.'

'*If* it's him,' I say. 'Innocent till proven guilty, right? Though, without meaning to big myself up, I honestly thought he was more interested in me than you.'

'Maybe it's a double bluff. Maybe he's using you to get to me. You just can't be too careful, Tay. I'm sorry if you think I'm paranoid, but after what happened . . .'

'No, I know. I know. Anyway. At least we know now why you're getting the calls.'

'Yeah, at least that,' she says, in a way that sounds like she's not pleased at all.

* * *

'So what was your fight with Jake about, if you don't mind me asking?' Anna says later as we weave our way in and out of the shops.

It's a weekday and the centre's not too busy. Anna's mood's improved, thank goodness, and we're having fun shopping for our new-mum essentials.

I try to laugh but the row is still raw and the sound comes out a little strangled.

'Was it about the bit when she tried to kiss him when you left?'

The words hit me like a punch. I take a breath then say lightly, 'What did you say?'

Anna clamps her hand over her mouth, her eyes wide. 'OMG, I'm sorry. You didn't see that?'

'No, I did not! Who told you?'

Anna looks sheepish. 'Caroline messaged me. Oh, don't get ideas – I think she still hates me but she was worried about you. She asked me to check on you.'

'She could have called me herself.'

'I know. But I think she likes having people to do her dirty work for her. Anyway, to be fair, she said Jake turned his head away so she missed, but that's not the point.' She pauses. 'So . . . can I tell her that your marriage is in ruins, you're a mess and your baby's now fatherless thanks to Sarah wanting jump your husband's bones?'

Despite myself, I laugh. 'Be my guest.'

'That's the spirit,' says Anna. 'You just have to trust him as he's away so much.' We're looking at eye creams and she holds one up. 'Have you tried this one? It's supposed to be amazing.'

I take the box from her and look at it. 'Wrinkles, dark circles, puffiness. How about a cream specifically for new mums?' I say. 'I guess they both had far too much to drink that night. That's all.'

'Do you think alcohol brings out the truth?' Anna looks sideways at me.

I put the eye cream back. 'We have so much together. We have a baby coming in a matter of weeks.' I look at her, pleading with my eyes for her to shut up: I'm on thin ice and I can hear it cracking. Anna stares back at me and, for a moment, I think she's guessed that something happened with Simon, but then she looks down. 'If I told you something, would you hold it against me?'

'Excuse me.' A woman tries to stretch past us to the shelf so Anna and I shuffle backwards a bit to allow her through. She stands right there in front of us, so we edge further down the aisle. Anna looks furtive, like a spy about to divulge a secret of significant importance.

'What is it?' I ask.

She sighs and rubs her forehead. 'I've been wondering whether or not to tell you, but Caroline also reckons something happened with him and Sarah in the kitchen that night.'

Suddenly the shelves seem to close in on me. Rows and rows of cosmetics tower over me: names, bottles, tubes, tubs, prices, buy-two get-one-free, three for £10. I can't breathe.

'When they were getting the cake or something?' Anna continues. 'She said Sarah was always trying to get him alone in the kitchen. That it was quite obvious. And pathetic. "Like hormone-crazed teenagers" were her exact words.'

I can't breathe. Anna reaches out and touches my hand. She has no idea of the pressure in my chest; no idea her words have hit me like machine-gun fire. 'I thought you might want to know,' she says. 'I'm sure it's nothing to worry about. But if I were you, I'd want to know.'

'No,' I say, and it refers to both: no, I don't want to know, and no, it didn't happen. 'She's just stirring up trouble. It's what she does.' I struggle to make my voice sound normal. The seed of doubt now bears a shiny, green shoot. It's not just me who thought something might have happened in the kitchen.

Anna smiles at me. 'Yes, you're right. Of course nothing happened. Come on.' She turns and starts to walk away down the aisle. 'I'm glad I've told you, though,' she says over her shoulder. 'Friends shouldn't keep secrets.'

Tears spring to my eyes. I'm suddenly damp and prickly hot,

and I rip at my scarf trying to get it off, and fan my face with my hand. Anna's still talking, then she turns and realizes I'm not behind her. She rushes back and puts her hand under my elbow.

'What's wrong? Are you okay? Oh my god, I didn't think you'd take it like this. You're right. Caroline's just stirring. It's okay.'

I can't stop the tears, so I turn to the shelf to try and hide my face both from Anna and from passers-by. Anna scrabbles in her bag and passes me a tissue. I rest my head on the edge of the shelf and gulp in as much air as I can get in the heat of the shop.

'I think they already kissed. The night they went out for dinner to discuss my birthday.' I tell her about the silence at the front door. 'It was a good few seconds.'

Anna rubs her hand over her mouth, then taps her lips, thinking. 'Some friend she's turning out to be. No wonder she asked you out for lunch. She probably wanted to get you onside before she went after your husband. What do they say? Keep your friends close, and your enemies closer?' She shudders.

I dissolve into tears again. 'The evidence is all there, isn't it?'

Anna sighs. 'Look, it's a difficult time for a man, seeing his wife pregnant. Maybe he feels insecure about how much attention the baby's going to get. Maybe he doesn't even know why he's doing it. All he knows is that when a pretty woman is giving him attention, it feels good. Men are basic creatures. Don't forget that.' She laughs and I try to smile but my lip wobbles. 'Look,' she says, 'it'll all be over in a couple of weeks. You'll have the baby and you'll be the centre of his universe again. You'll be the most amazing, wonderful person on the planet for giving birth to his child. I promise. This'll all blow over. It will. This is just a wobble. A tiny wobble.' She pats my back. 'Come on, come on, Tay. Let's get you outside. Find you somewhere to sit. I'm so sorry. This is all my fault. I shouldn't have said anything.'

I can't speak. I try to swallow but there's a lump in my throat. I blow my nose on what tiny corner of the tissue isn't saturated with tears. Anna leads me by the elbow to a bench in the mall, sits me on it and dashes back into Boots to get some water. I watch the people passing us by, hands full of carrier bags, going about their happy lives. Suddenly I feel alien, like a stranger in their midst. An aching for home – my real home – squeezes my insides and I honestly wish I could give up and go back to the States, back to my life there before it all got so . . . complicated.

'Right,' Anna says, handing me the bottle of water. 'Sip this. How are you feeling now?'

'He's cheated before,' I blurt. 'When we were in the States. It's why we moved here. A fresh start.' Like a sprinter off the blocks, my secret's gone. Anna's mouth hangs open, her eyes wide. 'What?'

'You heard.'

She blows out and leans back. 'Whoah. That puts it all in a completely different light.'

'I know. Once a cheat, always a cheat. Isn't that what they say?'

Anna doesn't reply but her face says it all. I wave my hands up and down to try and fan my face.

'God, this is embarrassing. I feel like such a failure. I'm a useless wife.'

'Or maybe he's a useless husband,' Anna says. 'Have you thought of it that way?'

I feel my spine sag as a ball of tension inside me dissolves. Honestly, I've never thought of it that way.

'Look,' Anna says, 'I don't know what happened but the one thing I know is that it isn't your fault.' She sits down next to me. 'I suspect Rob cheats as well. I've never actually caught him. It's harder because he's away from home for so long. But I've often suspected he has a girlfriend in Qatar.'

'What? How can you live with that?'

Anna shrugs and exhales through her teeth. 'Well, it's not as if I know for certain. And what can I do about it anyway? Short of flying over there and catching them, it's hard for me to check up. But there's been the odd thing that's made me stop and go "what the . . . ?"'

'Have you ever asked him?'

She shakes her head. 'I'm pregnant. I don't earn enough to bring up this baby alone. I need him. For now. That's the nuts and bolts of it.'

'So you ignore it?'

'I try not to think about it. That's what I do.'

We sit in silence for a moment, watching shoppers weave around us. I see a woman who's heavily pregnant, her enormous stomach protruding way in front of her. She's pushing a toddler in a pushchair and she looks happy, competent, in control, and I wonder if she has moments like this; if it's just me who's losing the plot the closer I get to giving birth.

'I blame myself for Jake straying,' I say. 'It's different for you as Rob practically lives away from you, but Jake's here at least fifty per cent of the time. I was so focused on conceiving . . .'

'His child!' Anna interrupts, her eyebrows raised, and I smile gratefully at her. Sometimes I forget it's his child too.

'It's a massive gift you're giving him. He should've been pandering to your every whim, worshipping the ground you walk on, not getting his end away elsewhere.' She shakes her head. 'And to think of all that you went through . . . the ones you lost – the heartbreak. Oh, you poor, poor thing.' She rubs my arm.

'Thank you.' I sniff. 'Thank you for saying that. But I blame myself. I carry that around with me all the time. I think about it at night when I can't sleep.'

'Why didn't you tell me?'

'We made a deal: London was a new start. We weren't going to talk about it. But now I've thrown it back at Jake, told Simon and now you.'

Anna stiffens. 'You told Simon? Umm, am I missing something?'

Irritation flares inside me. 'Oh, come on! He's not so bad.'

Anna facepalms.

'Look,' I say. 'I know he's a bit odd, but he's a full-time carer. He's lonely, and he's a computer guy. They're all a bit geeky, aren't they? Not the best social skills, but I think he's basically a sound guy.'

'Erm, no. We're going to have to agree to disagree on this one. He's got an agenda. I don't know what it is but I don't like it. I mean, look at the way he turned up at your house with those presents. You've got to admit that was odd. How did he even know where you live?' Anna sighs. 'And as for the business cards – don't you think it's very convenient he was the one who found them?' She shakes her head at me. 'You're such an innocent. I despair.'

'He used to be married,' I say. 'He almost had a baby.'

'What do you mean? How do you "almost" have a baby?'

I tell her Simon's story, and then it all comes tumbling out about him coming to the house and feeling my belly. I'd forgotten she didn't know about that. Anna listens with her hand over her mouth and her eyes wide.

'Okay,' she says when I'm done. 'Is there anything else you haven't told me? Tay . . .' She peers intently at me. 'Come on, spit it out. Something else happened, didn't it? I can read you like a book.'

'He kissed me,' I blurt.

'What? When?'

'That night we had dinner. We went for a walk down by the river, and . . .'

'And what? Did he have to hold you down? Because I would have poked his eyes out . . .' She looks at me, horror creeping across her face. 'Did you respond?'

'No. No, I . . .' Unbidden, the feel of his mouth on mine comes back to me. 'I stopped him.'

'Oh my god. Tay. I can't believe you didn't tell me this. It's harassment! You could go to the police. You *should* go to the police.'

I shake my head. Despite everything, I don't feel a sense of danger. Not like Anna does.

'No. I can't do that. It's fine. It's fine now. It was just a kiss, and

I stopped it. He apologized, and it won't happen again. I've seen him since, and it was fine.'

But Anna's shaking her head. 'You're so wrong about him. I've seen how he looks at you. He practically salivates when he sees you. Licks his lips like Hannibal Lecter. I don't know what he wants from either of us but it isn't good. There's something really creepy about him.'

'He was really apologetic. As soon as it happened. He said it would never happen again.'

'And you believe him?' Anna looks upwards. 'Dear God, help me make this woman see. I'll come with you to the police if you want to report him. What if he tries something else? He knows where you live. He knows Jake's away . . . He knows you're on your own. He could do anything.'

'I'm not going to the police.'

Anna takes a deep breath in and paces up and down, pushing her hands through her hair, then she sits back down next to me.

'I'm so glad you told me all this. You have to take it seriously. Trust me, I should know.' She looks pointedly at me. 'Right, here's what we're going to do. You're not to be on your own with him again. Okay? You hear me? If you want to go walking, we go together. We don't even need to go with the group; we'll go just the two of us. Okay? And you're not to tell him when Jake's away. If he turns up at your house, don't let him in. Make an excuse, say we're going out, say someone's coming over, say Jake's upstairs and he's a black belt – anything.' She looks into my eyes, imploring. 'Please, take this seriously. You know nothing about the guy. Nothing. He's a weird bloke, and he's always been weird around you. Remember I told you that that first day we went to Costa? I wasn't joking. I've a nose for things like this. Trust me. Promise me you'll take this seriously?'

I nod but, mentally, my fingers are crossed. I still can't help thinking she's overly paranoid because of what happened to her.

'Good,' she says. 'Because if you don't take it seriously, I'll tell Jake and I'll tell the police. They should know. I'm not losing another friend.'

Subconsciously, I put my fingers to my lips, remembering the feel of Simon's mouth on mine as I nod.

'Right, do you feel a bit better now?' Anna asks, standing up and stretching. 'Shall we get going?'

'If we must.' I stand up slowly, my muscles stiff. 'God, what a morning. I feel like I've done ten rounds with Mike Tyson.'

* * *

Later that evening, I pick up the phone to call Caroline. I want to hear it from her. But I hang up before she answers. She calls back within a minute.

'Taylor? It's Caroline. I have a missed call from you?' She sounds like the CEO of a multinational on a conference call. What was it she said she was? An architect?

'Thanks for calling back,' I say. 'I just wanted to ask if you . . .' I squirm. 'Oh god, this is so silly. Forget it. It's okay. Bye.'

'What's silly? What were you going to ask?'

'Oh, nothing.'

'Clearly not nothing or you wouldn't be twisting yourself inside out on the phone to me.' She pauses then exhales. 'Is this about Jake and Sarah?'

I sigh. 'Yes. You know him. Do you there's anything going on between them?'

There's a silence that stretches. Then Caroline speaks. 'Did Anna tell you that we spoke? Typical.' She sighs. 'Look, I don't know. What do you think? In my experience, wives with hunches are usually right about these things.'

'I don't know. I don't know what to think any more.'

'Well, here's a suggestion. The only people you're going to get an answer from are Jake and Sarah. Not me.' And with that, she hangs up.

33

The next book club was to be at Caroline's house, a detached, white-painted Victorian pile hidden behind its own wrought-iron gates. Jake was away. It was his last trip before the baby came, and it was longer than usual – bartered with me on a solemn promise that he'd be home for the next three months. Anna was also away, seeing Rob as he flew back to Qatar through London. I called up Caroline to tell her I couldn't go either, and suggested we take a raincheck.

'Is this about Sarah?' Caroline said on the phone, and I heard her take a swig of wine. 'Because if it is, you mustn't hide away. You need to face her. Show her. That's my opinion. So I'll see you at eight, okay?'

I took a cab.

'How's Jake?' Caroline asks after she's buzzed me through the gates and walked me across the hardwood floors to what she refers to as the drawing room. For all her support earlier, she looks too innocent and I wonder what she's up to. One minute nice, the next minute a bitch. I get the feeling she's enjoying the car crash of my life – sitting back with her popcorn, watching.

'He's away,' I say, and Caroline raises one arched eyebrow as she takes a sip of wine.

'When did you say the baby's due?'

'Two weeks, if it comes on time.'

'And when will he be back?'

'Before then,' I say with a smile that I hope says 'shut up' but she doesn't.

'I'm surprised you let him go,' she says, her voice dripping with meaning.

I shrug.

'He was always a drifter,' she says. 'At school. Never one to settle.' She stares thoughtfully into the middle distance. 'I never thought he would get married, actually. Men like him, they don't like to settle.' She looks at me and gives a little laugh. 'Maybe that's why he travels so much.'

'What are you implying?' I say.

Caroline closes her eyes slowly, breathes deeply in, and then opens them again – a lazy blink that implies she understands that I'm thick and that she can't possible explain more clearly.

Sarah comes back from the bathroom.

'Oh, hello!' she says, and I give her a weak smile.

'Didn't you say you were going away for work?' Caroline asks Sarah.

'Yes, to Leeds,' Sarah says. 'Tomorrow.' She looks at me with a little laugh but my blood has run cold. Jake's in Leeds.

'Really?' I say.

Sarah's looking too innocent. 'Yes. Why?'

Caroline looks from her to me and back. 'Oh, don't tell me,' she says. 'Is that where Jake is? How *cosy*.' She pauses theatrically and presses her lips together as if trying not to smile. 'I'm sure it's just a coincidence,' she says in a manner that implies she doesn't believe for a second that it's a coincidence. Then Sarah bursts out laughing.

'Oh, don't look like that, Taylor! I'm just joshing with you. I'm not going to Leeds! I'm going to Peterborough.'

It takes a moment for this to sink in, but I'm not as relieved as she thinks I should be. She said Leeds. She knows Jake's going to Leeds. I haven't told her that. He must have. When did they speak?

Have they been messaging? The paranoia leaps back. Every time I think I've got a grip on it, it grabs me from another angle.

'Very funny,' I say without a shred of amusement.

Caroline picks up the empty wine bottle. 'Right, let me get refills and the snacks – I'm afraid they're homemade tonight: I didn't have time to get out to Cook – and we should start on the books.'

She clicks across the wooden floor to the kitchen and I don't know what comes over me. Maybe it's the way Sarah's joke's left me feeling, but a wave of rage rises inside me, making my heart thud as if I've been running sprints. *I'm afraid they're homemade tonight: I didn't have time to get out to Cook.*

I've had enough of Caroline carping on; of her bitching and digging and putting people down. Without stopping to think, I shove myself up and follow her into the kitchen. She's standing by a tall wine fridge with her back to me but turns around when I click the door shut behind me.

'What do you think? Chablis or a Cortese?' She holds up two bottles. 'Or I have a white Rioja that's a bit bolder . . .'

I'm breathing hard, my blood pounding in my veins. I put my hands on my bump and lean on the door for support.

'Why are you such a goddamned cow?'

Caroline doesn't even flinch. She continues standing there holding the two wine bottles. 'I'm sorry?' she says.

'You heard me. Why are you such a bitch? Just look at you tonight: telling me to come here then sniping at me about Jake. And all that crap about not having time to buy from Cook, just to make Sarah feel bad.'

Caroline looks innocent. 'What exactly did I say? Nothing that wasn't true, I don't think?'

'Oh, come on! All those barbed comments. Don't think we don't know what you mean. You're nothing but a passive-aggressive bully and I see straight through you.'

She shrugs. 'But it's true. You can't deny it. Nowhere does hummus as good as my own. I've been perfecting it for years.'

'And then what you said about Jake not settling. He was eleven when you last saw him. *Eleven!* Are you telling me you were sizing up the marriage potential of the boys at junior school? Oh, come on! You're just a bitch who gets off on making other people feel smaller than you. Well, let me tell you, I'm not putting up with it one moment longer!' I stop for breath, while we eyeball each other. She's clearly not going to say anything so I carry on. 'What happened to you? What turned you into such a bitter, twisted, sorry excuse of a person?' I shake my head, the wind suddenly out of my sails. 'You know what, Caroline? You would actually be all right if you weren't such a cow to everyone.'

I shake my head and leave the kitchen, closing the door firmly behind me. My whole body is shaking. I don't do confrontation. I don't know what just happened.

Back in the drawing room, Sarah's sitting wide-eyed. It's clear from her face that she heard everything. She raises her hand and starts to slow-clap.

'Bravo.'

'Well,' I say, slumping onto a sofa. 'She had it coming and if you weren't going to say anything . . .'

'I'm sorry about the Leeds thing,' she says. She gets up and comes to sit next to me. 'I was just joking. There's absolutely nothing between Jake and me. He adores you.' She rubs my arm, then takes my hand and squeezes it. 'I'm really sorry about your birthday, too. I was drunk and out of order. I do it all the time. Truth is, I don't get out much. I've no excuse. I get dolled up, have a few drinks and get overexcited. Don't take this the wrong way but, apart from how good-looking he is, there's nothing special about Jake. It could have been anyone giving me a bit of attention, even the bin man. I'm sorry.'

I breathe in deeply. Somehow I believe her.

The drawing-room door opens and Caroline appears. She puts the wine carefully into the cooler on a side table then turns to face us. We look expectantly at her. She folds her arms.

'I suppose you heard that,' she says to Sarah. 'Do you agree? Do you think the same?'

Sarah looks at the floor.

Caroline pulls herself up straight, then speaks, her hands clasped in front of her. Her voice is quiet, but determined. She looks like a prime minister announcing that the country's gone to war.

'I had a son,' she says. I've barely registered her use of the past tense when she continues. 'He died.'

It's as if she's dropped a thermobaric bomb on the room. I can almost feel the shockwave spreading out, hitting us all, rendering us speechless. Sarah has her hand over her mouth and I know it's a cliché, but my stomach constricts and coldness slides through my veins.

'He was two,' Caroline says.

She bites her lip now and I see that the ice woman's actually fighting back tears. She yanks over a chair and sinks onto it, the muscles of her face struggling to stay straight, to push back the tears. She presses her hands to her face then looks at us, more composed.

'I've never talked about it.'

'I'm so sorry,' says Sarah quietly.

'I can't imagine,' I say and, forgive me for this, but I'm also wondering if she's making it up; if there's any way we can check. Let's face it, it's a good excuse for being a bitch.

'What happened?' Sarah asks, and I'm thinking of things that cause toddlers to die: meningitis, sepsis, road accident, cot death, and thinking, please god, no.

'He choked on a grape,' says Caroline, and there's another silence as we absorb the nonsense of this.

'Were you . . .' Sarah waves a hand at the room, 'at home?'

'He was at nursery,' Caroline says. 'You just don't imagine . . . do you?'

'Dropping off your child in the morning and never seeing them again,' Sarah says quietly.

Caroline presses her hand against her face, then looks up. 'He ate grapes all the time. He loved them. I used to cut them in half but that morning I was running late. He'd been throwing his cereal around and I was cross. God! I was cross with him!' She sobs then regains control, her hand on her throat. 'I was shouting at him, and I made that decision: I put the grapes in whole. I knew the risk. I thought he was old enough. It's my fault.' She stops for a minute. 'I'd be lying if I said I didn't think about it that morning, but I did. It crossed my mind that he might choke – you hear these things, don't you? But how much cotton wool do you wrap your child in? Where does it end? I wanted him to grow up to be tough, not a namby-pamby.' She takes a deep breath. 'Anyway. It's a decision I have to live with forever.'

'You can't blame yourself,' I say. 'It was an accident,' and Caroline just looks at me. I'd blame myself. I know I would.

'How long ago?' Sarah's voice is soft.

Caroline laughs bitterly. 'A year. Exactly one year the weekend we went to Brighton and bumped into her.' She nods at me. 'That's why we were there. Getting away. Making a break. Trying to get through that weekend as best we could.'

I have a flashback to her drinking that champagne like it was going out of fashion; drinking herself to oblivion. No wonder they were so keen for company that night.

'I'm so sorry,' I say. 'I had no idea.'

'None of us did,' says Sarah.

'Well,' says Caroline, and her whole body seems to collapse, as if her bones are made of jelly. Her face looks different, too – as if the armour has dropped; the polished perfection. She looks older; I see wrinkles now, and shadows where before I just saw make-up. 'Now you know.' She raises her hands in the air. 'So, if you think I'm a bitch, or I've got a chip on my shoulder, or I put people down – well, I'm sorry. I see only the bigger picture. I'm just trying to get through the day. Every day.'

We sit there in silence for a minute. In my head I'm going over the conversations I've had with Caroline, and starting to understand a little more: the superiority, the brittleness, the drinking – the defences she must use to protect herself against pregnant women like me. Mothers. Half of book club, in a nutshell. It must be torture for her.

'Well, some book club this turned out to be,' Caroline says. 'Top-up?' She gets up and opens the new bottle of wine, sloshes some into her glass, swigs a mouthful, then looks to Sarah.

Sarah goes over to her and touches her arm.

'Thank you for telling us. Why didn't you say something earlier?'

'I didn't know how. "Oh hi, thanks for inviting me to book club. By the way, I had a baby but he died."'

'We'd have understood,' says Sarah.

'Well, I also didn't want to upset her.' Caroline nods at me.

'Thank you,' I say.

But she has upset me. We move onto books and, despite our attempts to be cheery, the underlying mood is sombre as if we're all still processing what Caroline has told us, and I can't concentrate. All I can think about is Caroline in her perfect kitchen that morning. Caroline making the perfect little toddler snack for nursery: a cheese sandwich cut into a star shape; carrot and cucumber sticks; a fromage frais. She would have been an amazing mother: I can see that now. She would have been well informed, have the best of everything. No wonder she knew so much about pregnancy. I see her son in his high chair, chattering as toddlers do, and throwing around his Cheerios or whatever organic, sugar-free, do-good power cereal she lets him eat while she works at the countertop, and her frustrated that she'll have to pick it all up when she gets back from dropping him off. Maybe that's what she was doing at the moment he died. Perhaps the sun was shining; maybe it was raining, the drops sliding down the window panes. She must go over that morning in her head every day, thinking about that moment she decided to add the grapes to his snack box; wishing she'd cut them into halves, or put apple slices in instead. How such an insignificant decision can change our lives forever.

I realize that none of us even asked his name. I want to know. I do and I don't. I can't stay here any longer.

'I'm sorry, ladies,' I say, pushing my chair back. 'I'm going to have to call it a night.'

Sarah jumps to her feet, surprised but not really surprised. 'I'll drop you back.'

'It's okay. I'll get a cab.'

'Well, text me when you're safe indoors, all right?'

'I will.'

Mercifully the taxi comes quite quickly, and I can't get out of there fast enough. It's as if the bad luck that had cursed Caroline and Toby will rub off on me.

* * *

Back home, I light all the scented candles I have, and say a little prayer for Caroline's son. I'm not religious and I feel silly saying the words out loud but I also feel they need to be said, almost like an insurance for my own baby.

Then I put my hands on my belly and whisper to the baby. I tell him to hang in there till it's time to come. I tell him it's going to be confusing coming out and that it'll be bright and cold, and he might cry, but that I'll be there for him. I tell him it won't be long until he's in my arms and I can touch him and hold him. I tell him to grow up strong and healthy; to have a long and happy life. I tell him that I'll always be there for him; that I'll love him no matter what, and always try to do my best for him. I can't believe that, by the time book club rolls around again, he'll be here, and I'll be a mother. Yet the thought of how he's going to go from being a bump in my belly to a live baby in my arms is a huge black hole in my imagination; a leap of faith. I can't picture how it's going to happen.

I call Jake. The phone rings eight times before he picks up. He sounds out of breath.

I can't help myself. 'What were you doing?'

'Just got out of the shower. Sorry – dripping wet.'

I KNOW YOU

I tell him about Caroline's baby. 'I can't believe she didn't tell us that night at The Grand,' I say, skirting away from telling him how her story's made me feel. 'I thought we got on all right that night.'

Jake sighs. 'I don't know what I'd do in their place. Talk. Not talk. Who knows what goes on in your head when you lose a child? It shouldn't happen. It's one of those things that's not supposed to happen. Your children should outlive you.'

Suddenly I'm crying. Trying to do it silently.

'Tay? Are you there? Are you okay?'

I struggle to compose myself. 'I'm just so worried.' And another wave of tears hits me.

'Worried about what, hon? Whoah, are you crying?'

I can't answer that. I press my free hand into my eyes and sniff.

'Tay! Honey! It's okay. The baby's going to be just fine, and you're going to be the most amazing mummy.'

'How do you know that?' My voice is a sob, accusing.

'I just do. Trust me on this. Everything's going to be fine.'

'What if he's born with some incurable congenital problem and given only a few years to live? What then? What if he's still-born? What if we're in a car crash on the way home from hospital and the car explodes and there's a fire and we can't get him out of the car seat and we have to watch him burn to death? You've seen all those straps.' I realize my voice is rising. 'What if . . .'

'Tay. We've had the scans. We've had the tests. Everything's come back 100 per cent normal. And look, what happened to Caroline is not normal. Things like that don't happen to the majority of people. Really, they don't. Think about the number of kids there are running about, annoying people in restaurants and clogging up the streets at school pick-up time.' He tuts. 'I know it's upsetting. Caroline really shouldn't have told you at this point, but please don't dwell on it. Everything's going to be fine. I promise you.'

'How do you know that? *How?*' I wail.

'I just do,' he says. 'Relax.'

199

I KNOW WHAT YOU WANT
TO CALL YOUR BABY

Joseph.

A biblical name. How sweet.

I can just see you both lying in bed, him spread tactfully over the damp patch with his hand on your belly, when you say, 'So, hon, have you thought about names?' and he hums and haws, and then says out loud as if it's a question: 'I quite like Joseph for a boy?' and you cock your head and sound it out a couple of times, then you say in your chirpy little way, 'Yeah, I like it. My parents are religious. They'll love that. It's perfect. And we can call him Joe.'

And he gives you a squeeze and you say, 'What about for a girl?'

But while you're mulling over Emily, Jasmine and Sophia, he's not thinking about girls' names. He's remembering that kid Joseph at school. Of course he is.

He can't forget.

Just the two of them, out on the quarry. Two boys exploring, making camp fires, building dens, messing about like boys do.

Until . . .

There's him bending down to gather sticks for the fire. The flames crackling into life, him standing back, rubbing his hands together, pleased, as he starts to feel the heat, then a scrabbling sound behind him, a scream, and Joseph dangling out over a hundred-foot drop, his face blue-white with terror, his hands rigid knots clinging to the root of a tree.

At least, that's what he told the police.

Everyone knows he has a temper; I wouldn't be the first to wonder if they had a row and he got angry, gave poor Joseph a shove.

I suppose we'll never know.

But, with Joseph dangling, what can he do? He's only twelve. What can anyone do? He lies down flat, inches to the edge, and drops his hands down to Joseph. 'Take my hand!' he shrieks and, for a second or two, he gets Joseph's hands in both of his and it's a stalemate but, ultimately, Joseph's bigger than him, a strong boy, muscular, and he starts to slide towards the edge.

Either he lets go, or they both go down.

It's a tough decision when you're twelve.

It's no secret what happened out there at the quarry. But you don't know about it, do you? He hasn't told you, and I bet you haven't googled him, his school, the news from his home town that year, have you? You haven't checked news stories that involve the name Joseph; you haven't googled anything except cots, prams and pushchairs and that poncey car. Of course you haven't. Why worry your pretty little head? Not everyone's as thorough as I am.

Oh, and there's one more thing. It's not just the name of your soon-to-be-born child; it's his email password, too: Joseph87. And his bank password. He really should use something stronger. Did no one ever tell him that?

34

They say that the urge to nest is a primal instinct that goes back to the days of cavemen. I can believe that, given the urge I suddenly have to clean and tidy the house. And with it comes a burst of energy the likes of which I haven't felt since before I was pregnant. With Jake away, I find myself shifting the sofa, mopping and vacuuming under furniture and rugs, disinfecting everything, buying bleach sprays and anti-bacterial wipes. I'm desperate to weed out any dust, crumbs, cobwebs, filth that might be lurking. And, better still, being so busy seems to keep a cap on my paranoia. Tidy house, tidy mind, I guess.

But it's more than that. It's as if my body knows that for the next few months if not years I won't have much time for sorting things out. I have a desperate urge to get the house completely and utterly shipshape: every cupboard has to be arranged nicely, every shelf stacked neatly; everything in boxes, cleaned, labelled and marked. I also throw out a lot. I make a huge pile of things that no longer belong in my life, from damaged saucepans and chipped plates to shoes, clothes, vases and old electronics. The old DVD player that came with me from the States and has never worked here. The printer that'll photocopy but no longer prints. An electric juicer. Piles of novels. Half-used notebooks.

It's while I'm shoving it all into black plastic bags that the doorbell rings. I edge to the window to look who it is and see the familiar shape of Simon dressed in his green jacket and red cap, and my heart bangs with sudden panic as Anna's warning burns in my ears. Without thinking, I drop to my hands and knees and cower below the level of the window, while I think about what to do: do I let him in or not? He rings again, twice, a rude, intrusive sound: ding-dong, ding-dong, then the letterbox opens and I hear him shout.

'Taylor! Are you there? Only me! I've got something for you.'

I stand up, pressing my hands to my chest to try and calm the thumping of my heart, then I take a deep breath and open the door. Damn Anna for making me feel so scared.

'Simon. Sorry. I was just . . .' I wave my hand.

'No problem,' he says. 'I thought you must be in the bathroom: when you gotta go, you gotta go! Anyway, look . . .' He steps towards the front door but I use my not insignificant frame to fill the doorway.

'Sorry, I'm just about to, umm . . . I've got to go out in a sec,' I say.

Simon recoils. 'Sorry. Look.' He holds out a small package wrapped in tissue paper. 'This is for you. I just wanted to drop it off.'

I unwrap the tissue and pull out a tiny babygrow for 0–3 months. 'Thank you. It's lovely.'

'It was for my baby,' Simon says. 'I kept one. When everything happened.'

'Oh. Oh my word. I can't take this. You keep it.' I hold it out to him. 'I don't want you to regret it. Please. You keep it.'

But Simon backs away, his hands up. 'No. It's over. I need to move on. Please take it. I want you to have it.' He turns to open the gate, gives a cheery wave and is gone.

35

It was quite a bit later, when I'd sustained myself with tea and chocolate biscuits, that Anna called. I remember being pleased to see her name come up on my screen; I remember thinking that she must be psychic because I was about to call her to ask if she could help me take my black bags to the recycling centre – but Anna's voice was panicky.

'Can you come over?' she says without preamble. 'Please? The police have just left and I need to you to come.' Her voice breaks. 'As quick as you can.'

A chill undulates through me, making my shoulders shiver. 'Oh my god, what's happened? Is it . . .' I swallow. I can't even say the word 'Simon'.

'Please, can you just come? Now?'

'Yes. Of course. I'm on my way.'

'Call me when you're outside. I'm not answering the door.'

I grab my keys, bag and coat, and hurry to Anna's, arriving breathless and sweaty at her door. When she opens the door her face is pale and drawn, and her eyes red. Despite the pregnancy she looks thin and frail. She ushers me inside and the first thing I notice is that all the curtains are drawn. I give her a hug.

'Okay, tell me,' I say, as she paces the room, biting the skin around her fingernails, nervous energy spiking off her.

'Someone's been watching me.'

'What?'

'I went out to the shed. I needed to see if I had some shears to . . . you know.' She waves towards the garden. 'Someone's been sleeping there.'

'What? In the shed?'

Anna squeezes her hands to her face, but I see tears seeping through her fingers. When she takes her hands away to speak again, her face is a mess of snot and tears. She gulps.

'He was watching me. I was right! I told you I felt followed!'

'Are you sure it's a man? You called the police? What did they say?'

'Not a lot.' She presses her hand against her mouth as if to stop herself crying again and then she clutches her belly. 'Oh my god, this stress. It's not good for the baby. He's all over the place.' She gives a huge sob and I go over to her and lead her back to the sofa.

'Come on, sit down. Try to relax.' I rub her shoulders. 'Let me make you some tea. What would you like? Chamomile?'

I make her the tea and hand it to her. 'Can I look at the shed? Do you mind?'

She shrugs. 'Help yourself. But I'm not coming. I can't bear it.'

'Okay. Back in a tick.'

The key's in the door of the shed. I turn it and wrench open the door expecting to see . . . what? Your usual shed interior, I guess: a lawnmower, a rake, a broom and a few shelves home to nothing but dead spiders, wasps and flies, but immediately I see that, aside from a pile of empty plastic water bottles scattered in one corner, the inside of the shed is cleaner than I'd have imagined. The most obvious thing, however, is that there's a bed on the floor. Not a proper bed: just a thin, stained mattress, a dark-red sleeping bag, a rough blanket and a pillow which, together, give a good impression of being a bed. Next to these is a large plastic box.

Feeling as if I'm snooping on someone else's possessions, I open the box. Inside there's a drinking glass, a few small bottles of water, a dog-eared copy of a porn magazine, an opened packet of biscuits, a large bag of Cheetos, and a pair of binoculars.

I stand there with my hands on my hips and survey the scene. I have to agree with Anna: it does look as if someone's been sleeping in her shed. But why? I take out one of the biscuits and apply pressure till it snaps soggily: they've been there a while, then. Maybe this all dates back to before Anna moved in. Maybe it's something as simple as the last tenant's gardener slacking off. Or their teenage son's bolthole. Who knows?

I chew the inside of my lip while I look through the window at the back of the house: you can see into the kitchen window and, if you look closely, through to the lounge-diner. Upstairs you've got the nursery window with its curtains just visible, and the small frosted window of the bathroom. Next-door's house is identical – the whole street has the identical back view, except one, which has a small conservatory patched on, like some sort of glass blister bulging on the brickwork of the house.

Yet suddenly I'm aware of all the unseen people who could be watching from the back windows of their houses and it gives me the creeps. I stumble back up the path and into the house, locking the back door behind me and taking out the key.

'Do you think it's Simon?' Anna says as I drop the key on the dining table.

'It can't be,' I say, blowing out through my lips. 'He can't leave his dad alone without a carer.'

'How do you know?' Anna snaps. 'You're so bloody trusting! All you know is what he's told you, and you're such a sucker! You've never met the dad, have you? You don't even know where he lives. There might not even be a dad! It's a great alibi at surface value: it can't be him because he never gets out! Come on, Taylor, wise up!'

'But . . .' I want to tell her about the babygrow – what a sweet thing that was to do, but I know she'll shoot me down.

'How did he know where you lived?' she demands. 'That day when he came round to give you the presents?'

I shrug. 'Maybe he asked the walking group. We filled out those forms, remember?' I realize as I say it that it sounds a little stalkerish itself.

'God, if you'd been through what I have . . .' Anna's shoulders heave. 'It's not something I can ever forget.' She exhales, trying to get a grip on her emotions. 'I'm sorry but Simon's a weirdo. It wouldn't surprise me if he turns out to be a paedophile. I'm sorry to say it, but it's what I feel. He's got that creepy look about him.' She shudders. 'I don't know what his game is. Maybe he likes little boys. Maybe he's befriending us so he can be close to our babies as they grow up. Maybe there's more to why his wife left before she had the baby – maybe she knew something about him?' She pauses. 'And what about that anyway? Having your pregnant wife leave you? It's got to leave you damaged, especially if you're slightly off your rocker anyway, stuck at home being a full-time carer. You'd go crazy.' She pauses again. 'Mind you, we don't even know for sure that he *is* his dad's full-time carer.'

'He's got a job.'

'I thought he never went out.'

'He works from home.'

'Doing what? Running a paedophile ring?'

'He's a forensic hacker.'

Anna jerks back. 'What in god's name is that?'

'Oh, you know, he helps companies tighten their online security by trying to hack into their sites or something. I think.'

Anna folds her arms. 'And you're telling me you think this guy is normal? I think you've just answered the question about how he got your address.'

That gives me pause for thought, to be honest. I stare back at Anna and she holds my gaze.

'Do you see now?' she asks. 'Do you see why I'm so worried?'

'So what now? How did you leave it with the police?'

She gives a bitter little laugh. 'They're "making enquiries". I gave them Simon's details, FYI. Oh, don't look at me like that: it's innocent till proven guilty, remember? They're not going to say, "Well, thank you very much for that, Mrs Jones, we'll pick him up now and throw him in jail." They'll just investigate. Go and have a chat. See if there's anything to link him to the shed. But I'll sleep easier for knowing they've checked him out.' She pauses. 'And they also said that, just for my peace of mind, I should move out for a bit rather than be here on my own . . . I've been looking at hotels. There's the Holiday Inn Express . . .'

'Stay with me,' I blurt.

'Really?'

'Yes. Obviously the baby's due in two weeks, but while Jake's away you're very welcome. It's the least I can do.'

Anna smiles. 'On one condition: I'm the one on the sofa.' I open my mouth to protest but she holds up her hand. 'No arguments.'

* * *

And so Anna moved in with me. I didn't tell Jake about what was found in her shed. Looking back, I don't know why. It just didn't seem that relevant. I guess, deep down, I thought she was being melodramatic and, honestly, I was embarrassed for her.

I suggest we share my bed, and we try it but, with both of us with our bellies and our maternity pillows, we're squeezed in like sardines.

'Hmm,' Anna says, trying not to fall off the edge. 'Not ideal, is it?'

'We can top and tail if you like,' I say, so she shifts so her head's level with my feet.

'Any better?' I ask, raising my head to look at her.

She looks back at me and says, 'It's fine if you're used to sleeping with elephants,' and it's as if it's the funniest thing anyone's ever said. I get the giggles and then I can't stop laughing, clutching my stomach and gasping for breath because there really isn't much room for air in my lungs – at least that's how it feels.

'Elephant keepers would probably find it quite comfortable,' Anna says.

'Ow, ow, stop it!' I laugh till tears run down my face. Then Anna gets up and, each time I get a grip on myself, she does an impression of an elephant, waving her arm around like a trunk and trying to trumpet, 'Hello, I'm Taylor the elephant,' which sets me off again.

Finally I manage to haul myself up to sit on the edge of the bed. 'So, how about I sleep downstairs?'

But Anna won't have it. 'No. You're more pregnant than I am. Not to mention taller. Absolutely no way you're sleeping on the sofa.'

Maybe it's all the laughing, maybe it's the stress of the day, or maybe it's just that the baby's ready, but it's later that night that I go into labour – two weeks early.

36

Most little girls imagine their wedding day, don't they, when they're growing up? They put on white dresses, frilly veils and plastic slip-on high heels, and walk about singing 'here comes the bride'. Not so many imagine what it'll be like the day they give birth to their first child. And I was no different: I hadn't given much thought to what it would be like to give birth until I was actually pregnant and, even then, I didn't have a concrete birth plan. Ultimately, I was willing to follow the baby and do whatever had to be done to get him out safe and well.

And I'd be lying if I said that, as the due date grew closer, various scenarios – forceps, vacuum-assisted births or even emergency C-sections – hadn't played out in my head, but there was one constant in all of them: Jake. For all his faults, in every scenario he was there, holding my hand as I screamed and writhed. In my mind, he'd be mopping my brow; crying as the baby's head appeared between my legs like a crinkled walnut, or rubbing my forehead while the doctor cut into my abdomen. I never imagined, not even in the middle of the night, at that low, low point around 3 a.m., that he wouldn't be there. But, when it comes to my hours of need – while I walk and breathe my way through the pain – it's Anna, not Jake, who's there for me.

And she's amazing. She calls Jake and leaves a message when

he doesn't pick up; more messages as I become increasingly distressed. Then she helps me down the stairs so I can pace the living room when the contractions hit.

'I need Jake!' I wail. 'He's supposed to be here!'

'He'll get here,' Anna says, 'and, if he doesn't, I'm here. We'll get through this. Don't worry.'

Between contractions, she searches for a contraction-timing app and downloads it. 'Right. Perfect,' she says. 'Now we can tell your midwife exactly what's going on.'

And as it becomes apparent that Jake hasn't even seen his messages, it's Anna who's on the phone with the midwife. It's Anna who tells me when it's time to go to the birthing centre, and drives me there. Inevitably, it's Anna who's there when my son's born just three hours after I'm admitted, as the sun's changing the sky from black to grey to pink; it's Anna whose hand I'm squeezing when I give those final pushes and feel the head crowning, then his shoulders and body gushing out of me; when we hear that first precious cry.

When the midwife places my son gently on my chest, both Anna and I are crying. I'm overflowing with love: both for the baby who's suddenly here in the room with us, and for my friend who's got me through the most difficult and emotional experience of my life. I stare down at my baby's face, his eyes still squeezed shut, and the responsibility hits home: it's my job now, to look after this tiny thing – to make sure he's well fed, and happy and healthy and cared for, from now until – I can't even imagine a day when I might be able to let go.

'You need to tell Jake,' Anna says, breaking into my thoughts, so she takes a picture, and I send it to him before I put it on Instagram: 'Joseph says "Hello daddy." #Insta-love.'

37

When everything's calmed down, Anna goes home to shower and get some rest.

'Thank you,' I say before she leaves, and my voice breaks as the emotion of the night hits me. 'Thank you for everything.'

She brushes back my hair with her hand. 'Look at you so shattered. I did what anyone would do. You'd have done the same for me.'

'I would. I will,' I say, meaning it with every fibre of my being. 'If yours comes early and Rob's not here, I'll do the exact same for you.'

'I'll hold you to that.'

The nurse tells me to sleep when I can, but I'm too wired so I lie there staring at the tiny bundle in the bassinet and trying to sleep but failing. My head keeps replaying the labour and the birth: the hours of pacing in the living room, bending over the dining chair to get through the contractions; the pain – oh, the pain! The frantic drive to the centre; the pushing; and then the unbelievable fact that I'm finally a mum. Over and over in my head, it plays: 'I'm a mum. I'm a mum. Oh my god, I'm a mother. I have a baby. My son. My son.' It's as if I've left one species and joined another, so monumental is the change.

I pick up my phone to see if Jake's messaged – he should have got here by now – and see I have forty-eight new Likes on Instagram, as well as some messages – most from my friends in the States. But there's one from Caroline – 'congratulations' – and I stiffen as I see one from the random bunch of numbers I now know to be Simon.

'Can't wait to come and see you both,' he's put, with a kiss. I'm staring at this, wondering what to do about it when the door opens a little. I look up, expecting Jake, but it's Caroline.

'Knock knock,' she says, poking her head around the door, then easing her way into the room carrying a stunning bouquet of flowers, all in blues, mauves and whites, and already arranged in a square glass vase.

'From Sarah and me,' she says. 'She's at work. Sends her love. I hope I didn't wake you?'

'No, no, it's fine,' I say, taken aback to see her here; to see her being so nice. She places the flowers on the table then comes over to me and smiles.

'You look great. Well done. Is this him?' She tiptoes towards the bassinet where Joseph – healthy, perfect little Joe! – is sleeping. He's swaddled and has a hat on – all you can see is his tiny, crumpled face – a few centimetres of brand-new pink skin. Caroline stares at him then looks up at me. 'He's beautiful. Congratulations.'

'Thanks for coming. It means a lot.' I smile at her, thinking about how difficult it must be for her. 'Would you like to . . . hold him?'

Her eyes widen and I see her chest move as she breathes in and out, her jaw also clenching and unclenching. Then she says, 'Really? I'd really like that, if you're sure . . . but he's sleeping.'

Maybe it's my hormones but suddenly I'm overwhelmed with the desire for her to hold Joseph. I hope it heals her. I hope it makes her want to try again; to move on from the pain of losing her own child.

'It's okay. If you'd like to . . .' I say.

She hesitates by the bassinet, so I gently raise myself up in bed, slide my legs over the edge and stand, holding onto the bed for support. I didn't have an epidural, but I'm still wobbly on my feet. Together we stand looking at my son.

'So precious,' Caroline whispers.

'Go on,' I say, so she reaches down and gently picks him up, and settles him in the crook of her arm, her face close to his.

'Oh, the smell of him,' she whispers, closing her eyes. 'That baby smell. I wish they could bottle it.'

'Why don't you sit down with him? I need to use the bathroom.'

'Are you able to? Everything went . . . well?'

'Natural birth,' I say. 'Gas and air. But we'll see about the bathroom. The midwife said I should try if I could, so I will.'

'Okay, take your time,' Caroline says, and I watch as she walks over to the chair and settles herself, all the while gazing into Joseph's face. I have to say it suits her. Holding a baby suits her.

'Back in a minute,' I say. 'If he starts crying and you don't know what to do, just press the bell.'

'Okay,' she whispers and it's as if she's in a trance.

I shuffle off to the bathroom.

When I get back to the room, I know immediately that it's empty but, even so, I look around, look into the corners and under the bed as my brain fails to process the fact that both Caroline and Joseph have gone. My heart feels as if it's been ripped out of me; panic stampedes my senses. Not caring that I'm in a blood-smeared nightie, I rip open the room door and look down the empty corridor.

'Caroline!' I scream. And then I faint. Out cold on the floor.

38

'm only out for a minute. When I come around, a nurse is kneeling in front of me and I'm lying on my back on the floor with my legs propped up on a chair.

'Okay sweetheart,' she says. 'Don't move. You just had a funny turn. Get up too soon, did we?' She lifts my wrist and feels my pulse. With her other hand she feels my forehead, then looks into my eyes. 'How are you feeling?'

'The baby!' I say, struggling to sit up. 'Where's my baby?'

'Try to relax,' says the nurse. 'He was fretting a bit so your friend took him for a walk. I saw them leaving.'

'Leaving what? The hospital?'

The nurse tuts. 'No. The room. I'm sure they won't have gone far.'

I try again to sit up. 'Get him back. I need him back. My baby!'

'Shhh . . . shhh,' says the nurse, sliding a pillow under my head and gently easing me back down. 'Don't get up too quickly. Your baby's fine. We'll get him back in here before you're back in bed, don't you worry, but I don't want you fainting again, so we'll just take it easy, okay?'

Bit by bit, she helps me up and then back into the bed, but all the while my eyes are on the door. I'm sweating heavily. I can feel the wetness of it on my hairline, at my throat and behind my knees; my whole body is damp with it. What's Caroline doing with

Joseph? My baby should be in here with me. He was inside my body a couple of hours ago – now he's gone.

The nurse bustles around the room, settling me in the bed, taking my blood pressure, bringing me a glass of water and making sure I can reach the call button.

'Right. Try to stay put for a bit. I don't want a repeat of that. Remember what your body's just been through.'

She leaves the room and then I hear footsteps and the piercing cry of a baby. I've not had Joseph long enough to recognize his scream but something deep inside me tells me it's him and my body melts with relief.

'Here we go . . . Here's Mummy,' Caroline says, nudging the door open. 'I told you she was right here . . .'

'Oh my god,' I say as Caroline hands Joseph back to me, 'please don't do that again.'

'What? You thought . . . ?' She laughs. 'I forget how possessive new mums are. He was fussing. I thought a walk might help.'

I smile weakly. I'm whole again now I have my son's weight in my arms. I touch my lips to his forehead. We're both looking at him when the door opens and Jake walks in.

'Hello, hello,' he says to all of us. He comes over to me, kisses my head, then peers down at Joe. 'Oh my god, Tay! Is this him?'

'No, it's her pet llama,' Caroline says.

39

Having a baby wasn't as easy as I'd thought it would be. Nothing had prepared me for the huge responsibility I felt towards him. When he'd latch on to feed and I looked down at his tiny face and he looked back with those bright little eyes that looked like they knew all the secrets of the universe, I felt he was relying on me 100 per cent to take care of him; to feed him the right food; to keep him the right temperature; to make sure that he thrived – and I'd be lying if I said I didn't find it overwhelming.

He cried a lot. After those first couple of days, Joe found his voice, and boy did he use it. He didn't sleep much, either, his little naps between feeds barely long enough for me to shower, get something to eat and tidy up the house, let alone get some rest myself. I was jealous of the mums on my online forums whose babies slept for three or four hours at a stretch – what were they doing that I wasn't? Why was my baby so fractious, so demanding, so unreasonable?

And then there was the exhaustion. I'd never known anything like it; days lost in a haze of tiredness. There were times when I went upstairs and forgot why I was there; days when I found my mobile phone in the fridge; days when I woke up and cried with the bone-tired misery of having to get up and do it all again, having been up the best part of the night. Joe had colic in the early days. Every feed would be followed by screaming on his part, his face twisted in pain. I didn't know what to do. I felt like screaming back. Sometimes I did.

There was pain, too. No one told me about that: not just the physical tension in my shoulders from holding a baby, but the agony of the early days of breast-feeding. I got mastitis, and lay alternately shaking and sweating with fever until the antibiotics kicked in, my infected breast huge, red and throbbing like a beacon. I expressed milk using a double electric machine, my breasts sucked dry like a cow. In those early days, my sense of self was stripped to the bone. The person I was before Joe was born ceased to exist, and a new me – a shattered, careworn mother – evolved. The learning curve was steep; sometimes so steep I thought I'd fall right back down to the bottom.

Did Jake notice any of this? I doubt it. He wasn't travelling, but he did go back to work after a week and, once again, I found myself marooned at home. Only this time I wasn't bored – how can you be bored when there's a baby in the house? – but something was missing. There was an emptiness inside me that I couldn't explain; an emptiness that wouldn't go away, and I honestly think that Anna quite possibly saved my life. I don't mean to sound overly dramatic but she came over every morning, soon after Jake left, and she made herself indispensable, helping me with housework and making sure I kept up with the laundry. I expressed milk, and she took Joe out for long walks so I could sleep during the day. Despite her own worries, she kept Joe and me in a bubble of safety and support. She became my backbone, my moral support, my cheerleader. Everything, with hindsight, that Jake should have been.

* * *

'Do you know much about post-natal depression?' Anna asks me in the living room one day. She's folding muslin cloths and babygrows at the dining table while I'm doing a bit of ironing and Joe is, for once, asleep in the bassinet I keep in the living room. Anna's got a serious look on her face.

'Not much. Why?'

'Hmm,' she says. 'I was reading up about it the other day and, please don't take this the wrong way because I want to help, but I wonder if you might have a touch of it.'

'Really?'

'Yeah. You're not yourself. You seem down. You've lost your confidence.'

'I've no idea what I'm doing half the time, that's why.'

Anna shakes her head. 'It's more than that. You've lost all interest in life. You never want to go out.'

'Because I'm exhausted!'

'But you won't even take Joe for a walk to the park. It's so lovely to get out, get some fresh air – it'd do you no end of good, maybe help you sleep better at night – but you don't even want to do that.' Anna smiles to soften her words and I focus on the ironing. I'm doing one of Jake's shirts, trying hard not to put tramlines down the sleeve, even though I'm seeing double. Anna's right. I don't feel myself, but I'd put it down to tiredness. I sigh.

'I know I've been a bit subdued but I don't think I'm depressed. I'm hardly sitting about sobbing, am I? And it's not as if I want to kill myself and throw Joe out the window. I'm just tired. Really tired. Like you can't begin to imagine. You have all this to come.'

Anna looks at me in a way that makes me wonder what she sees. I know I've been skimping on the make-up lately so the black bags under my eyes are more obvious than usual, and my hair needs a wash, but what else?

'Maybe you should get a blood test or something,' Anna says. 'You look like a corpse, and I tell you that as a friend. You're also not eating. Don't think I haven't noticed. You're living on coffee, tinned soup and toast.'

'I've just had a baby,' I say. 'I think I'm a bit anaemic, and I'm not getting any sleep. Of course I'm exhausted. And I don't have time to cook like I used to. So yes, our diet is a bit hit and miss at the moment.'

'No, but above that. You look drained. Washed-out.' Anna looks thoughtful. 'When will your mum be able to travel?'

My mum had fallen and fractured her leg the day after Joe was born. With her entire leg in plaster, and instructions to keep it elevated as much as possible, her planned trip to stay with me had had to be put on hold.

I sigh. 'I think that one's not going to happen for some time. She's just not up to the flight.'

'What about Jake's parents?'

'His mum died years ago and his dad's old – he's in a home.'

'I see.' Anna frowns. 'What about a night nurse? Don't they have those nurses who come and do the night feeds so you can try to get your sleep back on track?'

I sigh again. 'All very well if you're married to royalty, but for us commoners it's a bit of a stretch.'

'What about Jake? Is he pulling his weight? Can he do some night feeds? You *are* expressing. He could help out.'

'He does occasionally on the weekends. But I feel guilty keeping him up all night during the week as he has to get up and do a full day's work. Specially as he does so much driving. At least I'm at home so I can sleep when the baby sleeps.'

'All very well in theory,' says Anna, 'but you don't, do you? I've seen you. As soon as he nods off, you're off doing the housework or catching up on the washing or something. And he doesn't sleep for that long, considering.'

Joe stirs and we both look over towards him, our tiny dictator swaddled in his blue dotty blanket.

'So much disruption for one so little,' I say when it becomes apparent he's not waking up, after all.

'But you love him?' Anna asks. 'Because, sometimes . . .'

'Of course I love him,' I snap. 'But he completely rules the house. Everything revolves around him. It's like he's the sun and we're the planets.'

'Good analogy.'

I let my head loll back on the sofa and close my eyes, feeling my eyeballs roll up ready for sleep, my head already heavy.

'Why don't you go and see your parents?' Anna breaks into my micro-nap.

'What? Take him to the States?'

'Why not?'

'I hadn't thought about it. Flying all that time on my own with a baby? Jake can't get any more time off. Not enough to go to the States, anyway.'

'I'll come with you.'

'You couldn't!'

'Why not? I have no ties here, with Rob in Qatar. I can do my work anywhere. Besides, I could really do with a break before my own baby comes.'

I look at Anna, searching her face and she looks back, eyes shining. She's sitting up really straight now, smiling, and I can see that she's plotting this trip in her head already.

'We could do it,' she says. 'Take turns with him on the flight so each of us gets some sleep. I could help feed him, hold him . . . and then you'd be with your mum. How nice would that be? To have her there for moral support. Don't worry about me – maybe Rob will join me there. He's been offered the job, by the way. So we could use some time to decide if we want to move back.'

This hits me like the proverbial tonne of bricks but I'm too excited by the thought of going home – of seeing my parents and showing them Joe – that I let it slip for now.

'When's your due date?'

'It's fine. I checked. I can fly up to thirty-six weeks and I'll be thirty-two next week. I'll get a "fit to fly" certificate from the doctor. I have no complications so it shouldn't be a problem.'

I purse my lips. 'My parents are desperate to see him.'

'Well, let's do it! It's probably easier to fly with a newborn than with a toddler who you've got to amuse.'

'Do you really think we could?'

'Yes!' says Anna. She's jumped up and is pacing the room. 'How soon do you think we can go? Rob's not coming back for another three weeks. If we went in the next few days . . .'

'Let me talk to Jake,' I say and, for the first time in a little while, my heart is full of hope.

40

It's difficult to look back on what happened next. This is the hardest part of the story to recount. Jake agreed that I should go. Of course he did. What kind of man would stop his wife from seeing her mother? Maybe he was also worried about me, because he was very glad to hand over the duty of care to my mum, I could see it in the way he smiled and his shoulders relaxed the moment I suggested it. Perhaps I didn't give him credit for how much he worried about me in those early days. It's hard to see it objectively now.

But he certainly didn't have any concerns about me flying to the States with Anna. Not one. He thought it was a great idea. I want that on paper at this point: he thought it was a great idea. We are both to blame – that's a fact that was forgotten in the aftermath, and I have to remind myself of it every time the guilt creeps up on me. But wait, I'm getting ahead of myself.

* * *

The trip is exactly what I need. Once the tickets are booked and my parents told to expect us, and I get my energy back, despite the lack of sleep, I plan for the trip like a soldier, trawling 'travelling with baby' websites and forums for tips and advice on flying long haul with a newborn. Anna gets her ESTA; I take out travel insurance; arrange a passport for Joe; pay extra for premium economy; check the regulations for flying with bottles of expressed milk. Nothing is left to chance. We're ready to go within a week of that first discussion. It's a frantic week, but a good one. For the first time in months, I feel like the real me: invincible. Joe is six weeks old.

The morning that we fly is etched into my memory. It's a dull, grey day that threatens rain, as if even the elements know what's about to happen. Had I been staying at home, I'd have been down at the thought of a late-March day being so miserable. As it is, I can't wait to be up high in the bright blue of the atmosphere, looking down at the clouds as we hurtle towards the sunshine of California, of home. Before he leaves for work, Jake pulls me into his arms and holds me tight.

'Look after yourself,' he says, 'and look after our son.' He kisses me longer and harder than usual, and it squeezes at my heart. I don't want to leave, but I do want to go.

'I'll message you when we're through passport control,' I say, and I wave at the car until he turns out of the end of the street.

Anna and I take a taxi to Heathrow. It comes at 10.15 a.m., plenty of time: I don't want there to be any rush, any stress. The driver helps me fix Joe's rear-facing car seat into the cab and load the luggage. Anna, giddy with excitement, Instagrams a picture of the cab. She and I both have backpacks stuffed with nappies, wipes, muslin squares, blankets, spare baby clothes and rattles for our hand luggage. We're at the airport before 11 a.m. The driver helps us haul the bags out of the cab and load them onto a trolley. I tip him.

'Cheers, love,' he says, and Anna starts pushing the trolley towards the terminal while I carry Joe in his car seat. I don't know if it's nerves or excitement about being back in an airport environment, the smell of jet fuel hanging in the air, but my insides flutter and cramp, and I realize I need the bathroom. I spot one right there, inside the terminal doors, and hand Joe to Anna.

'Sorry. Won't be long,' I say, but I'm wrong. I don't mean to go into too much detail – let's just say that my stomach was loose with nerves. I wash my hands in hot water and dry them with paper, but I'm impatient to get going so I'm running my hands down my jeans to finish the job as I walk out of the bathroom looking for Anna.

I'm going to describe what happens next in detail because I've gone over it so many times; told Jake and the police so many times. I'm smiling as I look around for Anna, half-expecting to see her sitting on a bench, dandling a rattle for Joe. The luggage trolley is there, by the wall, but Anna and Joe are not. My eyes skim over the people bustling past with their suitcases and carry-ons piled high, yanking wayward trolleys into line. I look left and right, and probably start to frown as my eyes move faster through the crowds, skimming over the bright reds, blues and yellows of the airline logos behind the banks of check-in desks. Outside, beyond the doors, taxis, cars and people-carriers pull up, disgorge passengers and leave. The electric doors whoosh open and closed, open and closed, bringing with them a blast of fresh air and the sound of car horns. Trolley wheels rattle; children cry.

I squint a little as I try to spot Anna. I walk a little to the left and run my hand through my hair, anxious now. I turn, and take a few steps the other way. Then I try to calm myself. Maybe she's gone to check in? I hurry over to the desks for our airline but she's not there – and neither can she check in without me being there: I have the tickets. I go back to the bathroom door. 'Stay here,' I tell myself. She'll come back to where she last saw you. So I stand with my back to the wall outside the Ladies, and I wait, but all the while I wait, my eyes are searching, searching. Where *are* they?

I take a deep breath in through my nose, and exhale it slowly through my mouth. I repeat this three times, maybe four, trying to calm myself. Then I wonder if maybe Joe's nappy needed changing. I imagine a poo so enormous it's squelched out of the nappy and into the sleepsuit; Joe's whole outfit needing a change. Maybe

Anna's locked in a cubicle, struggling to clean him up. I go back into the bathroom, but all the cubicles are empty.

'Anna!' I shout. 'Are you in here?'

Silence.

I position myself back outside the bathroom and check my phone. No messages. I dial her number and raise it to my ear, still looking for Anna while the number rings and rings. Now I'm not just confused; I'm angry. Where the hell is she? She knows we have a flight to catch. This is ridiculous.

I cross the area in front of the Ladies and look left and right into places I couldn't previously see; I look back at the Ladies from where I'm now standing, but it's as if Anna was never here. Then I hurry towards the bank of check-in desks and crane my neck as I look in turn at each desk, more carefully this time. Maybe I missed her? The desks aren't busy, and it doesn't take long to see that Anna really isn't there. Still, I look again, as if she might magically appear, and then I decide to go back to the Ladies and wait there, but this time I'm too agitated to stand still. I walk ten paces this way and ten paces that way. This way, that way. Up and down.

When my phone rings, I think I might vomit with relief. I rip it out of my back pocket but it's not Anna, it's Jake, just checking we reached the airport okay.

'I was worried about you,' he says and I hear a smile in his voice; relief that we've arrived safely.

'I can't find them! Anna and Joe – they've gone!' The words explode out of me with a sob.

'What do you mean "gone"? They'll be somewhere. They've just gone to the bathroom, or for a walk or something.'

'No! You don't understand! I've looked everywhere! They've been gone ages. They're nowhere. Something's happened!' I'm clutching at my head with my spare hand, trying to come up with a scenario that explains why my friend and my baby have disappeared out from under my eyes when we have a flight to catch.

I'm panicking but also, all the while, holding out that stupid, ridiculous hope that it's some sort of misunderstanding. A stubborn part of me still believes we'll make the flight.

'Calm down,' Jake says firmly. I can tell from his voice that he's gone into management mode. 'Taylor! Come on, think logically. When and where did you last see them?'

I talk to him through sobs, my eyes darting left and right across the concourse.

'Okay,' Jake says. 'But nobody's going to abduct an adult woman and a baby from an airport. Why would they? Things like that just don't happen. Someone would have noticed.'

'Where are they, then? Where? You tell me!' I shout. I pace frantically up and down outside the bathrooms, this way and that, scanning the crowds for a familiar flash of Joe's apple-green car seat.

'I don't know, Tay! But they'll be somewhere. I promise you! They can't just have disappeared. Maybe they went to get something to eat. Or left something in the taxi. Maybe they're outside calling the taxi back.'

'Why isn't she answering her phone, then? She'd tell me. I know she would. She knows I'd be frantic! Something's happened. She said she was being followed. Maybe someone had it in for her . . . Oh my god!' My knees go weak and I lean on the wall to stop myself from falling.

'Don't be ridiculous,' Jake says. 'People like her don't have enemies. This doesn't happen in real life.'

'Oh god, oh god,' I moan, and the whole sorry story comes tumbling out. How Anna felt she was being watched; how someone was sleeping in her shed; how she suspected it might be Simon.

Jake goes quiet. 'Why didn't you tell me? I'd never have let you go with her! What were you thinking?'

'So you're blaming me?' I snap.

I hear Jake take a deep breath, and picture him running his

hand through his hair. 'No. Look. Let's keep calm. Why don't you go to an information desk and ask them to put out a call for Anna? I'm sure they can do that.'

So I go over to the information desk. The lady there calls over another lady in a smart suit with an airport tag. She listens to me, nodding, then calls for a police officer. I explain to each of them in turn as calmly as I can that my friend and my baby have gone missing but, having handed me over to the police, the airport official gently melts back into the terminal, and, while the police officer is kind, I can see in his eyes that what he sees is a panicky new mum, a misunderstanding and a potential waste of his time as he asks me for a description of Anna and Joe.

'She's about five foot six, blonde hair, wearing a blue coat . . . No, hang on. She didn't have that on today . . . It was the Zara one. Oh god, just, like, a grey coat like this . . .' I try to show with my hands how long the coat was, how it did up with buttons. 'Umm, jeans, sneakers. Dark-blue Converse, I think.'

'And the baby? Can you describe him?'

'Six weeks old. Dark hair. Dark eyes. Oh my god, it's nearly time for his feed!' Fresh tears spring to my eyes. 'He's a baby, what else can I say?'

'What's he wearing? Any identifying marks?'

I shake my head. 'A sleepsuit. A navy one with white stars. A white blanket. He's in a car seat. At least he was. A Maxi-Cosi, you know the newborn car seats that you carry?' I mime holding it. 'Black and apple green, quite bright. They've been taken! I'm sure of it. She was being watched!'

The officer's writing everything down but nothing's actually happening. I want to shake him till his teeth rattle – make him realize the urgency of the situation. It's like a nightmare: one of those dreams when you want to run but your legs won't move, only this is real life and my mouth's dry and my words aren't coming out right, I'm gabbling, and I'm aware of how unstable I sound; how hysterical I look as I repeat myself. Then my head goes woozy and I'm out of my body, looking down on myself in the airport terminal, struggling to be taken seriously as I keep trying to get it through to the officer that my best friend and my baby have been snatched, but all he's doing is making notes and telling me to calm down, and I'm standing there at the information desk, scrubbing at my eyes with the back of my fist and, all the while, my baby's getting further and further away from me.

'Oh for god's sake! I can't stand here doing nothing!' I sob, snapping back into my body.

I spin around and run towards the check-in zones, my head swivelling left and right, searching for that flash of apple green.

'Have you seen a blonde woman with a baby in a green car seat?' I scream, my voice coming out thinner and reedier than I imagine it will. Still, the crowds part around me, a sea of startled faces and shaking heads. The airport's so big, there are so many people – I feel utterly hopeless, aware, too, that somehow the abductors might have fake passports; might have got Joe through security to the departure lounges, where the rest of the world lies in wait like a hungry wolf, jaws open to swallow him up.

I might never see Joe again.

The enormity of the thought overwhelms me and my legs give out, forcing me to sink to my knees, head in hands like the weight of what's happening is too heavy to bear. Footsteps thud. The officer kneels down in front of me.

'Mrs Watson.' He offers an arm but I ignore it. 'Mrs Watson, if your son is here, we will find him.'

'But you're not *doing* anything! Every minute is a minute he's further away. Don't you *understand*? They've been taken! Kidnapped. Abducted. Whatever you call it. Someone's taken them. We need to catch them before they leave the airport. What if they get on a flight? Can they stop them before they board? Can you tell all the airlines to watch out for a blonde woman with a small baby? Please? You've *got* to.' I tug at my hair. 'What about sniffer dogs? I've got luggage they can get a scent from.'

'We'll make enquiries.'

'Enquiries! I don't want enquiries. I want my son. You don't get it. This has been building up for weeks. It's a carefully orchestrated plan. I *know* it. Where are the police? Look!' I fling my arm at the terminal where no police are to be seen. 'Where are they? Why aren't they searching the terminal? If you're not going to do it, I will.' I stumble back to my feet and launch myself back into the fray, aware at a base level as I do so that I'm making a scene; that people are turning to look while others are scurrying away, heads down, not wanting to be a part of this; not wanting trouble to smear itself across the start of their holidays.

'Has anyone see a blonde woman with a baby? He's in a green car seat?' I scream. 'I've lost my baby. Help me!' But the officer grabs me.

'Mrs Watson. Please. The best thing you can do right now is to assist us with our enquiries. Please come with me.' He speaks into his radio and then leads me across the concourse, through a door marked 'Private' and down a back corridor until we reach a small room, which he indicates I should enter, and all the while I'm thinking how will this help? How will I find Joe if I'm stuck in a room, but the fight's going out of me as I realize that what's happened is bigger than me – bigger than me just being separated from Joe and Anna – and that I'm going to have to trust the police to do their job.

Inside the room there's a small sofa that's seen better days, a table and a couple of hard chairs. The officer leads me to the sofa and gets me a paper cup of water from a cooler. He sits on one of the hard chairs.

'I'm just waiting for a colleague, and then we'll ask you some questions. Is there anyone we can call for you?'

'My husband,' I whimper. 'Jake.'

41

In a few minutes, the door to the room opens again, and a police-woman enters and introduces herself as PC Manning. I instantly like the look of her: she seems brisk and capable – as if she deals with things like this every day of her life.

'Right,' she says with a small smile, 'I know this is a difficult time but, in our experience, a positive and constructive parental response in the first twenty-four hours is critical to success in finding missing minors. Ninety-nine times out of a hundred, it's some sort of misunderstanding, but we need all the help we can get from you. Do you think you can do that?'

I nod. She brings one of the chairs over and sits so she's facing me. The original officer, whose name I still don't know, remains at the table.

'Just to let you know, the CCTV is being checked as we speak.'

'Okay,' I say, overwhelmed that this is my life, not a television show.

'Now, who was with your son when you last saw him?' PC Manning's pen is poised over her notepad so I reel off Anna's name, address and phone number.

'She's my best friend. She was with me for the birth. I can't imagine what's happened for her to disappear with him. Something terrible . . .'

'We'll also need your address just to check she hasn't gone back there for some reason,' she says, and suddenly I imagine Anna realizing she's forgotten something vital to the trip and nipping home to pick it up. Hope leaps through me, its flames licking my heart and then extinguishing as I realize that's highly unlikely: she would have just waited for me to come out of the toilets and told me. Surely she would.

'Right,' says PC Manning after I've told her our address. 'Now we need to get as much background information as we can. Anything you think that might help with the search. I need to know about who's had contact with your baby: friends and family who've visited the house and so on.'

I lean forward, focused and eager to impart as much information as I can.

'My son is six weeks old. As I said, he was with Anna. We were travelling to the States together – she was helping me with the baby then going off on her own holiday. But – and I don't know if it's relevant – but for the last few weeks – months maybe? – she's been telling me she feels like she was being watched.'

PC Manning tilts her head. 'Okaay . . .' she says slowly. 'Anything concrete?' And there's something in her voice that puts me on edge. I'm aware that, from the outside, I must be sounding a little mad to this sensible, capable woman, but isn't the proof in the fact that Joe and Anna have gone missing? That's not something that happens every day. I take a deep breath to fight down the defensiveness springing up inside me. PC Manning represents my chance of getting Joe back. I need her to be on my side.

'I met Anna at a walking group in Croydon,' I say. 'We were both new to the area, and I joined to meet people – she was there and we hit it off.' I check to see that PC Manning is following. 'But we both also met a guy called Simon that day. Anna said that she started feeling like she was being watched ever since then, which was in early December.' I pause, wondering if that sounds like I'm accusing Simon and that by doing so, I might be giving the police a red herring because I honestly don't know if it was him, but PC Manning just waits for me to carry on.

'I don't know if it's relevant,' I shrug. 'I don't know if it's him or not, but Anna never felt comfortable around him. She thought he had, I don't know – an agenda of some sort?'

'I see,' says PC Manning. 'And did you share the same feeling about him?'

I exhale through my teeth. 'Oh god . . . I don't know. He's odd. You can't deny that. But I thought he was harmless – just lonely? But Anna pointed out all these things, like he knew where I lived when I didn't think I'd told him. And I . . . I thought she was over-reacting. She'd had a bad experience in the past and was suspicious of everything so I didn't take her that seriously.' I shrug. 'Maybe she was right.'

'Okay. I'll get his details and we'll make some enquiries. Anyone else you can think of?'

I start to shake my head but then I remember how Anna felt Caroline had something against her too, so I mention that.

'She'd have a motive for taking Joe,' I say, ice suddenly running through my veins as I remember her taking him from me at the hospital. 'She lost a child about a year ago.'

PC Manning nods. 'Okay, well, we'll check her out and we'll also need to know if there's anyone else who might wish you ill will – conflicts with neighbours, arguments, bitter exes, whether you've noticed anyone strange hanging around the house, following you . . . anything you can think of that might be relevant? Anything at all, however small you think it is.'

I shake my head. 'I can't think of anything. God, this is all to do with Anna, isn't it? Maybe someone had it in for her and Joe just got in the way?' I picture Anna murdered; Joe left squalling in the car seat, dumped in bushes, cold and hungry.

'What about Anna's passport? Who has that?' PC Manning asks, blocking that rabbit hole.

My heart skitters. 'She does.'

'And who bought the airline tickets?'

'We each bought our own,' I say, as the realization of what PC Manning's getting at oozes into my mind. 'We coordinated about the flight, but she booked her own ticket.'

'Did you ever see her passport?'

'No . . .'

PC Manning shakes her head. 'You didn't see her name on it?'

I shake my head in silence and PC Manning's lips form a straight line. 'Okay.' She taps her pen on the notepad and sighs while I try to imagine Anna planning all this but I just can't. There has to be some other explanation.

'Right. One last thing,' says PC Manning. 'Do you have a picture of her we can circulate?'

'Sure.'

I take a few deep breaths and start to scroll through the camera roll on my phone, realizing with the surety of lead sinking that I don't actually have a single photo of Anna. Not one. I go to her Instagram account but nothing comes up.

'I can't find it,' I say, stabbing at the phone with my finger. 'It's not loading.' It takes me a minute to comprehend why it's not loading: because the account no longer exists. I flick to Facebook and type 'Anna Jones' into the search window but her familiar avatar isn't there and her page doesn't come up. I stare at the screen, uncomprehending.

'What is it?' PC Manning asks.

'I can't find her Facebook. Or Instagram.' I try Twitter but it's the same story. Anna's been wiped off social media.

I look up at the officer. 'There's nothing,' I say, shaking my head. 'Absolutely nothing. Everything's been deleted.'

42

They find Anna's phone in a bin close to the toilets. A uniformed officer brings it in for me to identify while I'm still with PC Manning. She puts the phone on the table and asks me to ring the number to confirm, but I hardly need to. I've seen Anna's phone with its crack at the edge of the screen and its aqua-and-red watermelon case lying on the dining table so many times it's as familiar to me as my own.

'It's definitely hers,' I say as it rings. 'So what does that tell us?'

'It doesn't rule out anything,' says the officer. 'As I'm sure you appreciate, we need to investigate all angles.' He pauses and I know that they already feel that Anna's the guilty party here.

'Someone else could have deleted her social media,' I say hopefully. 'Whoever has her.'

They both look at me straight-faced and I realize how silly I sound. Fear spikes at my insides.

'Can I speak to my husband?' I ask.

'I believe he's with CID,' PC Manning says. 'At least, they were on their way to see him.'

'What do you mean "see him"?'

'Sorry: they need to talk to him, too. Just to see if he can shed any more light on things.'

'What? You think he . . . ?' I shake my head. 'We've had our differences but . . . no. No way!'

'It's just procedure,' says PC Manning. 'He might remember things that you don't. We don't think anything at this point. We're just trying to gather as much information as we can. It's a stressful time, but please bear with us.'

The other officer, who's been talking quietly on his phone, puts it down and looks at us.

'We've assigned a Family Liaison Officer to you. Her name's Jackie Dane. Her role is to help you through this. She'll meet you at your home,' he says.

PC Manning stands up, and I realize that the interview is over. I stand unsteadily. Mine and Anna's holiday baggage has been brought discreetly into the room. I look at the suitcases – reminders of what now seems another life.

'What happens now?' I look from one of them to the other. 'Do I just . . . What do I do?'

'I'll take you home,' says PC Manning. 'You'll meet your FLO, Jackie, then maybe try to get some rest. Jackie will guide you through the next steps.' She smiles. We're all standing when her phone rings. She looks at the number and picks it up with a sense of urgency.

'Yes,' she says. There's a long pause during which she nods and says, 'Mmm, I see,' and then, 'Yes. I see. Okay. Thank you.'

She closes the call and turns to us. 'We believe Anna's been spotted on the CCTV. They'd like you to come and view it for a positive identification.'

43

'm led down more back corridors to a surprisingly large room full of desks and screens. Waiting for us there is a man in shirt-sleeves and grey trousers, who introduces himself as Steve, along with two officers whom PC Manning introduces as DS Baldwin, who's apparently in charge of our investigation, and DC White. We're ushered over to a desk and seated in front of one of the monitors.

'This is the camera which was on the door in the departures area close to the Ladies,' says Steve. 'Ready?'

He presses play and, right there on the screen, I see Anna and me walking into the departures area with me carrying Joseph's car seat. Steve freezes it.

'Is that you?' DS Baldwin asks and all I can do is nod because I'm suddenly shaking. I want to be back in that moment; I want to jump into the screen and be once more in that precise moment when I had Joe in his car seat. I want to not go to the bathroom; to walk straight on through to check-in; to get through passport control and security and onto the plane without ever handing him to Anna. I want to be on the plane to California right now with my baby in my arms.

Steve presses play again and I see myself stop, then Anna turn to face me. She nods and I hand the car seat to her and enter the bathrooms without a backward glance. My heart shrinks inside my chest. That's the last time I saw Joe and I didn't even say good-bye – I just handed him over like a parcel. Steve pauses the frame again.

'Keep going!' I gasp. 'What happened? I need to see who took her!'

So Steve presses play again and then we see exactly what happened: straight after I go into the bathroom – probably before I'd even undone my trousers – Anna looks quickly left and right, then goes swiftly back out of the door we'd just come in, her arm already raised to hail one of the cabs that's just dropped a passenger.

I stare at the screen in shock. 'She took Joe herself? No one was with her?'

My hand clamps over my mouth and the piercing scream that echoes around the CCTV room is animal, guttural, and comes from the very heart of me.

HE STILL LOVES ME

I was only going to tell you ten things, and now I've used them all up. But I'm quite enjoying this, and there's still something worth saying: the most important thing of all, I suppose, so consider this a bonus. Something I'll give you for nothing.

He still loves me.

Oh, you think you have a happy marriage. You think you he's 'the one' for you – the man you trust to father your children. But I hate to break it to you, sweetie-pie: you're living in La-La Land.

Oh, come on, don't look at me like that. You don't believe me? Let's take a look at Croydon. Nothing against it, of course: it's my home and I love it. It's got art, culture and open spaces. But you left Santa fucking Monica in California, zip code 90401. You left the beach, and you moved to Croydon. Let that sink in for a minute.

Did you ever wonder why he ripped you from your perfect little existence there and dumped you here when he could have picked anywhere in Britain? Was it for the joys of the Whitgift Centre? For the rolling spaces of Lloyd Park?

No, shit-for-brains, it was for me.

I knew if I waited, he'd come back home. I knew it was just a matter of time. So I sat and I waited, I dreamed about him every night and, sure enough, just as planned, here he is.

What you never realize, sweetie-pie, is that men are simple

creatures. There's no point asking him about this because he prob-ably doesn't even know himself why he came back to Croydon – it happened subconsciously: like the tides being pulled by the moon, he was drawn to me; he chose to come back to where he last saw me without even realizing.

And when he sees me with his baby, it'll feel like coming home. He'll know then why he did what he did, and he'll come to me and be with me. We'll finally be a family: me, him and Joe. And you, my sweetie? You'll finally see what you've been up against; you'll see the monster that's always lurked under your marital bed. You'll let him go. You'll go back to your Yankee Doodle friends and your Yankee Doodle family. You'll get over this, and everyone will live happily ever after . . .

One day, you might even thank me.

44

Denial comes after the scream.

'There must be a reason!' I say, biting my lip as I shake my head. 'Something must have happened. She wouldn't just take Joe for no reason.' I lean back in the chair, thinking, thinking. 'Maybe she forgot something; maybe she went to get it and – I don't know – got into a car accident or something. Have you checked the hospitals?'

DS Baldwin nods, his arms folded.

'Maybe someone was waiting for her,' I say, aware from the way everyone's looking at me that they're already drawing conclusions I don't want to see – but I simply can't understand why Anna would have taken my son back out of the airport. 'Maybe someone bribed her. She wouldn't do this on her own. She wouldn't!'

'They've picked her up getting into a cab. We're tracing the cab right now.' DS Baldwin says. 'We've also checked the CCTV at the doors to the other terminals in case she entered a different one.'

'Why would she . . . ?' I gasp. 'You mean, to get a flight some-where else? Oh my god!' My voice rises hysterically and I clamp my hand over my mouth, my mind a maelstrom of babies snatched to order, of paedophile rings, and the drawn faces of Madeleine McCann's parents who never got their happy ever after.

'Let's take this one step at a time,' says PC Manning. 'It's positive that we have a sighting of her exiting the building and we don't yet have one of her re-entering a different building.'

My hand's still clasped over my mouth. How could this have happened? Why did I leave Joseph with Anna? *Because I always did. Because I trusted her!*

Because she made you trust her, says a little voice in my head and, metaphorically, I jump on it with both feet. But I can't stop my thoughts: *what if I hadn't gone to the bathroom? What if I'd run straight to the doors when I came out, instead of standing outside like a lemon? Would I have seen her getting into the cab? Would I have seen the back of her head in a cab as it drove off? How long did it take for her to get the cab? Did I miss her by seconds?* My insides twist at the thought that the decision I made – to stand outside the bathroom and wait – could have cost me my baby.

'We'll get to the bottom of this,' says DS Baldwin. 'But for now, it's best for you to be at home. She might try to get in contact with you there.'

Suddenly I see things in a different light. Whereas I'd wanted to remain at the airport because that's where I felt Joseph was, now I suddenly realize that home is exactly where Anna will look for me.

'Let's go!' I say, grabbing my bag. 'What are we waiting for? She's right. We need to be at home!'

And that's it. PC Manning leads me back down the warren of back corridors to the original questioning room, where I collect the luggage, and then we troop back into the hustle and bustle of the airport, where all the noise suddenly starts up again: announcements, children shouting, babies screaming, people rushing to check-in, clutching see-through baggies; checking their pockets and bags for liquids before they go through security; a mass of humanity hugging, crying and kissing their loved ones. We head towards the terminal doors and the car park.

'Just a minute,' I say. I thread back through the afternoon crowds over to the spot where I last saw our son, but all I see is people going about their daily business, catching flights and going on holidays, and I don't understand how they can when my baby has been taken from this very spot. In the distance, I see the information desk I went to when I realized Anna and Joe were missing. The same lady's still behind the counter, still smiling her customer-service smile. It seems years since I approached her, hoping – believing – I'd get Joe back quickly.

'It was here. Right here,' I say. 'This is the bathroom.' I look around, shaking my head, then I turn and look at the door through which we've just watched Anna exit with Joe. Doors that will be imprinted on my memory for life.

'If I'd only . . .' I can't finish the sentence. PC Manning touches my arm.

'Come on.'

'But . . .' I can't find the words to explain how it feels to stand on this spot – this spot where I last had Joseph with me; breathing air that he might have breathed himself. Leaving means accepting that he's gone. It makes it real. I'm no longer just 'separated' from my son at the airport. Leaving means admitting that there's nothing more I can do; that my six-week-old baby has left the airport without me. I close my eyes as I walk out of the door and, outside, I can't stop myself from looking behind every obstacle, pillar and stack of luggage trolleys, hoping that maybe Anna left him somewhere. That she put him down before she got into the taxi. She wouldn't take him.

'Come on,' says, PC Manning gently.

'I can't believe he's not here.'

'We'll find him. We have a strong lead.'

We make our way numbly to the squad car as cars and buses stream past us, picking up people and moving on.

'He could have been in any of these cars,' I whisper. 'Oh god! Why did she do this? There's got to be a reason why.'

45

The journey home seemed to take forever. PC Manning tried to make conversation, explaining that Jackie would have to have a look about the house to glean any 'extra information'. She said it was 'just procedure' and the fact that she said that put me on the defensive – I remember that. I remember thinking 'Are we suspects?' and wondering how Jake was taking to being questioned.

When PC Manning stopped talking, I slumped in the back seat, staring out of the window, hoping against all the odds that I'd see an Anna-shaped figure with a baby in the street. All the while in my head, there was a tangle of thoughts: *did she really take him? Why? There must be a misunderstanding. We'll laugh about this one day – one day when I have my baby back.* Hope is a cruel thing: I let myself picture Joseph back in my arms, the warmth of him snuggled against me, the milky, soft scent of his skin in my nostrils. *If I get him back, I'll be such a good mother,* I promised an invisible god. *If I get him back, I won't hand him to anyone. I won't trust anyone, I'll be the most hands-on goddamned tiger mum anyone's ever seen. I'll be his bodyguard, his champion, he'll sleep in my room, I'll watch over him 24/7.*

I noticed at that point that Jake wasn't in any of those images – I remember that, too. It was the first time I'd entertained the thought that we, as a couple, might not survive this – though I had no idea, of course, how badly things would actually turn out. *Just, please god, let me get my baby back* – that's what I thought all the way home.

Outside the house, I fiddle about, hunting for the keys, reluctant to go inside and face the reality. PC Manning heaves the luggage out of the boot while I stand on the street, unable to process the fact that it was only a few hours ago that Anna and I left from this very spot with me so excited to be going to see my parents.

I walk slowly up the path and unlock the front door. I can hear voices in the front room: a female one and the low rumble of Jake's, then Jake is suddenly at the edge of the hallway, still in his work suit, his tie loosened and hope plastered all over his grey face. He looks at me, and then at PC Manning, as if he expects Joe to be with us, like it was all a misunderstanding and we found him in the bathroom. I shake my head, my fist full of balled tissues, and Jake's face crumples as he turns away.

Behind him, there's a woman, burly and solid, with peachy cheeks and one of the kindest smiles I've seen.

'Hello,' she says, holding out her hand. 'I'm Jackie.'

'Jackie will be your Family Liaison Officer,' says PC Manning. 'She'll stay with you to support you over the next few days – hopefully until we find Joseph.'

'Please try not to worry,' says Jackie. 'We'll get you through this. I'm here to help in any way I can.'

'Thank you,' I say on autopilot.

'Can you get our baby back?' Jake asks abruptly from where he's standing, hands on hips, in the living room. 'Because that's all I want right now.'

'I know,' Jackie says smoothly. 'And we're working on it.

No one speaks, and I stand for a moment, just listening. The house has an empty feel to it, as if it has a baby-shaped hole in its very fabric. It's a desolate silence, one I'll remember as long as I live. I pause for a moment, breathing in, breathing out. How fleeting life is, I think. I had a son, the rest of my life mapped out as a mother, and now I don't. That could have been my only chance. Was I not worthy? Had some god I don't even believe in judged me and decided I was undeserving? Bad things I've done flick through my mind – things I did in college. Is there really a day of reckoning?

I step fully into the living room and then it hits me square in the guts: Joe's white bassinet stands accusing, and, although I know it's futile, I can't extinguish the hope that somehow, when I go over, I'll find him lying in it, asleep, while Anna makes a cup of tea in the kitchen. I drop a hand into bassinet and touch the sheet. It's too much. I turn away, my heart shrunken in my chest, a tight elastic ball of pain.

'All right?' asks Jackie gently. 'Can I make you a cup of tea?'

I nod yes and go and stand by the window, looking twitchily outside as if I might somehow find Joe. Jake prowls the room, like the caged tigers I've seen on TV. Jackie bustles in the kitchen then brings my tea.

'I'll just have a quick look around,' she says. 'It's just proce-dure.' She smiles and melts back out of the room.

'They said they saw Anna take him back out of the airport? On the CCTV?' Jake says.

'I saw it.'

'So you're definitely sure it was her?'

I nod. 'Sure.'

'But how?' Jake spins to face me. 'How did you let this happen?'

I look at him in disbelief. 'What? "Let it happen"? I went to the bathroom and . . .'

'Couldn't you have waited?' he says. 'You'd only just left home! If you'd have waited . . .' He breaks off.

I step back. 'You're blaming me?'

'Well, you can't blame me, can you?' he says smoothly. 'I never even met the woman. She was *your* friend!'

I put my hand on my heart. 'Oh my god. Unbelievable.'

Jake raises his eyebrows at me. 'Unbelievable? I'm just saying it as I see it.'

'*You* let me go with her!' The words blast out of me. '*You* didn't stop me. *You* didn't ask to meet her. *You* thought it was a good idea!'

'I trusted you. I trusted your judgement,' Jake says mildly. 'Why wouldn't I?'

But I'm defensive now. All the pent-up emotion comes bubbling up, a vortex that has to explode. I don't even care that Jackie may well be overhearing it.

'Why did you let your baby son go away – to the *States*! – with someone you've never met? Great fathering skills!' I snarl. 'In fact, you were keen to send me, as I remember. You didn't question anything. You just said yes! Oh, that was very convenient, wasn't it? It's almost as if you wanted me out of the way. Who were you meeting? Your *girlfriend*?'

Jake lunges for me and I think he's going to shake me, but he stops himself. Instead, he shoves his face close to mine.

'Will you give it a rest?' he hisses, then he steps back. 'You've got to stop throwing that back at me.'

I look at the floor. He cheats – and it's my fault for mentioning it?

'It's far more worrying that you never told me that Anna was being followed,' Jake says. 'That Jackie woman mentioned it?'

I look down.

'Why didn't you tell me? Oh, I know why,' he says pompously before I have a chance to answer. 'Because if you told me that, I'd never have let you go away with her! Am I right, or am I right?'

'No! I . . .'

'What? You what?' he shouts. 'Tell me because I'm dying to hear this one!'

'I didn't want to worry you. I . . .' I break off and take a deep breath. Why should I explain myself to him? 'The police were on it. I thought she was being a drama queen. I knew it was your last trip.' I shake my head: why hadn't I told him? 'It didn't seem that important.'

Jake forms a fist and slams it into the palm of his other hand. 'Not that important? If I'd known! If you'd thought to tell me she had a *stalker* living in her garden, we might still have our son.' He wipes spit from the corner of his mouth and glares at me.

My heartbeat quickens. 'We didn't know it was a stalker! Honestly, it looked like whoever it was was long gone. The police didn't seem too concerned.'

'There's evidence that someone's been sleeping in her shed and you don't think it's a reason for concern?' He forces the breath out of his lungs in exasperation.

I keep my voice steady. 'Jake, please. Don't be like this. She called the police. They came. They said it didn't look that recent. It might have been before she even moved in. It might have been the last family's gardener. And if you weren't "too busy" to meet her before you let me fly halfway around the world with her, she might have told you about it herself.'

'So all's well that ends well, hey? Everything turned out fine, did it? Don't try and throw it back at me. We both know you're the one at fault here.' Jake comes over and brings his face close to mine, glowering, and in that moment he looks like a complete stranger. 'So where's my son?' Jake snarls. He springs back up, goes over to the back window and looks out at the garden. 'He could have been in our shed, too. Right there! Sleeping at the bottom of our own fucking garden. Watching our every move. He could have seen you naked. How does that make you feel, Tay, honey? Wanking as he watched you.'

'Stop it!'

'I bet it was your mate Simon.' Jake grabs his jacket and keys. 'He had a thing for you. Any idiot could see.'

'Where are you going?'

'To ask him out for dinner! What do you think? Where does he live? Tell me!'

'I don't know! I never went to his house. Anyway it wasn't him. I'm sure it wasn't him. He just wouldn't.'

'Says the woman who let her best friend abduct her baby . . .'

'Stop it!' I slam my hands over my ears.

He scoffs out loud. 'Did it ever occur to you that your friend Anna might even have pretended she had a stalker to give us a red herring when she took our baby? Did it? How easy was it for her to put a few things in her garden shed? Would have taken half an hour max. Then there's a convenient suspect when she and our baby go missing. God, she was a sicko.'

'Of course she didn't do that. This isn't some American crime show. It's our lives.' But even as I say the words, I'm wondering if he's right. Everything I've thought about Anna to date has been wrong. I can't get past the fact that she deleted her social-media accounts. That tells me more than anything. It tells me what I don't want to know.

Jake and I stare at each other, each locked in our own vortex of desperation. I steady myself on the wall and try to take a couple of deep breaths. Upstairs, I hear the floorboards creak as Jackie moves around. Jake returns to his pacing. I stare at the floor, noticing the intricate details of the carpet. We remain in our positions, both of us stuck in a tableau: grieving parents of snatched baby. Jackie comes back down holding Joseph's little hairbrush, a few of his hairs stuck in the super-soft bristles, in a sealed baggie.

'DNA,' she says. 'If we need it.'

'I'm going upstairs,' I say. 'I'm allowed, aren't I? It's not a crime scene?'

'It's fine,' Jackie says. 'But just to warn you, CID will be over later to do another interview, and I'll be liaising with them regarding the press release. We'll need a photo of Joseph and, if you have it, the car seat he was in. The clothes, too, if you have a picture of him wearing them.'

'But she has a change of clothes for him in the bag,' I say.

'Okay, well, the more you can give us to go on, the better.'

I turn to the stairs and, as I climb them, clinging to the bannister for support, an irrational hope grows in me that I'll turn the corner and find Anna in the armchair, shushing me as Joe sleeps peacefully in his cot – but of course the room is empty, and I take it like a sucker-punch in the abdomen. In the cot, the blanket in which I'd swaddled Joe last night lies abandoned, testament to my excitement to get to the airport; on the mattress, a few of his dark hairs are stark against the white sheet. I grab the blanket and bury my face in it, inhaling the smell of my son while my heart constricts, and then I lift out the mattress, put it on the floor, and lie down on it, hugging my knees and the blanket, and pushing my face against the sheet that my baby was lying on just this very morning. It's cold to the touch now, the warmth of his little body long gone. Almost instantaneously, I feel the familiar tingle in my breasts that means my milk's letting down. I ignore it for a minute, but it's too uncomfortable, so I haul myself back to my feet and go back downstairs to get the sterilized bottles and tubes for the pump.

Jake's on the sofa. 'What were you doing up there?' he asks.

I turn and face him so he can see the wet patches on the front of my top. 'What does it look like?'

He shuts his eyes and runs his hand through his hair. 'Sorry. It's just . . .'

I take everything back upstairs and connect my breasts to the pump like an automaton. Then I sit in the chair and let the tears stream down my face while the rhythmic sound of the pump's push and pull fills the room, and the milk I've made for Joe is sucked out of my body.

* * *

I wake much later, slumped in the chair. It's dark outside, and the nursery curtains are still open. It takes a minute for me to come to; a moment in which my son's asleep in his cot before my brain processes where I am and what's happened. The heating's gone off, my neck's stiff where my head's fallen sideways, and my breasts are still exposed, although the suction cups are in my lap and the machine's off. I stretch slowly, then tidy everything up. From the landing, I see no lights in the house, just shapes highlighted in the sodium-yellow bath of the streetlights. I creep down the stairs with the pump parts and milk bottle in my hand, fully expecting to find Jake asleep on the sofa, but he's not there and there's no sign of Jackie either. Relieved, I switch on the light, blinking until my eyes get accustomed, then I throw out the milk as it has sat out for hours, wash the parts of the pump and leave them to sterilize, then I make some toast, suddenly aware that I'm ravenous. In the sink, a dirty bowl, spoon, plate and knife give evidence that Jake's eaten too.

Back upstairs, I look at him, asleep in our bed. His mouth's slightly open, one arm flung above his head, and he looks as if he has no cares in the world. Ironic, I think, that he suffered from insomnia when he had nothing to worry about but now our son's gone, he's sleeping like the figurative baby. After the way he's been today, I don't want to be anywhere near him. I take my things downstairs, and make a bed for myself on the sofa. And then I call my mum.

It's one of the hardest calls of my life.

46

Birds wake me the next morning: sparrows so close they must be on the windowsill itself. They're chirruping out their little lungs, loud as any alarm and, for a moment, I'm in a world where my son isn't missing, then the memory of the previous day's events floods back with a force that crushes me. I lie on the sofa for a few minutes, not moving a limb as the horror of what's happened washes over me all over again, effectively pinning me to the sofa. *If I don't move, maybe it's not true.* But eventually I realize I have to face the truth. I reach for my phone and my heart jumps: there's a message from Jackie telling me to call her when we wake up. Still lying down, I click her number, my breath coming fast.

'Any news?' I say the moment she picks up, and I'm simultaneously hoping for good news and steeling myself for bad news, honestly not knowing what to expect. If they had him, they'd just bring him here, wouldn't they? Unless . . . An image of a tiny baby in a hospital bassinet springs into my head and I push it back out.

'Some good news,' says Jackie. 'We've traced the cab.'

'Okay . . .'

'But it seems Anna didn't go far. She asked to go to Redhill Station, which is where the driver dropped her off.'

'And from there she could have got the train to . . . ?'

'Well, there's a sighting of her on the station CCTV going onto the northbound platform.'

'So she could be right here in Croydon?'

'We're studying the CCTV of every station that train went through but there's been another development.'

'What?' I can hardly breathe. 'Have they found Joe?'

'No, not that. But we need to speak to you this morning. When you're ready, CID need to come over and get some further detail on your relationship with Anna.'

'Okay . . . ?'

'Can you be ready in an hour?'

'Yes, of course.'

'Perfect, well, we'll see you then.'

* * *

It's a long hour till Jackie arrives with DS Baldwin and DC White. They fill the hallway and I back nervously into the living room, where I've done a quick dust and tidy-up, and plumped up the sofa cushions, feeling as if I'm hosting some sort of bizarre coffee morning.

'Please, sit down. What can I get you?' I ask.

'We're fine,' says DS Baldwin. 'Just a few minutes of your time.'

I pull over a couple of the dining chairs and everyone finds a place to sit – Jake and I are next to each other on the sofa, me with my hands in my lap, him with his arms folded, and then we wait expectantly.

'We wanted to ask you about your relationship with Anna,' says DS Baldwin.

'Okay,' I say. 'Anything specific?'

'If you could take us through how you met her, how long you've known her and so on.'

So I go through it all again and they listen attentively, throwing in extra questions.

'But neither of you had ever known her previously?' DS Baldwin asks when I get to the end.

'No. I'd never met her before.'

'She wasn't an old friend from school or anything? You know, dyed her hair, lost weight . . . ?'

I shake my head. 'I honestly have never met her before.'

'Long-lost relative? Old work colleague? Think hard. It's important.'

'Nothing,' I say.

'I've never met her at all,' says Jake. 'She was *her* friend.'

'You weren't aware of her on social media before you met her?'

'No. Why do you ask?'

'We searched her house and found certain . . . items that lead us to believe she knew you previously.'

My heart quickens. 'Like what? What did you find? Not . . .' They'd tell me if they'd found Joe, wouldn't they?

'We'd like you to come and take a look. Are you ready?'

Jake and I look at each other. 'Yes,' I say, but I'm thinking about the times I've been in Anna's house – what could it be that I hadn't spotted? Or did she leave something since she packed for the holiday? What could it be?

We all get up and troop outside. It's only a walk to Anna's but Jackie insists on driving us in her car.

'What have they found?' I ask her as she looks for a parking space outside Anna's.

'You'll see in a minute,' she says.

We get out of the car and the two officers lead us up the path to the door I remember knocking on for the first time what seems like years ago. I remember Anna opening it in her blue sweatshirt; me standing there with my bags from Costa, full of joy to be helping a new friend rearrange her furniture.

DS Baldwin opens the front door and we step inside. The familiar scent of the house brings back a visceral memory of happier times spent here: Anna and I pushing her furniture around, me playing the interior designer. On the table in the hallway is the reed diffuser I bought her, its fragrance not quite covering up the mustiness I smelled that first time I came over. I still have that ludicrous hope that Anna might be here with Joseph after all, that this is some sort of misunderstanding; or that it's a prank – a cruel prank – that they're going to jump out at me, shouting 'Surprise! Ha ha! Got you!' but I can tell from the depth of the silence that the place is empty. Even so, loyalty clings to me like seaweed: it feels wrong to be in her house without her knowledge.

We go into the living room and I'm struck, as always, by how similar to our own living room it is, from the positioning of the furniture to the colour scheme. She really took my advice on board. I look through towards the kitchen, wondering what it is that they want to show us but there's nothing there. It's a home that's been closed up for a couple of weeks while the occupant goes on holiday, everything spick and span, no taps dripping, the heating on a low constant. I shiver.

'Right,' says DS Baldwin. 'I presume you're familiar with the layout of the house?'

'Yes,' I say. 'I came over a good few times. As I said, I helped with the interior design.'

'And you went upstairs?'

'Yes. Into the bedroom. But not the nursery. She was keeping that private until her baby was born.'

DS Baldwin nods, his lips a thin line. 'Okay. Well, that's the room we need you to look at.'

'The nursery? I saw a picture of the cot she wanted on Instagram.'

'I'd like you to see it on your own first, if you'd like to lead the way,' DS Baldwin says. So, while Jake remains downstairs with DC White and Jackie, I walk nervously up the stairs and open the door to the nursery where I stop in my tracks, unable to take in what I'm seeing.

It's not a nursery at all.

47

The room looked like some sort of a control centre. That's the only thing I could think of as I stood, stunned, in the doorway. I'll never forget that moment, not as long as I live. It was like looking at an air-traffic control centre: there was a chair, and a long desk covered in equipment. There was a huge computer screen angled towards the chair, a stack of iPads and a digital SLR camera with a long lens on the desk. On the other wall, there was a bank of bookshelves with lockable doors. The curtains I'd seen that day from the bottom of Anna's garden were closed, and the air was stale. On the desk, there were used coffee cups, cereal bowls and plates with fetid remains of food. I was so shocked I didn't even notice the pinboards on the wall, not to begin with.

'Oh my god,' I say. 'What is this?' but DS Baldwin indicates that I should go further in.

On the floor there's something I don't immediately recognize. It looks like a flesh-coloured mound of rubber. I pick it up then drop it like a dead squid as I realize what it is: a prosthetic pregnancy bump. It's not big, maybe made to look like three or four months, and is attached to a flesh-coloured body suit. My mind can't compute it.

'Why does she have this? She was pregnant,' I say, and DS Baldwin shakes his head.

'It seems she wasn't.'

'Maybe her bump was too small?' I say. 'Maybe she wanted to make it look bigger?' But my subconscious is putting the pieces together and I don't want to know; I can't even begin to imagine. I think about the bump pictures she posted on Instagram. They looked so real.

'Have a look at those,' DS Baldwin says, nodding towards a pile of scrapbooks on the desk. I pick one up and gasp as I flick through it. I recognize every single picture: there's our house, our car, our road and our front yard in Croydon. Our apartment block in Santa Monica, and shots of our road there from both ends. A picture of the beach. Maps of the area. Some are my own Instagram shots; some have been taken by someone else; some look as if they've been taken from a distance using a long lens. One is of an empty box of pills I'll never forget. I look up at DS Baldwin, flustered, the book between us like it's glowing.

'What is this? How does she have all these pictures?'

'We were hoping you'd be able to shed some light on that.'

'Well, some are social media . . . They were out there . . . in the public domain, but not all of them . . . Some of these are . . . Oh my god. Who took these? Her?' My eyes flick to the long-lens camera.

I put the scrapbook down and pull out a ringbinder folder, my heart thumping a rhythm so crazy I feel it might explode. DS Baldwin watches closely as I flip through the pages, and nausea rises as I realize what I'm looking at: it's a printed record of my Twitter account. There's me announcing my pregnancy, me chatting about where to go on honeymoon; a few pictures I Tweeted from Mexico; an exchange of Tweets between me and Renault regarding issues I had with the new car; places I've eaten; people I've seen; things I've done in the UK. Anna's found and printed every single Tweet. Not just printed but laminated. I look up at DC Manning, appalled.

'She's been following me?'

'It certainly looks that way. Can you think of any reason why she might?'

'No . . . I . . .'

Feet thump up the stairs and Jake bursts into the room, then stops on the threshold just as I did. I'm standing motionless in the middle of the room, the folder still in my hands.

'What the . . . ?' he says as his eyes sweep over the room then stop on the rubber mass on the floor. He steps further into the room, picks it up and turns it the right way around.

'It's a pregnancy bump,' I say. 'Prosthetic.'

'Wasn't she pregnant?'

'I thought she was.'

Jake goes over to the wall and stares at one of the pinboards that I haven't yet reached.

'What the hell is this?' he asks DS Baldwin. 'Who put this here? You? Or her?'

'We found this here,' he says. 'We haven't touched it.'

I go over and stand next to Jake, craning my neck and standing on tiptoe to make out what he's looking at. It's a collage; scores of laminated photographs pinned together without any space between them. I know before I even absorb the images what they are: the images from my Instagram and Facebook accounts. Every. Single. One.

Bile rises and my diaphragm contracts. Clasping my hand over my mouth I run to the bathroom, rip up the toilet lid just in time to throw up. I reach for some loo roll and wipe my mouth, then rest my head against the coldness of the seat for a few moments, breathing hard before I get up slowly, rinse at the basin, and go back to the bedroom. Jake doesn't even ask if I'm all right; he turns on me, his face twisted in anger, and I'm suddenly glad for the police presence in the room.

'Jesus, Taylor, where did she get all this? Have you put all this online?' I stand there, taking his words like punches. 'You put our whole lives on display! Look at this! And this!' He jabs a finger at the picture he took of me ice-skating on our first date at the Rockerfeller Center in New York; then at the picture I took at the top of

Chichen Itza on our honeymoon; at the snap of the first positive pregnancy test I got – one I'd posted before I miscarried that first time; before I learned to be a little more circumspect about these things.

'You put this up?' His face is pinched. 'Do we not have any secrets? Nothing that's sacred? Does the whole world know everything about us? There's a reason I don't do social media and this is it.'

He shakes his head slowly at me, and a pit opens up at the bottom of my stomach. Suddenly I see it through his eyes.

'I'm sorry. I just didn't . . .' My voice fails and I just mouth the words.

'What? Think? You didn't think?'

I go over to Jake and try to touch him but he throws me off.

'Jake, please?'

'This is all your fault! All of it. All your stupid fucking oversharing has got our baby stolen,' Jake snorts. 'Yes, your "friend" took our baby right from under your nose and it's all your fault. Do you see that now? Look!' he shouts, jabbing at the first ever picture I took of Joe – the one I hashtagged 'Insta-love' and posted after I sent it to Jake.

'Even this! Our son had barely been alive two minutes and you put his face on fucking social media. What's wrong with you? What are you looking for? Some sort of validation? "Likes"? Am I not enough for you?'

'Jake, I . . .'

'Oh my god, you practically handed Joe to a psycho. No one's going to have any sympathy, not least the police. God, Taylor. *You* let her in. *You*!' He sinks against the wall, massaging his forehead.

I look at DS Baldwin. 'But why has she done this? What did she want with me? Why me? I don't understand. I mean, look at this! It's been going on for years! Look: there are pictures she's taken of our house in Santa Monica! She's been watching me for years. I don't know who she is.'

Jake's stroking his chin. 'How did you meet her, again?'

'At the walking group.' My voice is a whisper. I scan the board and find the Instagram I took as I approached the park that morning of the first walk: *Hiking – London-style! #lloydpark*. 'Here.'

'And you thought it was a happy coincidence she was there? When you put something like this up? For fuck's sake, Taylor. How naive can you be?'

'But . . .' I'm going to say that she was already there that morning but then I remember that she wasn't. I walked with Simon. Anna only appeared at the end of the walk. Long enough, I realize with a lurch, for her to have seen my Instagram post, got herself ready and got to the park by the time the walk finished.

'But what?' Jake says. His voice is cold, his eyes hard, flashing anger and, worse, disappointment I know is aimed at me. 'Nothing you can say is going to change this. The fact that you let a psycho into our lives. No, scrap that.' He holds up a hand. 'You *invited* a psycho into our lives, and now she's got our baby.'

I sink to my knees, and pick up the prosthetic belly. 'She wasn't pregnant,' I say, more to myself than to Jake.

'No. And there probably is no husband, either,' Jake says.

'But I saw his photo.'

'Photo? It could have been anyone! Brother, cousin, friend . . .'

'I saw his shirts in the wardrobe.'

'Oh please. That doesn't prove anything!' Jake says. 'They could be from the charity shop for all you know.'

'Right,' says DS Baldwin, who's been watching us with his eyes flicking from Jake to me and back, as if he's watching tennis. I get the feeling he's not missing a trick. 'I think we're finished here.'

48

The drive home is short and silent, the weight of Jake's blame hanging squarely over me. It's bad enough that Jake blames me, but I get the sense that Jackie does, too. Does that make me some sort of accomplice to what's happened? Have I 'aided and abetted' the abduction by providing so much information? I realize I have no idea how cyber laws view these things.

I get out of the car while Jackie's still undoing her seatbelt, barge up the path first, and unlock the front door. The smell of the house hits me and it's as if my breasts realize I should be home feeding my baby: the milk lets down with the familiar tingle. I dash into the kitchen and grab the pump.

'Sorry,' I say as I slip past Jake and Jackie and head up to the nursery.

After I'm done, I sit back in the nursing chair, gently pushing the rocker with my foot and going back over all that we saw this morning. I thought I was the one pushing for the friendship with Anna – from the very beginning I had the sense that if I pushed too much, she'd run scared. The phrase 'treat 'em mean and keep 'em keen' pops into my head: had she really planned it to that degree? She kept me wanting more; kept me feeling it was me driving the friendship when all along it was her manipulating me like a string puppet.

As I picture the pinboards and the scrapbooks a shudder runs through me . . . She was there, all along, watching us. Before Croydon, before the UK, before we even got married. I remember with a sense of shame the box of pills in one of the photos – I'll never forget that box nor what it represented. Anna was there the day I terminated Jake's baby; back when our relationship was new, when I was unsure of him, and the thought of having kids terrified me because of what it meant – how I'd have to stop flying. Sitting here in my chair with my baby missing – taken by her – the irony's not lost on me.

My phone pings and I pick it up, open the email application and honestly feel my heart stop. There in my inbox is her name: Anna Jones. Subject: 'FYI'. It must be some kind of joke – that's what I'm thinking even as I click on the email with hands that shake so much it's difficult for me to focus on the tiny screen. Attached to the email there's a load of Word documents – I wait, wait, wait while they download then I scroll through them – ten or more of them – pages and pages of bilious prose, not understanding what I'm seeing.

'Tea, Taylor?' Jackie shouts upstairs.

'*I know where you live,*' I read out loud. What is this? I keep scrolling: *I know what you read . . . I know how you met. Iceskating . . . Mexico . . . Disney . . . College . . . Joseph . . .* My heart's thudding now. *He'd be better off if you weren't having the baby.* What? My arms go weak; the pages shake along with the trembling in my hands, and I sink back onto the bed as I start to read.

It's my life in a document. Pivotal moments from my life, including things no one else could possibly know. Things I've never even told Jake. And things I don't even know myself: why Jake picked the name Joseph – because of a boy in his class who died? Oh my god. I press my hand over my mouth. I don't want to know these things but I can't stop myself from reading. We're in debt? Jake has a gambling problem?

He doesn't want the baby?

So much is true, why wouldn't the other bits be, too?

The phone drops into my lap and I close my eyes, waiting for my heart to slow. Outside I hear footsteps coming up the stairs. I nudge the phone out of sight and feign sleep, leaning back in the chair, my mouth slightly open. I hear the footsteps stop at the door, then retreat. Jackie's voice a moment later, in the lounge, telling Jake.

'Fast asleep. It's good. She needs it.'

I pick up my phone and read the document one more time, more slowly this time, trying to calm my breath; trying to take in more detail; trying to find two and two and make them add up to four; trying to figure out why Anna wrote this and why she's sent it to me.

He still loves me.

I shake my head in despair. They never even met.

Did you ever wonder why he ripped you from your perfect little existence in the States and dumped you here when he could have picked anywhere in Britain? Was it for the joys of the Whitgift Centre? For the rolling spaces of Lloyd Park?

No, shit-for-brains, it was for me.

But he doesn't know her.

And when he sees me with his baby, it'll feel like coming home . . . We'll finally be a family: me, him and Joe.

How can he not know her? Is she even crazier than we thought? Is this some sort of online obsession?

I sit and think for a long while, then I close the document and walk carefully down the stairs.

49

I find Jake and Jackie in the living room: Jake on the sofa and Jackie at the dining table, both nursing cups of tea. They each look at me as I enter the room and I have the sense that life's about to change; that what's said now will never be able to be unsaid. I think of my baby – my son – hidden somewhere without me, and draw strength from the thought I might finally be on the route to getting him back. But before I pass the email to the police, I want to ask Jake a few questions.

'Hey,' I say carefully.

'Good sleep?' asks Jake.

'I was exhausted,' I say.

Maybe I sound defensive because he says immediately, 'I'm not accusing you.'

I sit on the sofa and hug a cushion to me. 'I was just thinking about the name "Joseph". Do you remember who suggested it? Was it me or you?'

'I think I suggested it and you loved it,' Jake says.

'Yeah . . . I think you're right. What made you think of it? Is it a family name?'

He shrugs. 'No. I just . . . liked it, I guess?'

'Did you ever know any nice Josephs? I always find once I've known someone with a name, I always think of them when I hear that name.'

He shrugs again. 'No. Don't think I did.'

'Oh,' I say, my voice deliberately flat, willing him to hear that there's a lot at stake here; willing him to understand that he's being questioned; willing him not to lie. 'So you never knew a Joseph?'

'What is this?' Jake's voice is sharp. 'Twenty questions? No, I never knew anyone called Joseph. All right?' He picks up his phone and checks something on the screen.

I hold my hands up. 'Okay, okay.' I wait but no one says anything. 'I might have that tea after all.'

I get up and make myself a cup, using the time with my back to the room to compose myself. So he lied. The document contains so much truth that I believe it, not him. I turn back to the room and open my mouth to speak but Jackie's phone rings and we all jump. Jake and I stare at each other, suddenly drawn together in our hope, as Jackie moves to pick it up. She catches both our eyes before she says smoothly, 'Jackie Dane.'

We watch her, hanging on every monosyllabic word she says. In my mind I'm going over what I'm about to say; I only have one shot to see his reaction; to judge if he's lying.

Jackie hangs up her call.

'Nothing to report. Sorry. Just updates. They're just working on the press release to send out to the TV stations. When that goes live we might start to get some sightings.'

'Do you tend to get good responses to those appeals?' Jake asks, and I see through him now. Does he even really care that much about getting Joe back – the baby he didn't want in the first place?

'Depends,' Jackie says. 'Of course there are timewasters, but all we need is one person who genuinely saw Anna and we have a solid lead. It's worth a try.'

'I can't believe she could be right here in Croydon,' I say weakly.

'Can you think of anywhere she may have gone?' Jackie asks. 'Places you used to go with her? Places she talked about?'

I struggle to centre my thoughts. 'We only ever hung out at home, Costa and the shopping centre.'

'What about a hotel?' Jake asks. 'Is it worth checking hotels between Gatwick, Redhill and here?'

And I see it. This is my chance. I look at him through narrowed eyes.

'You tell me,' I say quietly, although I feel as if I'm jumping off a cliff. 'You know her. You promised her a baby, after all. So what do you think? Is she in a hotel? Or somewhere else?'

50

For a moment, everything in the room freezes, and then Jake's face creases into a scoff – an arrogant, pompous scoff.

'Have you gone completely insane?' he snorts.

'I know you know Anna,' I say. 'That you love her.' My voice starts dangerously low but crescendos quickly. 'What have you done with Joe?' I shout. 'I just want my baby back!' I launch myself at him and pummel his chest. 'That's all I want! How could you be so cruel? You might not want him but he needs me . . .' The emotion of my missing son swamps me and tears spill out of my eyes. 'He's only tiny. He needs me!' I sob, my blows getting weaker.

'What's got into you?' Jake shouts, shoving me off him and sending me stumbling backwards. 'If I knew where he was, don't you think I'd have said by now?'

Jackie leaps up and takes my arm. She extends her other arm to create space between Jake and me. 'There, come on, sit down.' She leads me to a chair, brings over a box of tissues.

'He knows! He knows something!' I sob.

'You're crazy,' Jake says. 'She's crazy. As if I know where they are! Do you honestly think I would be sitting here doing nothing in this house if I knew where they were? Do you?'

Jackie motions to him to calm down. 'Taylor?' she asks gently. 'What's going on?'

I take a deep breath. 'Anna wrote to me. I got an email. Just now, while I was upstairs.'

'What? What did she say?'

'A lot about you!' I spit. 'A lot about us. Things no one could know. And things about you and her.'

Jake's shaking his head. 'There is no "me and her"!'

'She told me why you chose the name Joseph. There was a boy in your class who died? When you were there?'

Jake's face goes pale. He turns away.

'Well?'

He turns back and I see that his eyes are closed. He rubs the bridge of his nose and is breathing heavily through his mouth, as if he's panting.

'Dear god. It's true, isn't it?' I say. 'So is it also true that we're nearly bankrupt?'

Jake's still holding the bridge of his nose, but he's shaking his head now too. It tells me everything I need to know.

'She says it's because you have a gambling habit,' I say.

Jake's knees buckle and he collapses onto the sofa.

'Here, let me read it out to you,' I say, tapping on the document called 'I Know He Can't Afford the Baby'. '"And he knows that pay-day loans aren't the answer. He does. But still he googles them; still he clicks through from the ads, working out ways to keep the car; keep the cash flowing; keep you from finding out." This is true? How, Jake? How did this happen?' The words explode out of me.

He shakes his head and it's as if the physical mass that makes up my husband has shrunk inside his clothes.

'I didn't mean for it to happen,' he says. 'It got out of control and I didn't know how to fix it. And then you wanted the car . . .'

'I thought we could afford the bloody car!'

'I wanted you to be happy.'

'So you gambled away our savings? In what crazy world did you think that would make me happy?' I shout, my voice tight.

Jake covers his face with his hands.

'And this isn't the half of it. Shall I carry on?'

As I start to read out loud, I can't keep the bitterness out of my tone.

'"And, all the while he's thinking one thing. He doesn't want to think it but I know he is. It's tormenting him. He's up at night chewing the skin around his nails,"' I break off to look at Jake. 'That's true, isn't it? You always were up at night – how does she know? *How does she know that?* "thinking the thought that makes him sick to his stomach. It'd all be okay if we weren't having the baby." Is she right about that too?'

My voice is deathly cold. Jackie's holding her phone up. I think she's recording. Even if it's illegal; even if it can never be used, I'm glad there'll be a record of what was said.

Jake's face is pale. He's shaking his head. If he could disappear down the back of the sofa cushions and never come back, I think he happily would. In fact, I'd push him down myself, stamp on him.

'You want more?' I say, my voice rising. 'Here: "I know your husband's going to miss the birth. I don't need a crystal ball or a pack of tarot cards to know that, when push literally comes to shove, he won't be in the delivery room with you." Anna wrote this. Yes! Anna! How did she know you weren't going to make it? Where were you anyway? Why didn't you answer my messages?'

My voice breaks and, for the first time in my life, I feel I could actually murder someone. I could put my hands on his neck and choke him to death; watch his eyes pop as he suffocates. I don't think I've ever hated anyone so much. I try to focus.

'And then she says that you promised her a baby,' I say. 'She thinks Joseph should be hers.' I break off to stare at him. 'Why would she think that? "He still loves me," she says. "Did you ever wonder why he ripped you from your perfect little existence in the States and dumped you here when he could have picked anywhere in Britain?" ... blah blah blah ... "No, shit-for-brains, it was for me ... And when he sees me with his baby, it'll feel like coming home ... We'll finally be a family: me, him and Joe."'

I look up at Jake's face and all I see is confusion. 'I don't get it,' he says. 'I just don't get it. She must be delusional. She's seen your pictures and created a fantasy where she's with me.'

'So why Croydon?'

'It's home.'

'She says you still love her.'

'I don't know what she's talking about. You've got to believe me,' he says, but there's a shadow in those eyes of his that makes me think there's something, something . . . I slam my fist into the sofa cushion. It's him who needs to connect the dots but he just won't do it. Is he hiding something, or does he genuinely not know what's going on? Suddenly I feel like the walls are closing in on me. I can't breathe.

'I need to get out. I'm going for a walk. That's allowed, isn't it? I won't be long. But I'm going to explode if I stay here any longer.' I turn to Jake. 'And you might want to have a think about all this, and figure out what the hell she's going on about.'

I forward the email to Jackie and slam the door as I leave the house.

51

stride off down the road, not sure of where I'm going until I get there. I pass the Italian – the place I had lunch with Sarah what feels like aeons ago. I look through the window, my eyes searching for the familiar shape of Anna, a pram, Joe's car seat – anything – but it's the usual crowd and no Anna to be seen. I march on to the park, scanning every single person on the street, and then I stop where I stopped that first day I went to the walking group and took that photo. The part of the park where the walking group meets is empty except for two little kids running about, chasing squirrels and birds and squealing while a woman, maybe their mum, smokes a cigarette on a bench. She's on her phone, not watching the kids, the eldest of whom can't be more than five years old. They scamper further and further from her bench and still she's unaware. I watch them for a bit, fury still thrumming in my veins. How careless she is: anyone could snatch her kids and she wouldn't even notice. Anger courses through me – I want to go over and shake her; I want to take the smallest child myself just to prove a point; to make her wake up to the real world the way I've had to.

I take a few deep breaths to try and calm myself, then I walk on, at a pace that makes my breath come faster. The monotonous act of putting my feet down left, right, left, right, helps get my thoughts in order and I feel calmer by the time I leave the park and head towards Costa – the branch where I had that first coffee with Anna. I think back to when I suggested it and she said she was too busy before relenting. I was desperate for her to say yes. She played me like a pro.

Inside, I order an orange juice and take it to the back, where I sit and watch the door, an absurd hope building in me that Anna will appear at the door with Joe; that she'll see me and rush over, thrilled to be able to give Joe back to me, full of what a misunderstanding it's been, and I won't even question her; I'll just take him back and ask nothing; just let her go; let her hide from the police – as long as she leaves us alone. I bask in that wonderful warm feeling of what it'll be like to have Joe back; to have him snuggle in my arms; root for my breast. To watch him sleep flat on his back with his arms above his head like a champion.

I've always thought positive; I've always looked for the best in situations. As I sit there with my juice, I start to believe so much that Joe and Anna are going to turn up that I startle when a mother with a baby in a carrier does appear at the door. She's bundled up against the cold wind but even so I can see immediately that it's not them and I take it like a slap in the face. Of course Anna's not going to come waltzing into Costa. She's wanted by the police; she's not going to be out buying fancy coffees with an abducted baby in her arms. My phone rings: Caroline.

'Hello?'

As usual Caroline doesn't bother with niceties. 'Taylor. The police called. I'm so sorry to hear what happened. How are you?' she says, and I realize that she's someone who understands the pain of losing a child. The thought of her empathy brings unexpected tears to my eyes.

'I'm . . .' I can't speak. I'm overcome. I flap my free hand up and down to try and stop the tears. It's embarrassing to be crying here in Costa. I press my hand to my nose and squeeze my eyes shut but the tears are still coming. 'I'm sorry,' I whisper. 'It's just . . .'

'It's okay,' comes Caroline's voice. 'Don't talk. Do you have an

FLO with you? Use her. They're a great support. And, look, I'm here for you if you need me. Any time, day or night.'

'Thanks. Thank you so much.'

'They'll find him. You know that, don't you?' She sounds so knowledgeable, so sure of herself.

'Thank you.' *Thank you for believing,* is what I want to say. She's the first person who's told me the only thing I need to hear. We hang up and I lose myself in a daydream of how I'll hear the news that they've found Joseph, imagining how I'll feel when I find out he's alive and well and on the way back to me. Maybe it'll be a phone call. Or maybe they've heard something at home already. I take a last swig of juice, throw the bottle in a bin, and push my way through the tables to the door. Time to go home.

52

'Hello there,' Jackie calls as I close the front door behind me. 'We're still here.'

I pull off my coat and shoes, and head into the lounge. It feels too small for the three of us. I don't know where to sit now Jackie's here occupying space that's usually empty, so I stand.

'Any developments?'

'I passed the email to CID, obviously, but other than that, no. We're just waiting for the mispers press release to come. Missing person,' she adds.

'Feeling better?' Jake asks.

I breathe in and out, constrained once more by the stuffy indoor air. 'Yeah.' I pause. 'Have you remembered anything yet?'

Jake sighs. 'She must have seen you somewhere – on a flight or something maybe? And become obsessed by you and stalked you – taken all your pictures off social media and imagined herself in your life,' he says. 'That's all I can think of. She's kidding herself I want to be with her. She's a fantasist.'

'It's possible,' says Jackie. 'Stranger things have happened.' Her phone pings and she looks at it. 'Ah brilliant. It's the press release. You want to take a look?'

She holds her phone out and I scan the document: they've zoomed in on Anna's face from the picture I saw in her bedroom of her and Rob. It's funny to see it in this setting – so familiar yet so strange. I scan the words, reading the facts as if they relate to someone else's life, then hold the phone out to Jake.

'Here.'

He takes the phone then does a double-take. 'What?'

He frowns and shakes his head at the screen.

'No,' he says. 'Where did they get that picture?'

'Her house. It was in her bedroom. It must be the only picture they could find.'

'No! That's impossible.' He points at the screen as if he's seen a ghost. 'That's not Anna.'

'Of course it's Anna!' I snap. 'And that's Rob, her husband, blocked out next to her.'

'No. I know that person. Her name's not Anna . . . Oh my god, oh my god!' Jake looks as if the life's been sucked out of him. His eyes are panicky and he's clutching at his chest. 'This can't be true.'

'I'm telling you, it's Anna! For god's sake, stop messing. This is difficult enough as it is.'

'No.' Jake starts walking this way and that, shaking his head with his hand pressed on his chest. 'Oh my god. Oh-my-god-oh-my-god-oh-my-god.'

'What's going on? You're scaring me!' I want to shake him.

Jake practically throws the phone back to Jackie, as if it's burning his hands.

'That's not Anna. It's Vivian. Oh god. It all makes sense now.'

'What do you mean? Vivian who?'

'It's Vivian Watson,' Jake says. He looks at me and his eyes are empty. 'Watson. As in "Mrs". That woman is not "Anna". It's my ex-wife.'

53

take a step back from him. 'You have an ex-wife?'

Jake closes his eyes. His head's buried in his hands. Jackie looks from one of us to the other. Then Jake snaps his head up and looks at me, somehow accusingly, as if this is my fault and, for some reason, I think of Keanu's eyes. He couldn't look further from Keanu at this point. Untrustworthy eyes, that's what he's got. Debts, gambling, lies, affairs, an ex-wife. I don't know my husband at all.

Jake takes a deep breath then exhales it. When he speaks, his voice is absolutely dead, as if the worst thing that could happen in the world has just happened.

'Yes, I know I should have told you. But I didn't want to dignify it. If I didn't admit it, I could move on. Pretend it never happened. Never mention it again.'

It's almost as if I feel all my organs collapse inside myself, such is the downward pull in my abdomen. But I inhale and control my exhale to beat down my anger. I want answers and I want my son back, and yelling isn't going to get me either.

'How long for?'

'Not long. Too long.'

'How long, Jake?'

He shakes his head. 'Couple of years.'

'When did you split up with her?' I feel like an investigator.

'Around the time we met.'

'Before or after?' I ask. *By the end of the session, he knows he wants to marry you,* Anna wrote.

'It's important,' I say.

Jake shakes his head. 'I don't recall. It's not so black and white. But when I met you I knew you were the one for me. Viv was a mistake.' The shortening of her name hits me like a punch. 'It wasn't working out. I'd been looking for a way out for ages.'

'And then I trotted into your life and you thought you could just forget everything? Well, clearly not. Our son's missing. Your ex-wife has our son.'

'It wasn't like that,' Jake says, and I notice the dull details of our living room: the fact that the surfaces could do with a dust; the soft furnishings I'm usually so proud of now looking so mundane, so pedestrian here in the midst of this drama that doesn't belong in my life. I want to shake Jake and scream: *'How was it then? Tell me!'* but I know that's not going to get me back my baby. Yes, Joe's *my* baby now, not *our* baby. Of this I'm sure: after we get Joe back, there is no more Jake and me.

'Can you think where she might have gone?' Jackie says. 'The main thing here is that we've identified her and now we need to find her.'

But Jake ignores her. He runs his hand through his hair, clutching at his scalp.

'Oh god. She wanted a baby. She was obsessed by the idea. But that was years ago.'

'And you never had one?' It seems ridiculous I have to ask, but five minutes ago I didn't know my husband had an ex-wife.

'Of course not!'

'So she's taken Joe because he's yours? Is that what this is?' I still can't process the fact that this is Anna – my friend Anna – we're talking about.

'Oh my god. She was so insecure, so needy. She wanted something that would love her unconditionally. I suggested we get a dog. It became an issue. She started tracking her fertility.' He looks at me, and I realize with a thud in my chest that I did exactly the same thing. 'I'd realized by then that she had a few screws loose; I'd realized I'd made a massive mistake. I was going to leave her anyway, before I met you. She didn't like that.' He gives a bitter laugh. 'She made my life a misery.'

'How?'

'Can I just interrupt?' Jackie says. 'I'm afraid we're going to have to get CID back. They'll need to ask you some more questions about this.'

'Sure,' says Jake.

'This Vivian woman – your ex-wife,' Jackie says to Jake. 'You were saying she made your life a misery? What sort of thing did she do?'

I don't know what I expect him to say – small, domestic struggles maybe: long silences, a sex ban, Jake sleeping on the sofa.

'She started harassing me,' he says. 'Proper mad stuff. Late-night phone calls, attention-seeking texts pretending she was about to kill herself, putting stuff through the door, emails . . . popping up outside my office.'

I close my eyes. How is this suddenly my life? Jake barks a laugh. 'God, she was clever. I wanted to get a restraining order but she never broke the law. Never did anything the police would be interested in. Just small things, psycho things that let me know she was watching me. I could handle it. But . . .' Jake closes his eyes and shakes his head.

'All this was happening while we were seeing each other? Why didn't you say anything?'

'You were in the States and I was here. You were my fresh, new future, so pure . . . I didn't want to ruin it. God, Taylor, you have to know how I felt about you. You gave me hope for the future; you were everything I wanted moving forward. That's why I didn't tell you about her. I didn't want to sully what we had. Tinge it. I wanted a clean break from all that craziness. Do you get that?'

I just stare at him. I, I, I – it's all about him. And I thought we were 'us'.

'This is why I was so glad to move to the States to be with you,' Jake says. 'I heard nothing after that. It all stopped. I thought that was the end of it. I assumed she'd got over it and we could get on with our lives. I put it to the back of my mind and – god, forgot, I suppose.'

'You're unbelievable. Didn't you think you owed it to me to tell me you were being stalked by a psycho ex-wife?'

Jake snorts. 'I didn't want it hanging over us. It was a mistake. Fix it. Move on. I didn't want to have to explain it to you. None of your business.'

'But now it is.' I close my eyes and massage my temples. 'And you didn't think to mention any of this when Joe went missing?'

'I didn't know "Anna" wasn't Anna!'

'It's your fault! You were never here.'

'She's the one who bailed on your birthday,' Jake shouts and a bubble of spit flies from his lips. 'I was supposed to meet her then – remember?'

That shuts me up as I think back to the excuses: she was sick, Rob was flying in, Rob was flying out – did she really plan this so Jake never got to meet her? I'm still furious at Jake but Joe is my priority. I need to focus on getting Joe back.

'Where would she go?' I ask.

Jake jumps up and goes to the window; lifts the lace curtain as if she'll be outside, watching, then lets it drop and turns to me.

'I don't know.'

'Come on!' I say. 'You must know! Think about the places you used to go with her . . . Is there anywhere she could have made a base? Anywhere she might have taken him? Where were your favourite places?'

'She could be anywhere.'

'But what if she's not? What if she's right here under our noses?'

'We used to live not far from here. A rented place. I doubt she's there, but . . .'

Suddenly I feel a flicker of hope. Now we know what we're dealing with, maybe we have a better chance of finding Joe.

'Is it worth a look?' I ask Jackie. I'm agitated now, standing up, adrenaline pumping through me. 'We should go and look. Can you come with us or do we have to wait for CID? We've got to do *something*!' Already I'm moving towards the door.

Jackie raises a hand. 'Slow down. They're already on their way over. We should wait. We need to do this properly.'

I stare at her: she's supposed to be a support, not a hindrance. I need to see this house; I need to see if my son's there. I also need to see it for murkier reasons: I want to know where Jake lived with his ex-wife. 'It's not far,' he'd said. Is that why he rented our house in this location? Has my entire time in England been based on this subconscious pull he felt to be back where he was when he was married to Vivian? He says he wanted to get away from her, but what if she was right all along?

'They'll be here very soon. Or I can send them straight to the house if you have the address?'

'Yes!' I say. 'Please. If he's there, I want him back. You can do the questions later. Please.'

So Jake gives Jackie the address and we listen while she tells someone on the phone.

'I guess we just wait now,' Jake says.

'I'm going upstairs,' I say. I stomp up the stairs, anger apparent in every thudding footstep, throw myself on the bed and picture how Joe would be found: the police banging on the door, storming in. Anna cowering, the cries of my son in another room – safe and well, of course – the detective scooping him up and bringing him, squalling, to me. Lying on the bed in a fetal position, I feel the familiar pricks of my milk letting down.

'Please let him be there, please let him be there, please let him be there.'

54

He wasn't there. Looking back, it would have been too easy. How neat it would have been to find him in the first place we looked. The house was apparently occupied by an Asian family now, any trace of the car crash that was Viv 'n' Jake long gone. The police told us all this with apologetic faces before getting down to the business of interviewing my husband about his psychopathic ex-wife. While I waited I planned my future in my head. I'd get Joe back, and then I'd go back to the States. I'd divorce Jake on the grounds of unreasonable behaviour – I mean, no judge could possibly argue that this web of lies and deceit, which led to my baby being snatched, was reasonable. I'd stay with my parents until I got my feet on the ground again, then I'd carve out a new life – and hopefully, one day, a new love – for me and Joe in California. Thank god, I remember thinking, that we don't have a joint bank account. His gambling debts, I hope, will remain his and his alone.

Funny how lies can make you care so little for someone you thought you loved.

* * *

I come down when the police arrive. It's DS Baldwin and DC Jones again. They nod and I take a seat at the dining table, a silent witness to the interview. They take Vivian's details, then they ask Jake, just as I did, for any leads and I watch as my husband paces the living room, trying to come up with a list of places he and Vivian used to go – places that meant something to them. There's a notepad in front of me and I pick up the pen lying next to it and start doodling. Boxy, angry doodles with lines and lots of hard shading. For god's sake, I'm thinking: how difficult can it be?

'Think back to when you first started going out,' DS Baldwin says. 'Who did she know? Did she mention any family, friends, colleagues? Where did she work? Who did she talk about?'

'Her parents lived in Bristol but she didn't have much to do with them when we were together,' Jake says, tapping his head. 'She used to go to her grandmother's sometimes.'

'What was her name? Do you have a number for her?'

'Granny Sue, it was. She lived somewhere in north London, I think. Acton? God, I had her number in my address book. I'm sure I did.'

Jake goes off and comes back with his old address book.

'Here it is. But maybe she's no longer with us. She was old, as I remember. In her late seventies even then.'

'Anyone else?'

Jake struggles through a few names but isn't sure about any of them. 'I can picture faces,' he says. 'God, I just can't remember the names. My memory . . .'

'Where did you used to hang out with her?' DS Baldwin asks.

Jake runs both his hands through his hair – a pastiche of a distressed man. 'We didn't go out a lot. She didn't like "sharing" me with other people, even strangers in restaurants. That's how mad she was. If we went to a restaurant, she'd be paranoid I was talking too much to the waitress, and we'd end up fighting. It was too stressful. We hung out at home. Watched movies. Got takeaways.'

'Love's young dream,' I say under my breath.

He whirls to face me. 'I told you she was nuts.'

'And you married her?'

We stare at each other: both accusing, both angry. It's him who looks away first.

'How about hotels?' DC White asks. 'Did you ever go for weekends away?'

'We camped,' he says, his voice flat. 'She's not going to have gone back to a campsite . . . is she?' He walks to the window, lifts the curtain and stares out, then he turns back to the room and perches on the window ledge, stroking his chin. The rain's got harder; the sky's an unrelenting, heavy grey. I can't bear to think of my baby in a tent in this weather.

'Oh god, anything's possible with her.' Jake presses his fingers to his temples. 'We used to camp down in Kent. There were a couple of farms there where you could pitch up. She liked horse-riding . . . near Maidstone they were, I think. I remember driving down the A20. And sometimes by the beach, near New Romney.'

'Did she like any of them enough to go back? Were any of the holidays particularly special?'

He closes his eyes. 'I don't know. Who knows what goes on in a mind like hers?'

'Have you got any photos?'

He laughs, a bitter bark. 'She kept them all.'

'Would you remember where they were?'

He shakes his head. 'Not without seeing pictures. Seen one campsite, seen 'em all.'

'Could you find them online?'

Jake tuts, but DS Baldwin asks for the iPad and calls up a map of Kent campsites, and Jake tries to remember all of the places he went with Vivian. After nearly an hour, there are five he's 'almost' certain about.

'We'll look into it,' says DS Baldwin. 'We've got a few leads to go on here.'

* * *

Jake closes the front door after everyone when they leave, and walks back into the living room. It feels odd to be just the two of us. I feel like I've been abandoned with a stranger. I look about the living room, noting escape routes to the front and back doors, then realize how absurd I'm being. Jake buries his head in his hands.

'We're never going to find her. She's created a new identity before. What's to stop her doing it again? She could be anyone . . . anywhere!'

We sit in silence for a minute or two. Blame hangs in the air – me blaming him; him blaming me.

'I can't believe "Anna" was Vivian,' Jake suddenly says. 'I can't get my head around the fact it was her you were spending all that time with . . . What was she like?'

I shrug. 'She was all right, actually. I can't deny it. I liked her.'

'She made you like her. She's clever like that. She knew everything about you and she made herself into something she knew you'd like.'

Shame slides over me: isn't that what I'd done to try and get her to like me? Look at the way I'd offered to help her design her living room, knowing that she'd just moved in.

'She must have given something away,' Jake says. 'She was always round our house. You knew her for three months. You stayed with her! And she gave nothing away in three months? Nothing that made you suspect?'

'No. I thought she was my friend.'

'Oh please!' Jake scoffs. 'Friend? If you weren't so desperate for friends, none of this would have happened. She saw you as an easy way in. You know that, don't you?' He shakes his head. 'God, you were such a soft target.'

'Hang on, hang on. You can't go throwing this back at me. After what you've done, you cannot seriously blame me for this.'

He holds up his hands. 'Sorry . . . But, god, couldn't you see she was a fucking nutcase?'

284

'And couldn't you "fucking" see that gambling was never going to solve our financial problems?'

We glare at each other, quits.

'I'm sorry,' he says. 'I'll sort it out, I promise. I'll talk to the bank and come up with a repayment plan. All right? I don't care if I have to work till I'm a hundred. I'll pay that money back, okay?'

I snort. 'How did it happen? I just don't get it.'

Jake shakes his head. 'I don't know. Bored. Hotel rooms. An ad on a website. It looked like fun. I had a few wins, got too confident.' He laughs bitterly. 'I guess that's how they sucker them all in.'

'I can't believe you fell for it. You of all people.'

We lapse into silence. I put my face in my hands as if I can wipe it all out. Open my eyes and find it was all . . . what? A dream? Jake sits on the sofa, staring at nothing.

'What did you talk about with her?' he asks after some time. 'Did she ask about me?'

I close my eyes, like, *do I really need to answer this?*

'She did, didn't she?' he says. 'What did she ask? Nothing can be worse than what's already happened.'

My eyes are still shut and I've got my hand over my mouth. I honestly feel as if I'm going to throw up again.

'What is it? You've got to tell me.'

'She wanted to know about our sex life.' My voice is a whisper.

Jake spins his head to face me. 'What?'

'You heard.'

'She asked you about our sex life and you didn't think that was odd?' Jake speaks slowly, as if he's explaining to a child.

'It was in context. To do with being pregnant. Women always talk about these things. It wasn't odd.'

But then I remember her questions about how Jake and I kept our love life alive . . . I remember that I told her about the kinky photos, about the role play, and I sink backwards on the sofa. What must she have thought? Did she do that with Jake, too?

'Well, it's not going to change anything now,' I say. 'What you need to do is figure out where she might be.'

Jake slams a fist into a sofa cushion.

'I don't know! I don't bloody know!' He lets his head slump down, and I realize that he's crying. More than twenty-four hours after our son was taken, my husband actually cries.

I file that thought away for the divorce court.

55

I don't know how either of us got any sleep that night but somehow, I guess, the body takes what it needs, even in times of stress. I was convinced there was no point in going to bed but did so just because what else was there to do? And the next thing I knew was Jake shaking me awake. He was crouched over me, his eyes sunken and lined, and thick, dark stubble making him look like some sort of runaway, his hair all over the place. Even though he was dressed, there was a rancid smell of sweat coming off him. I remember recoiling.

'What? Have they found him?' I ask, jolting awake.

'You got an email from Vivian! It's on the iPad.' I'm too shocked to worry about the fact he's been going through my email.

'What?' I'm upright now, rubbing sleep from my eyes. 'What does she say? Is Joe okay?'

He thrusts the iPad at me and I read: *I know you'll get over this. Yeah, I get that that sounds harsh, but don't forget the main thing here: I know you.*

I stop and look at Jake. He raises both eyebrows at me.

'You've read this?' I ask and he nods. I look back down at the words, finding my place again.

Sometimes, as I watch you floundering about in your pathetic life, worrying about pathetic Sarah coming on to your husband, I think I know you better than you know yourself. Actually, not sometimes: always.

I'm watching you pack for our States trip now, and I have to stop myself laughing. You're such an innocent; so easy to manipulate. You make my job too easy. 'Yes, Tay, course I'll carry a bag of essentials for Joe. Course I will, hon, it's no trouble.' You do realize you're packing me a bag so I can take his baby, don't you? Oh god, I have to look away lest I laugh. And I watch you planning for the flight and I want to laugh again: you're not going anywhere, sunshine. There'll be no flight for you.

But the thing is, Jake's baby should always have been mine. Did you know we were trying for a baby when he met you? Has he told you that yet?

So, this is all your fault. That day you sat on that fucking plane with him; that was the day you set the ball in motion. You could have ignored him. You could have put your fucking headphones on, watched a movie, gone to sleep, done anything except ruin my marriage.

But, you know what? Karma's a bitch and she's been chasing you. Did you feel her snapping at your heels as you met your new best friend? As you interior-designed her living room and invited her to join your book club? You take something from me, and I'll take something from you. It's how life works, honey. Tit for tat. An eye for an eye – isn't that what they say?

Oh, I had fun playing with you. I had fun winding you up about Sarah and making you think Simon was stalking me. Poor Simon. The police won't find anything on him. He was just a pawn. Collateral damage, if you like.

And you – yeah, you'll get over this. You barely knew Joe. It was me who took care of him, and me who loved him, not you. You never looked like you enjoyed being his mum, so let's say I'm giving you a second chance. Jake's son belongs with me.

It's the baby he promised me.

He's mine now. And, when he finds us, Jake will be mine too.

'She wants you to find her!' I say, dropping the iPad on my lap. 'Come on! Think! You've got to know where she is. She wants you!'

Jake is striding up and down the bedroom, a parody of 'man thinking'. At the window, the curtains are growing lighter as the first rays of the sun spider towards the horizon. Nearly dawn. And then the iPad pings and another email comes in. The name 'Anna Jones' right there on my screen. I open it and my heart stops: it's a photo, which opens in the body of the email.

'Joe!' Tears erupt from my eyes and I wipe them away as I stare at the photo, devouring it, desperate for clues. She's taken it since the airport. He's there in the same outfit, with the same blanket, lying flat on some sort of makeshift bed. He looks . . . okay. Smaller than I pictured in my mind – oh god, so small – but okay. The lighting is dim; it doesn't look like she's inside a house of any sort. I enlarge the picture as much as I can, raise the phone to my lips and kiss the screen.

'Show me,' Jake says and grabs the iPad from me. I watch as his eyes move over it, presumably taking in the same details as I did. He expands the picture, examines it, and then he looks upwards as if he's reading some invisible text written on the ceiling, and pumps the air with his fist.

'I've got it!'

'Got what?'

'Got it! I think I know where they are!'

'Where?'

'I can't explain, let's go.'

'Now? Shouldn't we wait for the police?'

'Sod the police. I know where she is!'

I jump out of bed and pull on yesterday's clothes while Jake runs downstairs. As I wash my face and drag a comb through my hair I can hear him jangling the keys in the hall downstairs.

'Come on, it's not a bloody fashion show,' he shouts.

I've got that slightly panicky feeling, slightly giddy, like my mind hasn't yet connected with my body. I look around the familiar room, not knowing what I'm looking for. Do I need to take anything? I clatter down the stairs, grab my coat from the hallway and follow Jake out of the front door, closing it behind me with a decisive bang. I feel underprepared without the pram, the car seat, the nappy bag. Underprepared, too, in thinking about what's going to happen if we find her. She's convinced he'll want to stay with her. What will I do when I get Joe back? Jake starts the car then blows on his hands and rubs them together.

'The heater'll come on soon.'

'Where are we going?'

'It's a warehouse. Not far.'

'A warehouse? What?'

But Jake just shakes his head.

The rush hour's starting and traffic isn't as thin as I'd have hoped. Jake drives badly, in a silence marred only by the metronomic swish of the wipers and the curses Jake throws at cars that pull out in front of him or traffic lights he misses. He under and overtakes where he can, cutting in to the front of queues, hooting and being hooted at. We start to leave the main part of town and head in a direction I don't know, into a more industrial area. The road widens and the houses give way to warehouses, set back from the road. Jake slows down, checking what we're passing on the left until he sees a turn and swerves into some sort of industrial estate. He takes a right and a left, then pulls up outside a warehouse and stops the engine.

'Right,' he says. 'It's a long shot, but it looked like she was here.'

I look at the warehouses all around. 'Do you actually know where we are?'

Jake nods forward. 'Just a bit further. There was a disused

warehouse here. We used to climb up the fire escape to the roof and look at the stars. You had a pretty good view of London, too. She liked to go up there and look at the skyline.'

Jealousy rises in me, and I try to scribble out images as fast as they form in my head: Anna and Jake climbing the fire escape – her running ahead, maybe, young and pretty, leading him to her special place. I know Anna, she'll have thought of everything – she'll have gone ahead and put a blanket up there, taken a bottle of wine. I see the two of them lying back to look at the stars – maybe even making love. Oh my god! It hasn't hit me till now, but the thought that Anna was married to Jake! Had sex. Went to bed together. Woke up together. That my best friend knew my husband so intimately. *But she's not my best friend,* I tell myself, with yet another sinking realization that the whole friendship was fake. All this passes through my head in a fraction of a second.

'I don't know if it's still disused – maybe someone's bought it – or if you can even still get up there. This was a good few years ago,' Jake says.

I exhale. 'You really think she might have come here?' I can't keep the doubt out of my voice.

'I can't think where else,' Jake snaps. 'If she wanted me to find her, this is where she'd come. It's where we . . .' His voice trails off and I complete the sentence in my head: first kissed? First slept together? Got engaged? Tiredness makes my eyes pop.

'Right,' says Jake. He unbuckles his car seat and I do the same. We get out and pull our hoods up: the rain is steady and cold. Jake indicates that we should walk in single file, sticking to the shadow of the warehouses. The sun's barely up.

'It's a little way,' he says, turning back to me. 'I didn't want her to see the car. If she's here, I don't want to scare her off. Who knows what state of mind she'll be in. She's not exactly stable.'

He turns another corner and then stops, holding his arm out to stop me, too. The building we're facing is derelict, the majority of its windows broken. There's graffiti daubed on its grey walls, weeds flourishing, and rubbish littered all around. The rain's already plastered my fringe to my head, and rain trickles down my face. I wipe at it with hands already stiff with cold.

'Is this it?' I mouth.

Jake nods. 'The fire escape's round the back.'

He starts to skirt around the perimeter of the building, picking his way through industrial rubbish: planks of wood, empty paint canisters, piles of bricks, lumps of broken concrete, decaying black bags, a snarl of barbed wire, a broken toilet, and piles of jagged boarding. I follow, gingerly, trying not to catch my clothes or twist my ankle. Up ahead, Jake stops and holds up his hand. I freeze, then shrug as he remains motionless. He puts his finger to his lips to shush me, then mimes listening towards a door to the ground floor of the warehouse. I strain but can't hear anything so I tiptoe closer until I'm standing slightly behind Jake. He's tilting his head towards the door, then he holds up his index finger, pointing towards the door, and turns to me questioningly. I shrug – I didn't hear anything. We both lean closer to the door and then, just as Jake raises his finger again, I hear it too: the murmur of a voice coming from inside. Jake and I look at each other, his face mirroring the panic that I feel. Is she inside? Suddenly I realize we have no plan. If it's Anna in there, and if she has Joe, will she simply hand him over? Jake and I stare at each other, our eyes hooked to each other, then he mouths 'Okay?' and I nod.

'Get Joe,' he mouths. I nod again, then he turns to the door, pushes it open and steps inside in one fast move. I'm right behind him, just in time to see Anna bend over Joe's car seat and scoop up Joe – my baby! Then there's a moment when everything freezes: Anna standing holding Joe to her shoulder, and Jake staring at her. She looks different without the pregnancy bump; the clothes she wore to the airport yesterday – the jeans and the Converse and the blue sweatshirt – are loose on her frame, giving her the look of a child. Her eyes are wide, panicky, mad.

'Vivian!' Jake yells and he launches himself across the room, oblivious to any danger there might be. Anna whirls around and runs towards a door on the other side of the space, Jake hot on her heels. I follow, noting Anna's backpack as I pass – the one she'd had filled with nappies, wipes and toys, ready to take to the States – and, even while I'm pleased she had supplies, it hits me how precisely she'd planned this.

Anna pushes open a door on the far side of the warehouse space and flies through it, shoving it closed behind her so Jake has to open it again. By the time I catch up, they're both clattering up a rickety metal staircase that zigzags up the side of the warehouse. Anna's already past the first floor, and Jake's running up the stairs two at a time behind her. Joe's crying now, and the sound makes my breasts tingle. Holding tight to the rail, I follow as fast as I can. When I get to the top of the stairs, Jake and Anna are already on the roof. Anna's clutching Joe to her chest.

'Don't come any closer!' she screams.

Jake stops where he is, his hands held up in a surrender. 'Vivian. Please just give me the baby.'

They stare at each other and I realize that Anna's dangerously near the edge; that whatever railing used to be there is long gone. My legs go weak at the thought of my baby so close to the edge, and I sway, grabbing onto the stair railing for support. Joe's wails build so he's barely sucking in enough breath to sustain the rhythmic cries that wrench right through to my uterus.

'Anna, please!' I yell, then try to calm myself, to speak evenly. 'It's okay. Whatever you want, it's okay. Just give us Joe. We'll do whatever you want. But please just give me back my son.' My voice breaks. 'He's hungry.' I look at the lightweight blanket she's got him in. 'He's cold!'

'He should be mine!' Anna shouts above the sound of his screams. 'He was meant to be mine! You don't want him!'

'You have to give him back!' Jake shouts. 'There's no other way out of this.'

'He's mine!' yells Anna. 'We were going to have a baby. You

and me! Remember? You promised! And then you left. You left me for her!' She sobs. 'This is only fair! It's fair that I get him. He was always mine. I was there for the birth – I was there for that pathetic bitch! I've looked after him ever since.' She strokes Joe's head then speaks in a baby voice that makes my skin crawl. 'There, there, Joe-Joe. Mummy's here.'

'Give him back!' I yell.

'Why should you have him? It's me he loves. It's me who looks after him. It's me who feeds him and rocks him and takes him to the park. You don't love him. You don't want him.'

'Please, Vivian. You have to give the baby to Taylor.' Jake's voice is calm and he edges towards Anna but she steps back, closer to the edge of the roof.

'Stop!' I scream at Jake. 'She'll fall!'

'All I ever wanted was your baby!' Anna shouts. 'All you had to do was give me that. We were so close, and then she,' she spits the word, 'came along.' The wind picks up and Joe screams louder, his blanket now almost saturated with rain. Anna's hair is plastered to her face and she looks so slight I worry a sudden gust might blow them both over the edge. 'You stopped me. You denied me the one thing I wanted. Well, now I've got him. He's mine. Your first son. He belongs with me. He always did.'

'Vivian, no! You're wrong. You'll go to jail for this. Give us the baby, and get on with your life.'

'If I can't have him, then neither can you.' She takes a step towards the edge, and I realize with a certainty that almost stops my heart that she's planning to jump with Joe in her arms. I launch myself across the roof towards her at the same time as Jake does.

'Stop!' Jake screams. 'He's not mine!'

I stumble to a halt just behind him, confused – of course he's Jake's – but his lie's hit the jackpot because it works. Anna turns away from the edge for a fraction of a second, and Jake seizes his chance. 'I can't have children. We used a donor.'

Anna's frozen, her face white. She holds Joe out in front of her. He's screaming non-stop now, at the top of his lungs.

'What?' Anna says. 'What did you say?' She gives Joe a little shake and I whimper.

'He's not my son,' Jake says, edging closer.

'You're lying! He looks like you. Look at him.' She shakes him again.

'It's the truth,' I shout.

'But I know everything about you. You never went to a fertility clinic. I'd have known.'

Anna stares at Joe's face as if trying to identify his father and, in that split second, Jake pounces towards her. There's a tussle, both of them on the edge of the roof, and I try to move but my limbs are frozen; I'm unable to look but equally unable to look away as Jake wrestles with Anna. Then suddenly he has Joe in his hands, and he screams 'Grab him!' as he turns to me and I'm there, my arms shooting out to grasp my son, but Anna's trying to grab him back and, instead, she gets a hold of Jake's jacket and swings him towards the edge of the building. Jake whacks her hand off him but she grabs his wrist and it's in a moment that seems to freeze forever in my mind that they struggle on the edge of the roof, then Jake shoves Anna and she falls backwards, clutching at him as she goes, and the last thing I see is her arms cartwheeling in the air as both of them plunge over the edge of the building, then almost instantaneously comes the sickening crunch of their bodies hitting the ground below.

I sink to my knees on the wet roof, clutching Joe to me, keening. But he's hungry, he's rooting for a nipple so I open my clothes, snuggle his wet little body under my jacket and let him latch on. He feeds hungrily, his body still convulsing as his sobs die down, his little fists opening and closing. I stroke his forehead with a finger, and touch my lips to his skin.

'There, there,' I say. 'It's all over. It's all over now.'

56

And in a way, I was right. In one way, it was all over. It didn't take me long to tie up the loose ends in London – to work my way through the red tape surrounding Jake's death, to sell the house, to get the shippers in and fly back to the States.

But in another way, it took much longer. Although I'd decided I was leaving Jake anyway, although he'd broken all the trust I'd ever had in him, there were still days when I woke up in the morning and, in that halfway haze between sleep and wakefulness, forgot all that had happened and reached out for him in bed, his absence sucker-punching me. You can snatch away the person, I suppose, but it takes longer to dissolve the emotional bonds of a marriage – no matter what wrongs were done.

I've come to terms now with the fact that my marriage was doomed from the start, but that doesn't stop me thanking God that it was that doomed marriage that brought me the light of my life: my son, Joe.

ACKNOWLEDGMENTS

There are many people I'd like to thank for the parts they've played in getting this book into your hands. The brilliant team at HQ: Lisa Milton, Kate Mills and Sally Williamson, as well as the sales, digital, PR and marketing teams who beaver away behind the scenes.

As always, my thanks go to Luigi and Alison Bonomi, who continue to guide me on my journey as an author. To Isobel Abulhoul and Yvette Judge of the Emirates Airline Festival of Literature, and to Charlie Nahaas of Montegrappa, the sponsor of the writing competition that propelled me to success, and one of the most inspirational people I have the pleasure of knowing.

Special thanks to Helen Kelly, Melanie Hellier and Rebecca Boldry for their technical advice on police procedure. Any mistakes are mine, not theirs.

To Rachel Hamilton for casting her expert and critical eye over the very first draft; to my author friends who are always there to share the ups and downs of this profession: B A Paris, Jessica Jarlvi, Charlotte Butterfield, Karen Osman and Alice Clark. To Jeremy Steane for all his help and film suggestions, and to my friends who support me every day perhaps without even realising: in particular, Valerie Myerscough, Rohini Gill, Zoe Dajani, Karen Connolly, Jacqueline Thorpe and Belinda Freeman.

ACKNOWLEDGMENTS

And finally, thanks to my mum, who believes I can do anything; to Sam for his unwavering belief in me, weekend child care and brilliant plot twists; and to Maia and Aiman, for reminding me (constantly) that there's a world beyond my office that keeps on turning.